UNCLEAR PURPOSES

JOAN HALL

PrimaCasa Press, Lower Burrell, PA15068
PrimaCasa Press is an imprint of AIW Press, LLC.
https://www.aiwpress.com

ISBN-13: 978-1-944938-29-1

DEDICATION

In memory of my cousins, Jack (United States Army) and Neil (United States Navy) who served our country in Vietnam

PROLOGUE

Presidio County, Texas
December 2012

Alyssa Weber stood in the large walk-in closet, eyeing the long row of garments. She reached for a black cocktail dress. Elegantly designed, it had a beaded neckline, tiered jacket and skirt, and above-the-knee hem. A pair of silver pumps and drop earrings were the only accessories needed.

If only.

She couldn't remember the last time she'd had an occasion to wear such a dress. But to wear black chiffon tonight would arouse suspicion. Travis had never indicated he doubted her, but she needed to be careful. As far as he was concerned, she was visiting her best friend, Sheri. She replaced the dress, then grabbed a pair of designer jeans and a red cowl-neck sweater.

It didn't matter. Jesse found her attractive no matter what she wore.

She dressed quickly, then walked back into the bathroom to check her make-up and run a brush through her hair. Satisfied with her appearance, she pulled on a pair of ankle boots and a leather jacket.

Taking a deep breath, she walked into the living room where Travis sat in his favorite chair beside the fireplace.

He looked up from the book he was reading when she entered the room.

At sixty-eight, Travis was the quintessential cowboy. Despite his age, many women found him attractive. His hair was now mostly silver, and the lines around his eyes from long days spent in the Texas sun.

Alyssa thought back to their first meeting ten years earlier at the Fort Worth Stock Show and Rodeo. She was a city-born, city-bred college senior, he a middle-aged rancher who looked much younger. Travis asked her out for drinks and dinner that evening. When the rodeo ended a few days later, they had become inseparable.

He invited her to spend spring break at his ranch. She was a bit hesitant at first, having already made plans to spend a week at the beach with friends, but it didn't take much persuasion. Having the attention of an older man was exciting. By the end of the visit, he had proposed. They were married three months later, shortly after her college graduation.

She pasted a smile on her face, "Planning to take it easy this evening?"

"What else is there to do? Thought I'd read." He rose and crossed the room, his gaze raking over her. "You look beautiful."

"Thanks. I'd better get going. I told Sheri I would be there around seven." She turned away to retrieve her purse when Travis's arms snaked around her.

He brushed her hair aside and bent to nuzzle the back of her neck. "Don't go. Stay with me tonight."

Alyssa had to force herself not to flinch from his embrace. She took a deep breath. "I promised Sheri I would come. She called this afternoon. It's been a bad day for her."

Travis pulled away and walked across the room to look out the patio door. "Sheri has become too dependent on you."

"I can't abandon my best friend. The entire fiasco with her ex-husband has been hard for her. She needs someone."

"It's been seven months since the divorce. Eventually, she's going to have to learn to be independent. You have a life. A husband and a home. Why don't I give her a call and—"

"No! You can't do that."

Travis wrinkled his brow. "And why not?"

"I'm sorry. I didn't mean to sound so abrupt. Talking to Sheri wouldn't be a good idea right now. It would probably make things worse. Her trust in men next to non-existent." Alyssa looked away, unable to meet his gaze, and silently praying he would believe her.

Travis sighed. "All right. Go if you must. But next Friday night will be for us. We'll leave town for the long weekend. Celebrate New Year's Eve in San Antonio on the River Walk."

"Don't you think it's kind of late to be making plans?"

"No time like the present."

"But everything will be booked, especially on the River Walk. It's okay if we stay home. We can always visit San Antonio another time."

"I would think you'd be excited about taking a trip. You're the one who's always complaining about never going anywhere. Besides, I have connections. I'll get us a suite, so be sure to tell your friend you won't be available."

Alyssa replayed the conversation as she left for Alpine. Travis's possessiveness had become extreme. She had no life. They never went anywhere these days. No more rodeos, no more stock shows, no fancy vacations. His life was wrapped around the ranch and had become her life too. If he had his way, she would never leave the place.

It came as no surprise that Travis was becoming suspicious. The way he emphasized the word friend confirmed it. Had he guessed she was seeing someone and was using Sheri as a cover? Why else would he suddenly plan a weekend away?

She had no other friends except for Sheri. Well, there was Jesse, but "friends" would hardly be the way to describe what they shared.

With Travis, she had what many women wanted—a rich husband, beautiful home, brand-new luxury SUV, a closet full of designer clothes, and expensive jewelry. Things many women only hope for. But that's all they were. Things.

Jesse gave her something Travis never could—love.

Alyssa's parents and siblings had been less than thrilled about her marriage. They didn't necessarily dislike Travis, but the age difference worried them.

Her brother had concerns about her emotional state. She was in a vulnerable place when she met Travis.

"Don't jump into anything," he had said. "You're emotionally fragile right now."

Alyssa denied his accusations, but the dispute strained their relationship to the point they rarely spoke to one another.

Now, ten years later, Alyssa had to admit her family had been at least partly correct. If she hadn't been in a delicate state of mind, she probably wouldn't have fallen for Travis so easily. And she wouldn't be in a miserable marriage now.

She drove quickly through town. Once she passed the Marfa Lights Viewing Area, she phoned Sheri and told her of the conversation. "I'm convinced Travis suspects something. I think he has someone following me. If he calls, tell him I phoned to say I'm running late and will be there soon."

"Don't worry. I'll cover for you. In fact, why don't the two of you meet here tonight? I can make myself scarce—"

"No. Don't do that. I'll be careful. Thanks for covering for me." Alyssa ended the call and glanced in the rearview mirror at a late model, dark colored sedan. Maybe she was becoming paranoid, but she was sure it had been following since she left Marfa.

What's more, she'd seen the same car a couple of times before, once parked on Jesse's street, and another time it followed her to Sheri's. Someone was tailing her. If Travis wasn't responsible, then who was and why? The police could probably find out quickly enough, but she couldn't report the incidents. They would ask questions she was unwilling to answer.

But if someone investigated it discretely…

Alyssa reached for her phone and called the once-familiar number, praying he would answer.

"Hello?"

"It's Alyssa. I need your help."

She felt guilty calling out of the blue, but time was important.

"Why do you suddenly feel the need to call me?"

"Because I think someone is following me." Then she told him everything that was going on, hoping he would understand.

But revealing her affair only made things worse. He'd always been morally above reproach, but when had he become so self-righteous?

After a few minutes, she'd heard enough.

"You know what, forget it. I'll deal with this myself." She ended the call, then slowed to turn off the main highway. The dark sedan continued to follow.

Alyssa took a few deep breaths and tried to ignore the queasiness in her stomach. She turned onto another street and looked in the mirror. The car was still behind her.

"This is not good." She didn't dare risk phoning Jesse. Travis had access to her cell phone records. It wouldn't be hard to trace the number. Rather than turning onto his street, she drove toward Sheri's house. The black car went in another direction, and Alyssa sighed in relief, then headed to Jesse's. She continued checking her mirror, but no one followed.

IT WAS after midnight when she left his house. The lonely stretch of road between Alpine and Marfa seemed even more deserted than usual. She hadn't passed another car for at least five miles.

Alyssa hated this part of the drive. The road curved through the mountains, and there weren't many signs of habitation outside of Alpine.

Her engine began to sputter. She frowned as she pulled to the side of the road. What could be wrong? The SUV was less than a year old. Travis was careful to have it serviced regularly.

She pressed the button for her cell. Phone service was often sporadic in this area. As luck would have it, she didn't have a signal. Sighing, she considered her options. Wait and hope someone would come along or get out of the car and walk back to town. Maybe if she went a short distance, she could pick up a cell phone signal.

Before she could decide, the lights of a car appeared around a curve. The dark sedan slowed and pulled behind her. Was this the car that followed her earlier? Uncertain of who it might be, Alyssa remained inside.

Her pulse quickened as she watched through the rearview mirror. The driver got out of the car and began walking toward her Lexus.

Sighing with relief at the familiar figure, she smiled and opened the door. "I'm glad to see you. Something is wrong with my SUV, and I can't get a cell phone signal."

"Car trouble? That's the least of your worries."

Alyssa's smile faded as she caught sight of the knife.

CHAPTER 1

Driscoll Lake, Texas
February 2015

*L*ate afternoon sun filtered through the tall pines as Christine Lawrence jogged along the wooded trail. The cloudless sky and gentle breeze energized her. The night promised to be a bit chilly, but spring was on its way. Peepers called from the nearby woods and lake. Tiny buds had already begun to form on the trees.

Only a few people remained at the park. Then again, it was Saturday. Most people had a social life. She didn't. Stopping to catch her breath, she bent over and rested her hands on her knees. Her biggest excitement in life was going home to a good book. When had that happened?

She scoffed at the thought. No need to ask herself that question.

More than three years had passed since Kyle's murder. His death had left a void in her life. One she began to doubt would ever be filled. Her heartache had eased with time, but there were days when the pain of losing her husband was still fresh.

Christine was grateful for the friends who supported her. Both Stephanie Bradford and Rachel Nichols had every right to be bitter about Kyle's actions, yet they were nothing but good to her. They were always careful to give her space when she needed it and were especially attentive near the anniversary of Kyle's death.

This past year, Rachel insisted the three of them get together for a "girls' night out." Christine had been hesitant at first. She often felt out of place. Like she didn't belong. Stephanie's and Rachel's husbands, Matt Bradford and Brian Nichols, were best friends, so both couples often socialized together. She was widowed and alone. Both families had young children. Christine's only daughter was a typical seventeen-year-old.

Despite her reservations, she accepted Rachel's invitation. She and Stephanie were linked in a nearly-tragic way. Had it not been for Curtis Lawrence's intervention, Kyle wouldn't have been the only one killed. Both women would both be dead. Matt and Brian would have been unable to reach them in time.

Ironic. The event that cost Christine her husband was the catalyst that brought Stephanie and Rachel to find theirs.

When a solitary tear slipped from her eye, she hurriedly wiped it from her cheek. Putting aside her thoughts, she straightened and began to stroll along the lakeside path, taking note of her surroundings. A flock of ducks swam near the shore. Squirrels scampered among the branches of the still bare oak trees.

Spring used to be her favorite season. Now she wasn't sure she had a favorite time of year. Winters were cold and lonely, she'd gotten engaged in the spring, their wedding anniversary had been in the summer, and Kyle died in the fall. Autumn only served to remind her of what she had lost.

She had always loathed self-pity. Lately, she seemed to wallow in it. Time to stop. But her mind drifted back to a conversation with Stephanie and Rachel when they met for lunch a few days earlier. Last fall, they began encouraging her to have more of a social life. Neither had resorted to matchmaking, but they'd upped the stakes.

Stephanie spoke first. "I know you miss Kyle. No one can take his place, but you're still young. You shouldn't be alone the rest of your life."

Rachel was quick to agree. "It's been three years. Time for you to start dating. I'm with Stephanie. You're much too young to stop living."

She wasn't opposed to a relationship. *If* the right man came along. So far, he hadn't. Maybe she was too picky.

It wasn't as if she hadn't dated anyone since Kyle's death. She'd been out a few times with a couple of men. One was a colleague from school, the other a local business owner. Both acted as if she needed a man around to watch after her and seemed eager to rush into a commitment—something she didn't want right away. After she ended things with the second man, she'd been reluctant to go out with anyone else.

Her biggest problem was the thought of betraying Kyle. The two of them began dating in high school and had gotten married in college. It wasn't easy to let go of something that lasted almost two decades. But she couldn't—wouldn't—admit her thoughts to anyone.

Instead, she said, "I'm doing fine, but thanks for the concern."

Stephanie hesitated as if trying to choose her words. "We're not trying to interfere. It's just…"

"We want you to be happy," Rachel said. "And right now, you're lonely."

"I am not. I have Emily."

Rachel shook her head. "A child isn't a partner."

She couldn't argue with that. No matter how much she loved her daughter, Emily could never take Kyle's place in her heart.

"Besides, Emily will graduate in a couple of years and be off to college."

Christine hated to admit it, but the closeness she once shared with her daughter had dwindled. Emily acted like a different person since her father's death. First, she became shy and withdrawn—very different from the carefree and outgoing teenager she had been.

Later, she resented Kyle, not only for dying but for withholding information that ultimately led to his death. These days she was temperamental and often disrespectful. If rebellion was one of the stages of grief, Emily was in that phase now.

Sighing, Christine straightened and pulled her cell phone from her pocket, hoping for a text from her daughter. Why was she kidding herself? Emily never called or texted unless she needed something. And that didn't happen very often. She hit the speed dial button for Emily's number.

The phone rang once. Twice. Three times. Surprisingly, Emily answered. "Yeah, Mom? I'm kind of busy right now. What do you want?"

Christine's shoulders stooped, and she blinked her eyes to ward off the tears. What had happened to her loving daughter?

"Wanted to know what you'd like for dinner. I'm at the park right now. Went for a long run. If you want, I'll pick up something in town. Or do you want to go out? Maybe grab a bite to eat in Brewster, then do some shopping too."

"Can't. Gigi invited me to spend the night. She's ordering pizza, and we're going to watch movies."

She sighed, unsure of how she felt about her mother-in-law's sudden appearance in their lives. Darla Martell had shown up a few months ago, shortly after her third husband passed away, and announced she was moving to Driscoll Lake.

She supposed she should be grateful Emily had one grandparent nearby. Her parents lived out of state. Curtis Lawrence had never been closely involved in his granddaughter's life. After learning about the judge's involvement and cover-up in the incident with Stephanie's father, both Christine and Emily broke off all contact with him. His death had been more of a relief than anything.

But Darla was hardly the nurturing type. She had abandoned her own son, choosing instead to live a Bohemian lifestyle.

Had it not been for Kyle initiating contact with her when he was a teenager, Christine doubted she would have ever met the woman. Darla seemed to care about Emily, but she wasn't the typical grand-mother. Until recently, Darla appeared to be still a part of the sixties.

"You're sure spending a lot of time with her. Gigi may get tired of you coming over so often. Besides, we never—"

"She doesn't mind. Bethany's coming too."

"Did her mother say it was okay?"

"No, Mom. Bethany decided to do it, anyway."

Christine could picture Emily rolling her eyes as she spoke.

"Of course, she's okay with it. Bethany called her earlier."

"Well, you didn't bother to ask me. Why don't I get the same courtesy?"

"Mom, can I spend the night at Gigi's?"

It was useless to say no. If she refused, Emily would stay in her room and sulk the entire weekend. No chance of the two of them having some quality time. "Okay, but you need to be home tomorrow afternoon. No spending the night anywhere tomorrow."

"Whatever." The line clicked dead.

Christine slid the phone back into her pocket. She probably should have protested. But Bethany was the only person Emily allowed to penetrate the wall she'd built around herself. The Austins were a respectable family. Myra, the mother, seemed to be a good influence on both girls. The way Christine figured, any time Emily spent with Bethany was good for her, even if it was at Darla's house.

The sun had started to dip below the horizon. It would be dark soon. She had already run her usual number of miles for the day, but additional exercise would help clear her mind. The lakeside trail was a favorite of hers. She had time for at least one lap around the lake. There were always a few runners or walkers who stayed late, so she felt safe. Shrugging, Christine started along the path. It wasn't as if she had anyone waiting for her at home.

VINCE GREEN PAUSED beside the jogging trail and took a deep breath of the fresh air. It was getting late. Only a few cars remained in the parking lot. He'd be lucky to run a mile before darkness fell. Probably should have gone to the gym and done his regular workout. Not only would he have been able to use the treadmill, but he could have done some weight lifting, too.

That had been his original plan. He'd driven there after spending the afternoon in his new office. Had even parked and started walking toward the building when he saw the same manager he had spoken with a couple of nights earlier. Before the man spotted him, he made an about-face, got back into his car, and drove away.

Without conscious thought, he'd ended up at Cameron Park. Stopping to take a few stretches, Vince reflected on that conversation from a couple of nights ago.

"Congratulations, Vince. You're one of our top members this month." The manager pointed to a board with several names. His name was at the top.

"How's that?"

"We base it on the number of visits from the previous month. Except for two days, you were here every evening."

That's what happens when your life outside your job consists of having an occasional beer with the guys. Vince stopped himself before saying the words aloud.

"We like members who are dedicated to fitness."

"Yeah, well, I try." He shrugged. Sure, he worked to stay physically fit—he always had. During his years with the FBI, he had to stay in shape or risk losing his job. Special agents were required to maintain a high level of fitness. Not always the easiest task, given he spent most of his time behind a desk.

"You set a good example for other members."

"I don't know about that. Just trying to keep in shape."

He turned away and went over to the weight benches. Finished his workout in record time and decided to cut back on the number of times he visited the fitness center. Driscoll Lake had several places where he could run. One thing was certain. He wasn't going to the gym on a Saturday evening and announcing to everyone he had nothing better to do.

Something about his conversation with the manager bothered him. More than he wanted to admit. Maybe it was because it made him aware of the present state of his life. Thirty-eight years old, never married, and no serious relationship.

Being single had never bothered him before. For years, he had been "married" to his job. He took pride in his work. In his opinion, being single served to make him a better agent. No ties. No commitments. Nothing to keep him from accepting tough assignments.

But he'd spent most of the last few years pushing papers. It wasn't like this area had high rates of crime that called for the bureau's involvement.

There was a time when he wanted to be at the top. Would have given his eyetooth to be stationed at headquarters in Washington. But things change. The FBI was no longer a part of his life.

Shaking off his thoughts, he finished stretching and started along the trail. He ran faster than usual, his feet pounding the pavement as if doing so he could rid himself of his feelings. Maybe the fresh air was what he needed. Free from the confines of four walls and others nearby. Free from people wanting to strike up a mindless conversation. Maybe coming here this late in the day wasn't such a bad idea, after all.

He hadn't gone far when he saw a woman running along the trail toward him. Her long strawberry-blonde hair was pulled back in a low ponytail, and it swung from side to side as she ran. Vince couldn't help but notice her long, shapely legs. Too bad he never saw her at the gym.

As she drew nearer, he was able to see her face. It was one he would recognize anywhere. The sprinkling of freckles across her nose. The dimple in her chin. The china blue eyes. Christine Lawrence.

Vince slowed his steps as she approached.

"Christine. Didn't know you were a runner." Stupid remark. Why would he know anything about her other than her husband was murdered three years earlier, and her father-in-law was a crook?

"Yeah," she panted breathlessly. "Started a couple of years ago."

"You're out of breath." Another stupid thing to say.

Christine shrugged. "Running faster than usual. Trying to finish for the day. Didn't know you were back in this area."

"Yeah, moved back a couple of months ago." Vince looked toward the lake. "It's nice out here."

"It is. I'd better get going if I want to make it around the lake before dark."

"You're going the entire distance?"

Christine crossed her arms. "I'm perfectly capable."

"Sorry. Didn't mean to insinuate you aren't. But should you be running alone this time of the evening? I could run with you."

"I have a cell phone and this." She pulled a container of pepper spray from her pocket. "Besides, you would have to double back. I'll be fine."

"Thought I'd offer."

"Thanks, but I'm okay."

"Maybe I'll see you around sometime."

"Maybe." Christine smiled before trotting off at a slower pace.

AFTER HER ENCOUNTER WITH VINCE, Christine couldn't seem to regain her momentum. To say she was surprised to see him would be an understatement.

She met him during the investigation into her father-in-law's alleged involvement in Phillip Denton's embezzlement scheme. After Curtis Lawrence went to prison on charges of obstruction of justice and assault, Vince called a few times to check on her. He seemed nice enough. Never pushy.

A year later, they had shared a few dances at Matt and Stephanie's wedding. Christine couldn't deny Vince was attractive. Tall, light brown hair, hazel eyes. She had noticed the envious looks she'd received from several women.

She'd found herself hoping he would call to ask her out. But he never did. Not long after assisting Matt in capturing the arsonist that had targeted Brian Nichols, Vince had dropped off the radar.

She often wanted to ask Stephanie if Matt knew anything about him, but she didn't dare. Knowing her friend, she would believe the questions to be more than idle curiosity and attempt to play match-maker. After her dinner with Stephanie and Rachel a couple of nights ago, Christine was glad she hadn't asked. The two of them would be in full-conspiratorial mode.

Looking back, she realized Rachel had been prepared to do a bit of matchmaking even back then. Vince had worn a business suit most of the time, but he'd looked great that night in jeans and boots. She liked the casual look.

His hair was a bit longer now than the almost military-like style he once wore. And now that she'd seen him in running shorts and a t-shirt…

No sense in wondering what might have been. If Vince had been interested, he wouldn't have left town without telling her. He'd been back for two months and hadn't attempted to contact her. So much for anything developing between them. He obviously wasn't interested.

Christine slowed to a walk when she neared the parking area. The sun had already dipped below the horizon. She debated on calling it quits, but it wouldn't take too much longer to finish the entire loop.

Determined to continue, she picked up her speed. But as she crossed the dam on the far side of the lake, she began to have second thoughts. The path curved slightly away from the water and through a grove of tall pines. Twilight had descended. Security lights on this side of the lake were few and far between. Christine wished now she'd taken Vince's offer to run together. Since he was running the same trail in the opposite direction, they should meet up soon. No point in turning back now.

As she rounded a curve, she noticed something large beside the trail and slowed her pace. An animal? Not likely. Too large for a coyote or dog. Bears and mountain lions weren't native to this part of the state.

Even a predatory animal would move. This object was perfectly still. Fighting the desire to flee, she pressed forward and came to an abrupt stop.

A woman's body lay at the edge of the woods, her back toward the trail. It was hard to see in the dim light, but her clothes appeared to be covered in dark stains.

Blood?

Christine screamed, her body trembling. *Oh, my God.*

She clutched her chest, unable to move. Blood rushed in her ears, drowning out everything but the sound of footfalls—fast-paced and getting louder.

Someone was racing straight for her.

CHAPTER 2

*V*ince admitted there was something to be said about outdoor exercise. Fresh, clean air. The whisper of a gentle breeze in the pines. The smell of the earth as it began to warm with the oncoming of spring.

Most of all, he enjoyed the feeling of openness. Far different from running on a treadmill inside a stuffy building where music played too loud, and people often crowded too close.

But next time he'd make a point to get an earlier start. The light had faded, leaving behind shadows and dark patches along the ground. While he appreciated the efforts to keep the park as natural as possible, right now he wished there were a few lights around. Running in the dark, even though the path was smooth, wasn't the safest thing to do.

Had it not been for Christine's insistence on upon running alone, he would have turned back before now. Unless she had changed her mind, he would be meeting up with her soon. He wasn't about to leave her on the dark trail alone even though she insisted she could take care of herself.

He'd often thought of Christine after he left Driscoll Lake. They had become acquainted when her husband died. He found her attractive, but the timing was wrong. She needed time to grieve. A year later, he'd spent a little time with her during Matt Bradford's wedding reception. She'd still seemed a bit withdrawn. He'd planned to call and ask her out, but a few months after the wedding, his world fell apart.

All the training he had received at the academy didn't prepare him for what happened. Some people tended to think of FBI agents as hardened individuals, immune to feelings and emotions. Diane, his one serious relationship since joining the agency, often accused him of being cold-hearted and uncaring.

After being together a couple of years, she walked in one day and announced it was over. Said she was no longer willing to share him with anyone, least of all the FBI. He later learned the real reason she chose to leave.

Sure, he could have been more attentive. Maybe if he had been, she wouldn't have had a reason to leave. He was younger then. Wanted to make a good impression with his superiors. Determined to be the best in his profession. Becoming involved in a serious relationship had been foolish. He didn't make that mistake again. Maybe Diane had been right. He was without emotion.

No, that came later. Everything changed in one night. A night he wanted to forget. A night that should have never happened.

A rustling sound interrupted his thoughts. He tensed, looked around. Laughed at himself when a raccoon scampered across the path toward the lake. He was starting to relax when a scream sliced through the silence. A woman's scream.

Christine? Vince doubted a small animal would frighten her. Maybe startle her, but that wasn't a startled cry. It was the shriek of someone who was terrified. It was primal. Urgent.

He doubled his speed until he spotted her near the edge of the path, her silhouette barely visible in the dark. She appeared to be looking down at something crumpled beside the trail.

As Vince drew closer, he could tell she was visibly shaken. Arms clamped around her waist. Lips and chin quivering. Eyes wide and unblinking.

She pointed to the ground.

"It's a woman. She's… I… I think she's dead."

Taking care not to disturb a possible crime scene, Vince placed his fingertips on the woman's carotid artery. No pulse.

"Is that blood?"

"Yes. Get your cell phone and turn on the flashlight."

Her hands shook as she pulled the phone from her pocket and pointed the light toward the ground. Long blonde hair cascaded down the woman's back. She was covered in blood and appeared to have been stabbed multiple times.

Vince clenched his jaw. Another victim of a violent crime. So similar...

"Someone killed her?"

"Yes."

Christine's voice quivered. "What if... what if the killer is still close?"

"Not likely. Too big a risk of being seen."

"But... He could be. We've got to get out of here." Sobbing, she began to back away.

Vince put his hands on her shoulders, careful not frighten her further. "Hey, it will be all right. Take a few deep breaths. They'll help calm you down."

When he sensed she had begun to regain control, he said, "There. That's better. You okay now?"

She sniffled. "Yeah, I guess."

"Good. We need to call 9-1-1. You're right. This is murder."

MATT BRADFORD PULLED his pickup through the service entrance of Cameron Park after the young officer guarding the gate waved him through. A crowd had already gathered outside. He rolled his eyes. Didn't take long for word to spread.

He had grown up in Driscoll Lake, but it never ceased to amaze him how people reacted to things. Small town folk tended to be overly curious. He supposed he couldn't blame them. It wasn't as if a murder happened here every day.

To make matters worse, the editor of the *Driscoll Lake Reporter* was at the scene. Tami Sutton had been out of town for several weeks. Matt wished she was still away. The two of them had disagreed on more than one occasion, the first being her decision to continue a weekly police report column.

"Might as well face it," she had said, "the column is boring, but so little excitement happens around here. People in this town want to know things. Why not let me in on a little more? Your officers are too closed-mouth."

Matt was adamant. "Which I support. If you think the column is boring, then drop it. I'm sure you can find other things to fill the space."

But she hadn't. Tami continued to publish the column.

So, it came as no surprise when she called out to him.

"Chief Bradford, my sources say a young woman was murdered. What can you tell us?"

"No comment at this time."

"Come now. Surely you know something."

"I only arrived a couple of minutes ago. Haven't even been to the crime scene. Someone will give a statement later." He turned away before she could protest.

Matt walked the short distance to the sealed-off area. Detective Jason Montgomery was already on the scene. He should be. It was his job. But this wasn't the first time Matt found himself wishing Carlos Gonzales hadn't retired. Matt trusted the veteran detective. Carlos had years of experience and wisdom.

Jason had yet to prove himself. He liked to do things his way and wasn't good at taking orders. Matt often regretted hiring him, but he was the most experienced of the three candidates who'd applied for the position. It wasn't like many seasoned detectives were breaking down the door to work in a small town like Driscoll Lake.

Jason looked up as Matt approached. "Boss, what are you doing here?"

He inwardly cringed at the word. Jason had taken to referring to him as boss a few weeks ago, and he hated it, which was why the term stuck. But Matt wasn't about to give him the satisfaction of showing his annoyance.

"Last time I checked, I was still the police chief."

"And the last time I checked, I was hired as a detective. Don't think I'm capable of handling this one?"

Matt ignored the question. "What have you got?"

"Female, approximately thirty years of age, multiple stab wounds. Couldn't have been dead long before the body was discovered."

"ID?"

"Got a name. Had an out of state drivers license, but Officer Tyson thinks she worked in one of those shops in Cameron Place."

"Oh, yeah? Who found her?"

"Couple of runners." Jason nodded to a park bench about twenty feet away. Matt immediately recognized Vince and Christine.

"They're the ones who found the body?"

"Yeah. You know them?"

"Friends of mine. Vince Green and Christine Lawrence. What did they say?"

"Officer Tyson was the first on the scene. Told them to wait over there. I only asked a couple of general questions and explained I would speak to them soon."

"Why wait?"

"I've been busy. I'll get to them when I get to them."

"Did it occur to you they might have other things to do than to sit around and wait? Or that she might be a little anxious?"

"No."

Matt took a deep breath, trying to squelch his anger. "Courtesy goes a long way in this town."

"Maybe so, but this is my investigation."

"That it is."

"Glad you agree."

"By the way, if you'd bothered talking with them when you first arrived, you might already have a positive ID on the victim. Christine's mother-in-law owns an art gallery at Cameron Place. Maybe she knows something. But since you're sure of what you're doing, I'll leave you to do your job." Matt started toward Christine and Vince, but not before he caught the look in Jason's eyes. And he wasn't sure he liked what he saw.

CHRISTINE STOOD in the small windowless room, wishing she were anywhere else. Why did Detective Montgomery feel the need to talk with her and Vince at the police station? In an interrogation room? Separately? Did he consider them to be suspects?

When he first spoke to them, he seemed arrogant but gave no indication his questions would be anything other than routine. Something happened between then and when Montgomery came back to talk to them. His demeanor had changed completely.

"I need the two of you to come down to the station."

"Why?" Vince asked.

"I have quite a few questions. It's getting late. Better to do it there."

"Tonight? I don't see why—"

"Do you have a problem with it, Mr. Green?"

"Christine—Ms. Lawrence—has been through a lot today. She also has a teenage daughter. and I'm sure she's anxious to get home to her."

Christine shook her head. "Emily is with my mother-in—her grandmother."

"Then it's not a problem," Jason said.

Vince persisted. "Why the rush? We told your officer everything we know. I don't see how our going to the police station would help anything. Whatever you need to know can wait until morning."

"I'm afraid it can't. We can do this the easy way or—"

"Is that a threat, Detective?"

Christine placed her hand on Vince's arm to calm him. "It's okay, Vince. I'd rather get this over with."

"Are you sure?"

She nodded. "But my SUV is in the far lot on the other side of the lake."

"Mine's closer. I'll drive you."

Jason Montgomery was quick to speak. "Not necessary. Officer Tyson can take you both to the station."

"In a squad car?" Christine didn't like that idea.

"Ma'am, I'll take you to your vehicle," the young officer said. "That way you won't have to come back for it later."

Montgomery didn't look pleased with the idea, but Tyson reminded him it's what Chief Bradford would have him do.

The detective relented, but only with the stipulation the officer follow her. Now she waited. Montgomery hadn't even given her time to change clothes. After darkness fell, the temperature began to drop. Too cold for shorts and a tank top. Fortunately, she had a pair of sweatpants and a jacket in her car and was able to slip them on before entering the station.

She knew Matt wouldn't believe she and Vince had anything to do with the killing. So, what was going on? And why was the detective making her wait? Had he already spoken to Vince?

The door opened, and Jason Montgomery entered the room carrying a cup of coffee and a legal pad. "Something to drink?"

Christine shook her head. "Can we get on with this?"

The detective sat down at the end of the table and nodded for her to take a seat. "Tell me what happened."

She repeated the same things she said to Officer Tyson. Yes, she found the body first. No, she didn't plan to meet Vince at the park. Yes, she had seen him earlier because they were running the trail in opposite directions. No, she didn't hear or see anyone nearby.

"How long have you known Vince Green?"

"I met him when my husband was killed three years ago."

"You've become close friends since then?"

Christine took a deep breath, trying to control her anger. What was this guy insinuating? "And why would that be any of your business?"

"Just answer the question."

"I consider Vince a friend, but I wouldn't say we're close."

"Meeting him at the park was a coincidence?"

"Yes. Today is the first time I've seen him in a couple of years."

Jason smirked. "Interesting. Did you know the victim?"

"To be honest, I didn't look at her face."

"Tell me about the relationship with your mother-in-law."

"My mother-in-law? What's she got to do with this?"

"How close are the two of you?"

"We're not."

"You said earlier your daughter was with her. Sounds like you've got some type of rapport if you allow your daughter to visit her."

"Emily spends a lot of time with her grandmother, but I barely know the woman. Darla walked out on my husband Kyle when he was young. I only saw her a couple of times before he died. She moved to Driscoll Lake about a year ago."

"Does the name Jenny Allen mean anything to you?"

"Should it?

"You tell me. She worked for your mother-in-law at the art gallery."

"I've only been to the gallery a couple of times."

Jason tapped his pen on the legal pad. "Let me get this straight. Jenny worked for your mother-in-law, but you didn't know her name because you aren't a frequent visitor to the gallery."

As I said, Darla and I don't exactly have a close relationship. What does all this have to do with a murder investigation?"

"Because," Jason paused for a moment. "Your mother-in-law's employee is the murder victim."

THE DEED WAS DONE. Finished. The rush of adrenaline had passed. It was time to relax. Savor the moment.

What were the odds of Jenny moving to Driscoll Lake? Had to be fate. Luring her to the park had been easy. She was so unsuspecting. So naive of things to come. The look on her face when she realized she was about to die. Reminiscent of another time and another place.

By now, someone would have found the body. Police would investigate. People would wonder if there would be another killing. Women would fear they would be the next victim. They needn't worry. There was no reason for alarm, but no one could know that.

One thing was certain. Jenny Allen wouldn't hurt anyone ever again.

∽

VINCE PACED the floor of the police station lobby. Years of training had taught him to keep calm and collected, but tonight's questioning by that sorry excuse for a detective was enough to try the patience of a saint. And Vince was a long way from sainthood.

Who did the guy think he was? Jason Montgomery hadn't bothered to ask him anything about his background. Otherwise, he probably wouldn't have acted overconfident. It might have been amusing to see the look on the detective's face upon learning he was talking to a former FBI agent.

He waited for Jason to finish questioning Christine. No way would he leave her here alone, even though she insisted she could handle it. She was upset enough without having to endure a barrage of questions by the arrogant detective.

Vince turned at the sound of a door opening. One look at Christine made him glad he stayed. She looked a bit shaken as she walked toward him.

"You're still here."

"Told you I wasn't going anywhere. What happened in there?"

"Most of what he asked I had already told Officer Tyson. Except—"

Vince lowered his voice. "Hold that thought until we get outside. Montgomery is watching—and listening."

Christine nodded and managed a faint smile when Vince held the door. They walked in silence until they reached her car. "Did he tell you they've identified the woman? Her name is Jenny Allen."

"Yes. Asked me if I knew her. Told him I recently returned to this area. He backed off after that."

"He asked me the same things. Then he started questioning me about Darla."

"Who's Darla?"

"Kyle's mother. She moved here a few months ago. Opened an art gallery at the factory."

"Where?"

"I mean Cameron Place. Hard to think of it by that name."

Vince nodded in acknowledgment. Many of Driscoll Lake's long-time residents still thought of the buildings that once housed Cameron Manufacturing as the old factory even though the business closed in the 1990s. By the time he moved to this area, the building had been vacant for years until Brian Nichols purchased the property and revitalized it. Cameron Place now boasted a selection of desirable restaurants and specialty shops.

"Anyway, Jenny worked at the gallery. The detective kept asking me if Darla and I have a close relationship."

"Do you?"

Christine shook her head. "Emily spends a lot of time with her. It's hard for me to forgive the woman who left her young son because she wanted to live a carefree lifestyle."

"I can understand. Don't imagine it was easy for Kyle."

"No, it wasn't. Especially having to live with someone like Curtis Lawrence. But I don't want to talk about the judge."

Vince glanced at his watch. It was getting late, and he hadn't eaten since lunch. Christine probably hadn't either. "Want to go somewhere and grab a cup of coffee or something to eat? Might help get your mind off things."

"Thanks, but I'm exhausted. All I want to do is go home, get a hot shower, and try to relax. Maybe I'll open a can of soup or something."

"Want me to follow you home?"

"Appreciate the offer, but I'm fine."

"If you're sure."

"Yes. I'll be okay. Ready to put this behind me."

"That's one thing we can agree on. I'll call you tomorrow."

CHAPTER 3

*A*fter leaving the police station, Vince decided to drive straight to his house. It had been a long day. Christine had the right idea about relaxing at home.

He showered, then put on shorts and a t-shirt. Went into the kitchen and rummaged through the refrigerator and cabinets. He had the ingredients for an omelet, but that didn't sound appealing right now.

Not only that, he was restless. He had tried to remain calm for Christine's sake, but the murder of Jenny Allen had shaken him. A senseless crime. Who killed her and why? Would the police be able to find the killer? Doubtful if the only investigator was Jason Montgomery.

Hard to believe Matt would hire someone so inept. Or maybe it was an act. Surely someone in Montgomery's position couldn't be that stupid. Vince made a mental note to talk with Matt on Monday.

So much for relaxing. He needed to get out of the house, so he went back into the bedroom and dressed in jeans, boots, and a long-sleeved Henley shirt. It was almost eleven. Even the restaurants that stayed open late on weekends would close at midnight. The only options were fast food places and a couple of twenty-four-hour diners near the interstate.

He grabbed his keys, then hurried outside, where he climbed into his BMW. He fiddled with the radio until he found a station playing jazz. Not his usual choice of music, but he needed something calming. The soft sounds had a soothing effect.

Vince drove slowly through the quiet streets. Deciding he didn't want fast food, he headed to one of the diners, then parked next to a red Corvette that entered the parking lot ahead of him.

He immediately recognized the driver and waved when he got out of the car. "Hey, Brian."

Brian Nichols nodded in recognition. "Vince! Matt told me you were back in town. Figured I would have seen you before now."

"Still getting settled in. But I'm surprised to see you out this late."

"Rachel and Dylan are with her family this weekend. Radical played at an event tonight. Going to grab a bite to eat before going home. You meeting anyone?"

"No. Here alone."

"Want to join me?"

"Sure."

Once they were seated, the server brought menus. "What can I get you to drink?"

"Coffee. Decaf," Vince said.

"I'll have a root beer."

"Coming right up." The server walked away.

Brian waited until she was out of earshot. "I think the last time I saw you was two years ago at Pinnacle. Never got a chance to say thanks for wrestling the gun from Clay. You probably saved Rachel's life."

"Glad I was there to help."

"You still with the agency?"

Vince shook his head. "Left about eighteen months ago. Lived in Dallas for a while. Grew tired of the big city, got my PI license. Decided to move back here and open an office."

Brian's jaw dropped. "You left the FBI? Figured you'd transferred somewhere else. What happened?"

Vince looked away for a moment. "Life. Things happen you don't expect. Something I really don't want to talk about."

"Sorry. Didn't mean to pry, but somehow I can't imagine you not being an FBI agent."

"And I never imagined you having a wife and child."

Brian smiled. "Point taken. But I wouldn't trade my life for anything right now."

When the server returned, Brian ordered a burger and fries. Vince decided on a sausage and mushroom omelet. He chuckled as she walked away.

"What's so funny?"

"I was going to make an omelet at home. Decided I didn't want one. Guess what I needed was to get out of the house."

"Rough day?"

"You can't imagine. It started okay until I happened to run into Christine at Cameron Park."

"And that's a problem?"

"Seeing Christine? No. It's what happened afterward." Vince relayed the events of the evening to Brian, including his dislike of how Jason Montgomery handled the situation.

"Not surprising. Matt's had trouble with him before. Jason wasn't the ideal candidate, but he had few to choose from. City council wanted Matt to hire someone right away, rather than wait."

"Poor decision on their part if you ask me."

"You should talk to Matt. Tell him what happened."

"I'd already considered it."

"Do it. He'd want to know."

VINCE VISITED with Brian for over an hour. It was good to catch up. He hadn't realized how much he'd missed the laid-back atmosphere of Driscoll Lake. Being here was like coming home. Living in a big city no longer held its appeal.

One advantage of the city was the ability to blend in with the crowd. Go virtually unnoticed. Often useful in his line of work. Not so in a small town.

Maybe that was the reason he couldn't completely relax during dinner. His instincts said someone was watching him. But who and why? The diner wasn't crowded. A couple of DPS officers had stopped in for a while. Two truck drivers were in a booth near the door. Another man sat at the counter, drinking a cup of coffee.

A young couple finished their meal, then walked to the motel next door. The only other customer was a woman seated near the back. She read while she ate, keeping her head down most of the time.

No reason to suspect anyone.

He and Brian paid their check, then walked outside together. By then, the diner was empty.

"Driving the 'Vette, huh?"

"Yeah. Rachel couldn't bring herself to sell it, so I get it out of the garage on occasion. Nice set of wheels you have." Brian nodded toward the BMW.

"Thanks. I—" Vince couldn't shake the feeling of being watched. He took a glance around the parking lot but didn't see anyone.

"Something wrong?"

Vince shook his head. "Nah. Feeling a little edgy."

"Understandable, given what happened today."

"Yeah, I guess. I'd better get out of here. See you around?"

"You bet." Brian smiled as he got into his car.

Vince's uneasiness didn't subside until he reached his house. Strange. A good investigator didn't allow feelings to cloud his judgment. If he'd been working a case... On the other hand, his instincts had served to keep him alive on more than one occasion.

But why would having a casual meal with a friend set him on edge?

THE TWO MEN got into the sports cars, then drove away in opposite directions. It had been so easy to watch without being seen. Neither one of them was the wiser.

It would have been nice to hear their conversation. To get an idea of what was happening. But patience was a virtue. The time would come.

They would meet again.

CHAPTER 4

*B*right sunshine streamed through the bedroom window when Christine awoke the following morning. She had tossed and turned the first part of the night, replaying the day's events in her mind. Even the glass of wine she drank before going to bed did little to soothe her restlessness. It was well after midnight before sleep overtook her.

After a long stretch, she rolled over to look at the clock and was surprised to see it was almost nine. It had been a long time since she'd slept this late. The wine must have done the trick after all. She got out of bed, then dressed quickly in a t-shirt and pair of sweats before going into the kitchen.

A few minutes later, she sat down in the sunroom with a cup of coffee. She had always loved the atmosphere with its light, airy feel. On spring and summer evenings, she often opened the floor-to-ceiling windows and enjoyed the natural breeze. In the winter, a wood-burning stove kept the area warm and cozy.

It used to be her favorite place to sit and read or relax. These days she spent most of the time in her bedroom. There, she had a haven. A place away from Emily's frequent tirades and too loud music.

The house was peaceful this morning. A welcome reprieve. Christine supposed she should feel a little guilty, but she was glad Emily was with Darla. It wasn't often she was able to enjoy a quiet morning alone. But now she had time to reflect upon her life. When had she allowed herself to become a prisoner in her own home?

Something had to change. Maybe Rachel and Stephanie were right. It was time she began dating. But who? Vince? The idea brought a smile to her face. Why had she been opposed to the two of them running together yesterday? Why was it so important for her to show her independent streak?

When Kyle died, Vince had to question her about her father-in-law's involvement with Phillip Denton. He'd acted as if he'd rather wait until she'd had time to come to terms with Kyle's murder, but he never gave the impression he believed she couldn't take care of herself.

If she had taken him up on his offer to run together, they might have decided to take a different trail. They could have gone for a cup of coffee or a bite to eat afterward. She wouldn't have found that poor woman's body.

Vince had been right. She shouldn't have been running alone so close to dark. If this was a random killing, she could have easily been the victim. She closed her eyes and shook her head to ward off the thought.

Her phone rang, and she glanced at the caller ID before answering. Darla. "Hello?"

"I hope you don't mind, but I allowed Emily to attend church with Bethany. Myra Austin will bring her home after lunch."

Christine wasn't opposed to the idea, but she would have liked to have been consulted first. But she welcomed any positive influence in Emily's life. "That's fine."

"The reason I allowed her to go is that I got a call from a Detective Montgomery this morning. He's coming by the house to question me about something. Said he talked to you last night. Any idea what it's about?"

"Yeah, I do. A woman was murdered yesterday evening in Cameron Park when I was out jogging. I found the body."

"Oh, no, darling. Are you all right? You should have called me. You must have been terrified."

"I was okay. Vince offered to follow me home."

"Vince? Who's that?"

"A friend. He's the FBI agent who worked Curtis's case. Happened to be running nearby and came when I screamed."

"Lucky for you. Who better to have around than the FBI when a murder has been committed?"

"True, but it's not his investigation. The detective questioned both of us. Acted as if we were suspects."

"You're kidding. Why?"

"Montgomery didn't tell you?"

"Tell me what?"

"The victim's name. Darla, it was the woman who worked in your gallery."

"Jenny? It can't be."

"I'm afraid it's true."

"When did it happen?"

"Not sure. She hadn't been dead long when I found her."

"I can't believe it. Jenny volunteered to stay and close the gallery so that I could leave early. But what's that have to do with you? Other than you were the person to find her?"

"Montgomery became suspicious when he connected me to Jenny through you."

"Why?"

"You'll have to ask him. I'm surprised he didn't drag you down to the station last night."

"He should be here any minute. I don't know what I can tell him. I was here most of the evening with Emily and Bethany."

"I'm sure he'll want to verify that. He's a bit, well, I should say he's downright arrogant and pushy."

"I can handle people like him."

No doubt about that. Darla Martell wasn't the type to allow anyone to push her around. Probably one of the reasons her marriage to Curtis Lawrence failed. "I'm sure you can, but don't say I didn't warn you."

The doorbell rang. "I've got to go. Someone's at the door. Let me know what happens." Christine stood, then walked to the front of the house.

Looking out the window, she saw a late model BMW parked in the driveway. *Vince. Great. And here I am slouching around with no make-up. Oh well, he saw me yesterday all sweaty from running. I've got to look better now than then.*

Christine glanced in the mirror, smoothed her hair, then opened the door. "Vince, I'm surprised to see you this morning."

"I, uh… I was in the neighborhood. You okay?"

Christine exhaled slowly. "Getting there. Have time for a cup of coffee?"

"Sure." Vince followed her into the kitchen. "Nice place you have here."

"Thanks. It's bigger than I need. I've thought about selling but… I don't know."

"Memories?"

"Yeah. Emily will leave for college next year. Good time for a change, I guess." She poured coffee into a mug then handed it to Vince. "Cream or sugar?"

"Black is fine."

"Have a seat." Christine refilled her own cup before joining Vince at the table.

"So, were you able to rest?"

"A little. I think it was sometime around three when I finally fell asleep. You?"

Vince took a sip of coffee. "I was restless. Went home but didn't stay. Ended up at one of those all-night diners near the interstate. Happened to see Brian Nichols. We talked for a while."

"Brian was there? Alone?"

"Yeah. The band had finished playing at some function, and he was there to grab a bite to eat."

"That's right. I forgot Rachel is in Austin this weekend."

"What did you think of Driscoll Lake's new detective?"

"Don't ask."

"Officer Tyson seemed embarrassed by Montgomery's actions."

Christine shrugged. "It wasn't his fault. He was caught in the middle. Montgomery, on the other hand, needs to change his ways if he wants people in this town to accept him."

"Well, he's young. Cocky. Eventually, something will happen to deflate his ego."

"One can only hope." She smiled. "Say, have you eaten breakfast? I was about to make pancakes before you arrived. You're welcome to join me."

"I haven't eaten, and I'd very much like to join you."

Christine and Vince ate a leisurely breakfast. Afterward, he helped her clean up the kitchen. She enjoyed his company. They chatted about various things, catching up on the past couple of years.

She had been surprised to learn he was no longer with the FBI. When she asked why he seemed reluctant to discuss the matter.

"I always wanted to be a private investigator. Everyone needs a change now and then." He quickly changed the subject. "Tell me about you. How is your daughter?"

"Typical teenage girl. What more can I say?"

Christine had finished loading the dishwasher when the doorbell rang. Too soon for Emily. Even so, she wouldn't ring the bell. She would use her key.

"If you're expecting someone, I can leave," Vince said.

"No. Please, wait here. I'll be right back." She went to the door to find Darla standing on the front step.

Without waiting to be invited in, she barged into the hallway and threw her hands in the air. "I can't believe the nerve of that man."

"Who?"

"I have a mind to call Matt Bradford and report him."

"You must be talking about Detective Montgomery."

"Whatever his name is. He's got gall. I'll give him that. Practically accused me of being involved in Jenny's murder." Darla continued walking toward the kitchen. "Do you have some iced tea, dear? I need something to drink, and it's too early in the day for something stronger."

Christine hurried to follow. Vince stood as the two women entered the room.

"Oh, dear. I'm sorry. Didn't know you had company. Hope I didn't interrupt anything." Darla gave Vince the once over, then turned back to Christine and winked.

Christine's face grew warm. What was Darla thinking? "You didn't interrupt. We just finished breakfast. This is my friend Vince Green. He's the one who was at the park yesterday and stopped by this morning to check on me. Vince, this is Emily's grandmother, Darla Martell."

"Oh, I see. So, you're the FBI agent."

Vince extended his hand. "Used to be. I'm a private investigator now."

Darla pulled a pitcher from the refrigerator, filled a glass with ice, then poured tea.

"Got any limes?"

Christine shook her head.

Darla sat down at the table, then took a sip of the ice-cold beverage. "As I was saying, Montgomery has some nerve. Pi— Made me angry from the start. I suppose he thought he was acting nice by questioning me in my home. But insinuating I was elderly caused my blood to boil. I may not be thirty-something, but I can run circles around that pompous jackass."

Christine didn't doubt Darla's words. She never revealed her age, but Christine estimated around sixty-five, though she looked much younger. Her ash blonde hair was short and smartly styled. Her clothes fashionable.

Today Darla wore a pair of black slacks and a teal blouse with long sleeves that flared at the elbows. It looked like something someone would have worn in the early seventies, but Christine knew she only shopped at the finest stores.

A few years ago, she had worn a long flowery dress to Kyle's funeral. Her hair was longer then and not styled. These days Darla dressed more professionally—maybe because she'd become a business owner and felt she needed to look the part.

On the other hand, it could be because she was seeing a banker from Brewster. Her last husband was an artist. A holdover from the sixties. The banker was more conservative.

Seemed Darla dressed to match her lifestyle.

Christine quickly banished the thought. It wasn't as if Darla had a string of men in her life. She had been married to Andrew Morgan for more than twenty years when he died. Her second husband was a bit of a mystery, but no one could blame her for divorcing Curtis Lawrence.

Darla continued to rant. "The more I think about it, the more determined I am to talk to Matt."

"Come on. Did he actually say you were old?" Christine looked at Vince as she spoke. He appeared to be trying to suppress a grin.

"Not in so many words. Told me he came to the house as a 'convenience' to me. Said it would prevent me from having to make a trip to the police station. Like it's a thousand miles or something. Huh! I could have easily walked there."

"Be glad Montgomery didn't drag you to police headquarters."

"He made you go into the station?"

Christine nodded. "Vince, too. Questioned us separately."

"And Matt allowed this?"

"I don't think he was aware. He was only at the murder site for a brief time."

Darla pursed her lips. "Then he needs to know."

Vince spoke up. "I've considered talking to him. How did Montgomery treat you? Did he insinuate you might be involved?"

"At first, it seemed he wanted to pin it on me. Asked where I was between five and seven. After I told him I was home with the girls, and could easily verify it, he backed off. He wanted to know when I last saw Jenny. What I knew about her friends and family. Things like that."

Vince shrugged. "Standard questions."

"Then he asked me to accompany him to the morgue to identify the body." Darla lowered her gaze as she spoke.

Christine reached for Darla's hand. "I'm sorry. That must have been difficult for you."

"There wasn't anyone else to do it."

"What did you know about her? I only saw her once or twice. She seemed quiet and reserved whenever I was in the gallery," Christine said.

"She was quiet, but she knew about art. That's why I hired her. She never talked about her family. Said she moved here from San Antonio. That's about it. Can't know much about someone who had only been in town a month."

"Wonder what brought her to Driscoll Lake."

"What brings anyone to this place? I would have never left Marfa if not for you and Emily."

"Marfa? You lived in *Marfa?*" Vince asked.

"Almost fifteen years. Why do you ask?"

Vince cleared his throat. "No particular reason. I, uh… I once knew someone who was with the border patrol near Alpine."

"It's possible I know them. Marfa is a small town. Does your friend still live in the area?"

"No." He lowered his voice. "Not anymore."

CHAPTER 5

*M*onday morning came all too soon for Christine. Having an extra day to recover from the weekend would have been nice. She needed more time to reflect on everything that had happened.

Vince had seemed somewhat melancholy after Darla's departure. Christine wasn't sure what brought about the difference in his mood, but after the mention of his changing careers, he acted differently. The other possibility was the reference to Marfa.

There was a reason for his reaction, and Christine would be willing to bet it involved more than knowing someone with the border patrol.

Whatever the case, Vince had been reluctant to discuss either situation. He left not long after Darla, saying he had some things to do.

Christine had a few precious moments alone, then Emily barged through the door. But instead of launching into one of her frequent outbursts, she acted empathetic toward her mother.

"Mom, I heard what happened. Are you okay?"

"I'm fine."

"It must have been terrible for you. Finding that woman's body. I can't imagine something like that."

"How did you know it was me? Did Gigi tell you?"

"She didn't have to. Everyone is talking about it."

Christine rolled her eyes. It didn't take the news long to spread. She would have to face a bombardment of questions at work.

Emily's calm demeanor didn't last long. When Christine asked if she had homework, her reply was short and sarcastic. "Don't I always?"

"And how much of it have you completed?"

"Some."

"Don't you think you'd better start working on it?"

"Whatever." Emily stormed out of the den and shut herself in her bedroom. Didn't bother to eat dinner or even leave her room until almost nine. Then it was only to announce she had finished all her work. "You can relax now."

Her mood hadn't improved the following morning. She sulked through breakfast, barely saying two words. Afterward, she grabbed her backpack, then went to the car a good ten minutes before Christine was ready to leave.

Emily's actions did nothing to improve Christine's mood. She could have used some help carrying things to the car—not that her daughter offered. Two trips later, she had everything loaded. As she backed out of the driveway, she realized she had left the front door unlocked.

What else could go wrong today? She pulled into the circular drive, parked, then hurried toward the house. Had almost reached the entrance when she heard her next-door neighbor call out.

Libby Gordon had moved to Driscoll Lake near the end of summer and was now the new high school art teacher. Emily was in one of her classes. The woman was friendly enough, but pretty much kept to herself. Despite her quiet demeanor, Emily seemed to like her as well as the class. At least Christine thought so. Hard to tell what her daughter liked and didn't like these days.

"Good morning, Christine. Looks like it's going to be a nice day." She smiled as she approached.

"I hadn't even noticed," Christine said. "One of those mornings."

Libby looked toward the SUV where Emily sat with her earbuds. "Let me guess. Your daughter?"

"Among other things. Sometimes I don't know how to reach her. We once had a close relationship. But her father was murdered a few years ago, and since his death, Emily and I seem to have drifted apart."

"I heard about it. I'm sure it was hard for both of you."

"It was. Not only did I have to face my husband's death, but I've had to live with knowing he kept a secret for twenty years. One that affected my two best friends." Why was she telling this to a woman who was practically a stranger? The maxim must be true—it was easier to talk to someone you don't know than to someone with whom you were vulnerable.

Libby nodded her head. "I had heard talk, but I didn't want to ask."

"Long story." She'd already said too much. "Anyway, sorry for unloading on you about my daughter."

"It's okay. I teach teenagers, remember?"

"Something I don't envy."

"She's a good kid. She'll come around."

"Wish I could be as optimistic as you."

When Tami Sutton arrived at the office of the Driscoll Lake Reporter, long-time employee Madge Sinclair's car was already in the parking lot. Tami admired the older woman, who came highly recommended by the former editor, Pat Turner.

At almost seventy, Madge still worked every day. She ran the office with the speed and efficiency of someone half her age, was friendly with customers, and had a good rapport with the other staff members.

Pat Turner, the previous editor, was a lifelong resident of Driscoll Lake—which Tami saw as an asset, and most everyone respected her. Tami found it difficult to fill her shoes. Madge helped ease the transition.

She was once a notorious gossip. Pat said she could dig up information on anyone and once referred to her as a walking newspaper. But she was quick to point out the older woman had changed her ways.

Too bad. Tami could use some inside information. No doubt her employee had heard about the murder. Probably knew something about the victim's background. At the very least, Madge would know of someone who could provide more information.

A police spokesperson had given a brief statement Sunday morning. Gave the standard answers. The gender and approximate age of the victim. The cause of death. According to the police, at this point there was no reason to believe this was anything other than a random killing.

No suspects but the investigation was ongoing. Name withheld pending notification of next of kin.

Tami hadn't been able to question the detective in charge of the investigation. Apparently, he was too busy to bother with members of the news media, or he had been given orders not to talk.

It was clear she wasn't going to learn anything more from the police. Matt Bradford ran a tight ship. Someone on the force might let something slip to a familiar face but not to Tami. She'd burned that bridge shortly after her arrival in Driscoll Lake.

After the press conference, she went to a popular café. Many locals gathered there every day to talk about everything from the weather to world politics. It was also one of the best places to hear all the latest local gossip. All Tami had to do was sit at a nearby table and listen.

It didn't take long to overhear someone say the victim had only lived in Driscoll Lake for a short time. Still, she wanted to know more. Most likely, Madge had heard things. Persuading her to talk would be another matter.

Tami took a deep breath, then smiled as she entered the building. "Good morning, Madge."

"Welcome back, Tami. How are things with your stepfather?"

"Making progress, but it's a slow process. The surgery was more in-depth than the doctor anticipated. He'll be in a rehab facility for another week, but the doctor is optimistic he'll make a full recovery."

"That's good news."

"Yeah. Mom isn't coping well with the situation. It took me two weeks to convince her they needed someone to help when Thomas comes home. Another week and a half to find a person who suited her."

"Sounds like your mother is pretty independent."

"Headstrong. Mom can't take care of my stepfather by herself and still run the business. But enough about my parents. I trust you had a good weekend."

"Yes, I did."

"I'm sure you heard what happened in Cameron Park."

"Unfortunately, yes. My heart goes out to the poor girl's family."

"Oh, so you knew them?"

"No. Don't know anything about her."

"Well, I assumed from what you said you must have heard something. Maybe her parents. A boyfriend. An ex-husband."

Madge shook her head. "From what I understand, she had only lived here a few weeks. Worked at the new art gallery."

Tami hadn't heard that bit of information, only that the victim had was at one of the new businesses located in Cameron Place. This could be the opening she needed. "She worked for Darla Martell?"

"Only art gallery I know of around here."

"Interesting. Darla's daughter-in-law found the body. Makes one wonder."

Madge frowned. "I can assure you it was pure chance. Christine wouldn't hurt anyone."

"Wasn't talking about her. What do you know about Darla? I understand she abandoned her young son. When Kyle worked here, I'm sure he told you something about her."

"He didn't talk about his personal life."

"You know something."

"Tami, I know what you're trying to do. It's true I once was one of the biggest blabbermouths in Driscoll Lake, but I learned my lesson. I'll continue to do my job if you want me here, but if you're looking for gossip, you'll have to talk to someone else."

"Sorry, Madge. Of course, you don't spread rumors. Don't worry. I need you here. Let's forget about this conversation, okay?"

"Gladly."

Tami went into her office and closed the door. Her tactic didn't work with Madge. She would have to get the information she wanted from someone else. The paper went to press tomorrow. As of now, all she had for the story was a victim no one seemed to know anything about and no suspect.

∽

VINCE WAS deep in thought as he unlocked the door to his small office. Located on Hudson Avenue a block from Main Street, the building was close to the former law office of Parker and Davis.

When Miles Parker retired, and Alan Davis left town in shame, a new attorney moved into the space. Vince heard good things about the man and made it a point to introduce himself when he first returned to Driscoll Lake. Attorneys often needed private investigators. The way Vince figured it, having his office nearby was a win-win situation.

He turned on the lights. Walked to the coffee maker. Placed a filter in the brew basket, then added a generous amount of a dark roast blend. He needed something strong this morning. Shrugging, he added an extra scoop.

After hitting the brew switch, he walked into the smaller room that housed his private office. With his business being new, he didn't need a receptionist but felt many clients would value privacy, hence the reason for his office being behind a closed door.

Vince checked for any new phone messages, not surprised there were none. It would take a while to build a clientele, and he had planned accordingly. Financially, he was sound for the next several months, thanks to some wise investments. He had given himself a year to establish his business.

He grinned in wry amusement. This line of work wasn't so different from what he'd done with the FBI—no murder investigations or kidnappings. He'd worked an insurance fraud case and conducted a couple of minor investigations for the attorney, but so far, that was it.

It was as he expected—things were more easygoing in Driscoll Lake. The area had a low crime rate. Violent crimes were almost non-existent. At least, not until the past weekend.

Vince had been unable to get the young woman's murder off his mind. The similarities between…

He shook his head. No reason to dwell on the past. On what might have been or what he might have done differently. He didn't want to remember the incident that was ultimately responsible for him leaving the FBI.

His thoughts drifted to Christine. Her expression when she heard he was no longer with the bureau. He supposed he owed her an explanation. It wasn't a secret. He was surprised she hadn't heard the news from someone else. Saturday was the first time he'd seen her since his return. It wasn't as if they were involved, but he wished he could have told her under different circumstances.

He walked back to the other room, poured a large mug of coffee, then took a sip. It was strong enough to clear the cobwebs from his head—and then some.

Sitting at his desk, he reached for the phone but quickly drew his hand away. He'd debated on whether to tell Matt about Jason Montgomery's actions on Saturday. What purpose would it serve? The detective was young and a bit inexperienced, but he had a job to do. One Vince didn't envy—learning the identity of a killer.

He might not agree with Jason's methods, but it wasn't for him to decide. Best to leave it alone. He'd given his story. Time to put the incident behind and move on.

An hour later, the outside door opened. Vince looked up to see Matt Bradford.

"Hey, Matt. What's going on?"

"Got a few minutes?"

"Sure. What's up?"

"Wanted to talk to you about Saturday. I heard what happened."

"You mean with Montgomery?"

"Yeah."

"Darla decided to talk to you after all."

Matt frowned. "Darla? No, Stephanie talked to Christine last night. Jason had to need to have you go to the station. Should have taken your statements and talked to you later if necessary."

"Can't say I approve of the way he handled it, but he does have an investigation to complete."

"True, but he shouldn't have questioned you and Christine like you were suspects."

"I agree." Vince shrugged. "He has a lot to learn."

"I'll say. I wouldn't have allowed him to act that way if I'd been there. Sorry I didn't hang around, but I had to take Stephanie to the hospital."

"Is she okay?"

"Fine now. Stephanie is pregnant. She had some cramping on Saturday. We didn't want to take any chances."

"Hey, congrats man."

Matt grinned. "Thanks. We didn't plan for it to happen. Abby is only a year old."

"Those things happen."

"Yeah. Anyway, I'd better get to the station. Again, sorry about Jason. I'm going to talk with him."

"Don't do it on my account."

"It's not only that. The guy is..." Matt shook his head. "Times like these I miss having Carlos around. Or someone with the experience to conduct a proper investigation." Matt glanced around the room before looking back at Vince. "Someone like you."

THE DISPATCHER GREETED Matt as he entered the police station. "Good morning, Chief."

"Hey, Sandra. Is Jason around?"

"No. He hasn't come in yet."

Matt glanced at his watch. Almost nine-thirty. Jason's job didn't require him to be in the office on a set schedule, but the past few weeks he'd been arriving later each day. Matt didn't have a problem with it as long as he stayed late enough to complete his work. On at least two occasions the previous week, Jason had come in late and left early. And he wasn't in the field working a case.

"When he arrives, tell him I want to see him first thing."

"I'll tell him."

Matt went to the breakroom and poured himself a cup of coffee before going to his office. After closing the door, he sat down at his desk and pinched the bridge of his nose. The beginning of a headache was blooming behind his eyes.

Now for the bigger headache. Confronting Jason Montgomery. Matt powered up his computer, intending to complete some reports while he waited.

It was almost an hour later when he looked at his watch. Still no sign of Montgomery. He picked up the phone and called the dispatcher's extension. "Sandra, isn't Jason here yet?"

"Arrived about fifteen minutes ago. He hasn't been to see you?"

"No."

"I told him you needed to talk to him as soon as he arrived."

"Thanks. I'll take care of it." Matt hung up the phone then started toward Jason's office when he heard laughter in the breakroom. He changed course. At the door, he found Jason and the newest female officer engaged in conversation.

The woman was at the coffee maker, and Jason stood behind her—close enough that their bodies were almost touching. The man was a flirt. Shortly after he arrived in town, Matt had to call him into his office when one of the female dispatchers complained.

"Why don't we meet for drinks after work?" Jason's voice was low and suggestive.

Matt cleared his throat, and the two of them jumped apart.

"Got nothing better to do, Daniels? Thought you were supposed to be on patrol."

Turning toward the door, she said, "No, sir. I mean, yes sir. I'm leaving."

Jason leaned toward her and spoke in a low tone, a smirk on his face. "Our boss would have made a good drill sergeant."

"Montgomery! In my office. NOW!"

At the sound of Matt's voice, everyone stopped what they were doing. A blush crept across Officer Daniel's face as she hurried from the room.

Jason shrugged, then strutted down the hall to Matt's office.

Matt took a few deep breaths before following him. Closed the door, then sat down at his desk. He nodded at Jason. "Have a seat."

"I prefer to stand."

"Sit. Down." So much for trying to calm himself.

Jason shrugged, then settled in one of the chairs beside Matt's desk. "Why do you need to see me?"

"You're supposed to be working a murder investigation. Update me."

"Nothing new to report."

"And why is that?"

"Not much there."

"Tell me what you do know."

"Darla Martell identified the body and confirmed the victim was the person who worked in her gallery. Said her name was Jenny Allen. She'd only lived in Driscoll Lake a few weeks. Didn't have any information about family or friends."

"What brought her here?"

"No idea. Darla said she moved from San Antonio."

"Did she have a house? Rent an apartment?"

"Lived in a garage apartment on Sycamore Street."

"Find anything when you searched the place?"

"I haven't been there yet."

"Why not?"

"Yesterday was Sunday. It was my day off. Bad enough I spent the morning interviewing Ms. Martell and accompanying her to the morgue."

"Day off? Do I need to remind you crime doesn't take a day of rest? You should have gone there first thing yesterday morning. At the latest."

Jason shrugged. "She lived alone. I figured there was no hurry."

"There's a killer on the loose, we have a victim we can identify by name only, and you figure you don't need to rush. That's rich."

"Didn't see you working yesterday."

"Can the smart-aleck attitude. If you aren't capable of handling this, I'll be more than happy to call the Texas Rangers for assistance."

"No. This is my investigation. I do things my way."

"As long as you're working for me, you'll do things the right way. Speaking of which, I don't appreciate the way you treated Vince Green and Christine Lawrence. They weren't suspects. You had no reason to drag them down here for questioning."

"I had my reasons.

"Not good enough."

"Don't you think it's odd that Darla Martell was the last person to see Jenny Allen alive and then her daughter-in-law was the one who found the body? Or that her 'friend' happened to be close by?"

"No, I don't think it's odd. And by the way, the 'friend' as you say is a former FBI agent."

"And that precludes him from being a killer?"

Matt's jaw twitched. "Hold it right there. You have no reason to believe that. And if you do, I will have you removed from this investigation."

"Oh, I forgot. They're your friends. So of course, we need to treat them like VIPs."

His vision tinged red. "That is uncalled for. I'm not asking you to give them special treatment. I do want you to treat them, as well as any other witness, with courtesy and respect."

"Like I said, you have your ways. I have mine."

"I'm warning you, Montgomery. I'm the police chief, and you answer to me. A few more comments like that, and you're out of here."

"Yeah? And what do you think the city council will say about it? From what I hear, they're the ones who insisted you hire me."

"City council be damned. You will conduct this investigation professionally, or I'll have you replaced. Have I made myself clear?"

Jason clenched his teeth. "Perfectly."

"Good. Now get out of my office and do what you need to do. I expect an updated report no later than five this evening."

The young detective rose from the chair. As he opened the door, Matt called out to him.

"By the way. Who you see or what you do in your own time is none of my business. But I don't ever want to see a repeat of what happened earlier in the breakroom. Understood?"

Jason started to leave but stopped and looked over his shoulder. "Whatever you say. Boss."

CHAPTER 6

*C*hristine parked her SUV in the garage—glad to be home after a long and trying day. She got out and began gathering things from the back seat when she remembered she'd failed to check the mailbox.

"Emily, will you see if we have any mail?"

A slamming door met her words. The moody teenager hadn't wasted any time getting inside the house. So much for that idea.

Sighing, Christine walked the short distance to the end of the driveway. Almost everyone she had encountered wanted to talk about Saturday night. Even some of her students had given her curious looks but refrained from asking questions.

She couldn't even escape during her off period. Another teacher, one who hardly gave Christine the time of day, approached her in the teacher's lounge.

"I'm glad I caught you. Can't believe what happened. Tell me about it."

That was it. She was tired of being polite. "You know, I might as well talk to the principal and see if he'll let me use the auditorium for a question and answer session. Then I could get it over with and inform the entire faculty at once."

"No need to be rude. Everyone is concerned. They'll stop asking questions in a day or two."

"Yeah, well if people care so much, why hasn't anyone asked how it affected me? All they want is to hear the gory details. You included."

Christine had hurried from the teacher's lounge, not caring what anyone thought. Now, she wanted nothing more than to retreat to the sanctuary of her home. Emily could take her loud music into the bedroom. She wasn't in the mood to put up with an ill-tempered teenager.

When she looked inside the mailbox, she found mostly junk mail. Nothing that couldn't have waited. Lost in thought, she didn't hear Libby walk up.

"I heard about Saturday night. Such a terrible thing. No wonder you weren't in a good mood this morning."

Libby, too? The woman hadn't been this talkative since she moved next door.

Pasting a smile on her face, she said, "Not exactly what I expected when I went running."

"Can't imagine what I would have done if I had been in your place. You must have been devastated. Is there anything I can do?"

"No, I'll be okay. Everyone at school kept asking me questions. Right now, I'm tired, and I want to be alone."

"I can understand. If you need someone to talk to, I'm right next door."

"Thanks. I appreciate it."

"Glad to help. After all, that's what neighbors are for."

Christine entered her house through the garage. Much to her surprise, it was quiet. Emily's door was closed. After placing the mail on the kitchen counter, she opened the refrigerator to grab a package of hamburger but changed her mind. Dinner could wait.

Instead, she reached for a bottle of wine, poured a glass, then went into the sunroom. The day may not have started well, but she was determined it would end on a different note.

It wasn't long before Emily rushed into the room. "When will dinner be ready?"

"In a little while. I've had a long day, and I need to relax. Grab something to snack. I'll cook later."

"But I'm hungry."

Christine's cell phone rang. She recognized Vince's number. Her day was about to get much better. Ignoring Emily's protest, she answered the call. "Hello, Vince."

She barely noticed when Emily stormed away.

MATT LOOKED up from his desk to see Jason Montgomery standing in the doorway with a file folder in his hand. The past few days, he'd acted professionally. There hadn't been any repeats of Monday's incident in the break room.

Officer Daniels apologized for her behavior and assured him it wouldn't happen again. Not surprising Jason hadn't acknowledged any wrongdoing on his part, but at times he seemed almost amiable.

Matt didn't expect things would remain as is. Jason's sarcastic attitude and deplorable behavior would likely return. A leopard couldn't change its spots.

"Got a minute? I need to discuss something with you regarding the Allen murder."

Matt nodded. "Come in."

Jason closed the office door before sitting down opposite Matt. "We know robbery wasn't a motive. The victim still had her wallet on her, and it had a debit card, three credit cards, and more than a couple hundred dollars cash inside. I spoke with neighbors, people who worked near the gallery, and her landlord. I haven't been able to learn anything about her family or friends."

"Didn't turn up anything from searching her apartment?"

"Nothing. No photos. No personal items or letters. Sent her computer to the FBI lab. So far, they've found nothing. She didn't engage in social media and apparently didn't even have an email account."

"In this day and age?"

"I know. Strange. The FBI is also trying to unlock her cell phone. Maybe she'll have contacts listed there. Something that will give us a clue."

"Cell phone records?"

"In the process of obtaining those. When I talked to her neighbors, everyone said she always smiled and was cordial, but otherwise kept to herself. No one was aware if she had regular visitors."

"What else have you learned?"

"She had a New Mexico driver's license with a Santa Fe address, but when I checked, she hadn't lived there in over a year. She moved to Texas about a year ago."

"What about her landlord? Did they do a background check?"

"Rented from a woman named Phyllis Chambers. Allowed her to pay six months in advance and didn't dig into her past."

Matt shook his head. "Well, Phyllis has always been a trusting soul."

"Jenny also provided a letter of recommendation from the manager of the apartment complex where she lived in San Antonio. Here's a copy." Jason opened the folder and handed the letter to Matt. "As you can see, he gave her a glowing recommendation."

"Interesting." Matt's chair squeaked as he leaned forward to return the letter to Jason. "Paid her rent on or ahead of schedule. Model tenant. Had a chance to speak to the manager?"

"This morning. He confirmed everything. And here's the clincher. When she moved there, she paid six month's rent in place of a credit check. Also gave the manager a hefty security deposit. Didn't provide any contacts, relatives, or references."

Matt frowned. "Strange. We have a woman with enough money to pay rent months in advance. Doesn't provide any background information. No one knows anything about friends or family, and except for her working in the gallery, she keeps to herself. Almost makes me wonder if she was in the witness protection program."

"The thought crossed my mind. If she was, we'll have a hard time getting any information."

"Right. We may never learn anything."

By mid-week, Driscoll Lake was abuzz with talk about the murder of Jenny Allen. The police hadn't released her name, but it was almost impossible for anyone not to know. People discussed it at coffee shops, in hair salons, and with their neighbors.

With the killer still at large, many women were afraid to be alone at night. The local fitness centers saw an increase in business after several women refused to run in Cameron Park or other outdoor areas.

Tami Sutton sat at her desk, looking at the latest edition of the *Driscoll Lake Reporter*. She wasn't pleased with the story but had printed what little information she had. The evening before, she had gone to Casey's, a favorite Driscoll Lake restaurant.

Detective Jason Montgomery had been sitting at the bar. She'd sidled up to the empty seat beside him.

"Good evening, detective."

Jason glanced in her direction, nodded, then turned his attention back to the big screen TV across the room.

Tami refused to be put off. She would persuade him to talk.

"What can I get you?" the bartender asked.

"Bloody Mary, please."

"Right away."

"She turned toward Jason. "How are things with you?"

He took a sip of his beer and shrugged. "Okay, I guess."

"Tough day?"

"You could say that."

"I'm sure. With the murder investigation. So many uncertainties. What are the odds of someone who recently moved to this town becoming a murder victim? Think it was a coincidence? Or did someone target her?"

"I know what you're trying to do. But I'm not talking to you or any member of the press. I'm out of here." Jason stood up and threw a few bills on the counter. After a brief nod to the bartender, he whirled then walked away.

She'd struck out on that one.

Tami drummed her fingers on her desk, trying to figure out what she could have done differently. Like everyone else at police headquarters, Jason wouldn't talk.

A few drinks tended to loosen lips. If she had waited for him to drink a couple more beers, then brought up the murder, he might have been more receptive.

She wasn't beyond using her feminine charms to get a story.

The grapevine had plenty to say about Jason Montgomery. He liked women and loved to flirt. According to the rumor mill, he had already been in trouble a couple of times with some coworkers.

Tami was two or three years older than Jason but wasn't unattractive. She could easily pass for someone a few years younger. Charming a man like him would have been easy. She'd missed that opportunity. At least, for now.

Madge Sinclair hadn't been any help, either. She wouldn't budge in her resolve not to discuss the situation except to say it was an unfortunate event and insist, "You know as much as I do."

Tami needed another plan of action. But what? An idea struck her. Time for a different source. She grabbed her purse, walked out of her office, then paused at Madge's desk.

"I'm going to the new sandwich shop in Cameron Place. If anyone calls for me, I won't be back until around two. You have my cell phone in case of an emergency."

"Okay. Enjoy your lunch."

"Thanks. I'm sure I will.

DARLA SMILED at the middle-aged couple as they entered the gallery. She had been around the art world long enough to recognize window shoppers and those who were serious about purchasing quality pieces. This couple fell into the latter category.

After a few minutes of conversation, she learned what they were looking for and guided them to a section of framed canvases. "I think I have something that would interest you. Some of the paintings are by locals, but I also have some high-quality selections by artists from other areas."

The woman glanced around and said, "Yes, I can see you do."

"Why don't I leave the two of you to browse? If you have any questions, I'll be right over here." She nodded toward a small desk.

Business was slow today. The idea of an art gallery in Driscoll Lake hadn't caught on yet, but Darla realized how much she missed having an assistant around. Jenny had been perfect for the job. She knew art and was friendly with customers but never intrusive. Had she been here today, she would have treated the couple in the same manner.

Such a sad situation. A young woman whose life was needlessly cut short. Who and why? Darla tended to believe Jenny's murder was a random act—wrong place, wrong time. She shuddered to think it could have easily been her daughter-in-law. If Christine had been a few minutes earlier…

No need to speculate on what-ifs. Christine was safe. Alive to raise her daughter. Darla wasn't sure Emily could handle losing another parent.

Which brought to mind another issue. She'd seen how Emily acted around her mother. Part of her attitude was that of a typical teenager, but some of it was the expression of unresolved issues related to her father's death. Neither was an excuse to be disrespectful to Christine, who had nothing to do with Kyle's murder and had her own grief to deal with.

Darla made a mental note to talk with Emily. It was time the girl made an attitude adjustment.

Christine needed to have a more active social life. She was young. Too young to remain a widow. Darla knew what it was like to lose the love of your life, but it wasn't an excuse to stop living.

Seeing her with Vince on Sunday had been promising, even though she had insisted he was only a friend.

Darla made a second resolution. She would encourage her daughter-in-law to begin dating. Years ago, she had allowed Curtis Lawrence to separate her from her son. No one was going to keep her from helping his wife and daughter.

Wrapped up in her thoughts, she forgot about the couple browsing the gallery until the woman approached her.

"We're interested in one of the landscapes. The large one of the desert southwest."

Darla stood up. She immediately knew which canvas the woman was referring to. Jenny Allen had also been drawn to it. "Ah, yes. The Saldana painting. Good choice."

"I'm ready to buy it now, but my husband wants to look at a couple of galleries in Dallas. Could you hold it for us until we've had time to check some other places? We'll be glad to pay a deposit, if necessary."

Darla made a split decision. It wasn't likely anyone else would buy the painting in the next few days. These people would probably be repeat customers. Possibly send more potential buyers her way, too. She took one of her business cards and handed it to the woman.

"Tell you what. Write your name and phone number on the back of this card. If anyone else shows interest in the painting, I'll explain a sale is pending and give you a call to see if you're still interested."

"Sounds fair. We'll let you know one way or the other by early next week."

"Perfect."

"Do you happen to know the artist?"

"I did. Unfortunately, he died last year." Darla shook her head. "It's a shame, too. So young. Had a promising career ahead of him."

AFTER THE COUPLE LEFT, Darla phoned her favorite deli to place a delivery order. Was it only a week ago when she and Jenny shared a meal from the same place?

Jenny had been in good spirits. Darla thought she might finally open up and tell her a bit about the past. Neither of them would have imagined she had only two more days to live.

Maybe it was the memories or the couple's interest in the painting, and Jenny's love for it, but Darla's ordinarily cheerful mood became melancholy. Someone had lost a daughter, a sister, a wife, or girlfriend. And they didn't even know it.

When the bell tingled, she blinked her eyes to ward off her tears. It was too soon for the deli. Gathering her composure, she turned to greet the visitor and was surprised to see the newspaper editor.

Tami Sutton had never been inside the gallery before, even though Darla had seen her frequently visiting other nearby shops.

Some people didn't have an appreciation for art, and that was okay. Most likely, the editor was there to snoop about Jenny.

"Hello." She forced a smile, determined to be nice. "How can I help you?"

Tami tucked a strand of shoulder-length blonde hair behind her ear. "I'm not here to shop. I was hoping we could talk."

"Then I assume this is about Jenny Allen. Afraid I can't tell you much. She only worked for me a few weeks."

"You must know something about her."

"Jenny was a private person. Didn't talk about her past. Never mentioned friends or family."

"Didn't you find it strange?"

Darla shrugged. "Not especially. Some people are reserved at first. Once they get to know you, they open up more."

"I suppose. So, in spite of the fact she was quiet, you still hired her. Wouldn't it have been better to have someone more outgoing?"

"Art galleries tend to attract a different type of clientele. They don't need a chatty salesperson to follow them around, but they do need someone who knows about art. And Jenny knew her stuff."

Tami nodded. "I see. You must miss her."

"Yeah, I do. This entire week has been a whirlwind. It's just starting to set in she won't be coming back. Before you came in, I was thinking about one of the last times I saw her. She was happy. Laughing and talking. She even convinced me to snap a selfie of the two of us."

"She did? Would you mind if I see it? I've heard a lot of things about this young woman the past few days, but I've yet to learn what she looked like. Having been out of town for almost a month, I never met her. Would be nice to put a face with a name."

"I don't mind at all." Darla retrieved her cell phone from the desk, opened the photo app, and scrolled to the picture of her and Jenny. "Here you go."

Tami took the phone from Darla. She gasped, then covered her mouth with her hand. "Oh, no."

"What's wrong, dear?"

Her voice trembled as she spoke. "This…this is Jenny?"

"Yes. Do you recognize her?"

Tami's eyes filled with tears. She nodded. "Jenny is…*was*, my stepsister."

CHAPTER 7

For the second time in a week, Darla found herself subjected to Jason Montgomery's scrutiny. She closed the gallery for the afternoon to accompany Tami to the police station. After the surprising discovery about her stepsister being the murdered woman, Tami needed a friend. And while she didn't exactly fit the bill, having just met the woman, she could offer support. Tami definitely needed that.

Darla didn't care much for the smug detective or his methods. He would probably treat Tami like a suspect, much like he did Christine and Vince. The last thing the poor woman needed was for Jason upset her even more.

When Darla asked if she could stay with Tami, Jason protested, insisting he needed to question her alone. Darla was about to give him a piece of her mind when Matt entered the room.

"Why alone? She isn't a suspect. There's no reason why Ms. Martell can't be in the room." He sat down opposite Jason.

"Guess you're planning to stay, too."

"I am."

Jason shrugged. "You're the boss."

Darla shook her head. The man had a complete lack of respect for authority. At the least, someone needed to take him down a notch or two. At best, Matt should probably fire the guy. But people like him eventually received their just punishment. No doubt one day he would get what was coming to him. Maybe more.

Jason looked at some notes scribbled on a legal pad before turning to Tami. "Let me get this straight. The victim, Jenny Allen, was your stepsister."

"Correct. My mother married her father ten years ago."

"You went to Ms. Martell looking for information on the victim. Why?"

"Wasn't getting anything from you, so I decided to look elsewhere."

"But why the curiosity? Did you know your stepsister was here in Driscoll Lake?"

"To answer your first question, I'm a newspaper reporter. I needed information to run the story. Regarding the second one, I haven't seen or spoken with Jenny in years. I was away for a month because my stepfather had major surgery. From what I've heard, she showed up here about the same time I left. There's no way I could have known."

"Your parents weren't in contact with her?"

"Jennifer…Jenny moved away from home when she was eighteen to attend college. About five years ago, she broke off all contact with the family. We lost track of her. The last we knew, she was living in Taos, New Mexico. Apparently, she either married or changed her last name. If Darla hadn't shown me a photo, I never would have suspected anything."

"Why was she estranged from your family?"

"Does it matter?"

"Yes. It might help lead us to her killer."

"I hope you're not suggesting I, or any member of my family, had anything to do with Jenny's death. Because if you are, this conversation is over." Tami stood and squared her shoulders.

Darla glared at Jason before turning to Tami. "Relax, honey. His methods may leave a little to be desired, but I'm sure he has his reasons for wanting to know."

Matt cleared his throat. "Ms. Martell is right. Anything you can tell us about her background might be important. Her friends. Her lifestyle. Do you know if she was involved with someone? We're trying to put together pieces of the puzzle."

Tami took a deep breath and sat again. "My stepfather owns a chain of restaurants. Thomas is a good man, but he had some preconceived ideas about Jenny's career path. He thought she would take over the business one day. Set about trying to groom her for that role. Decided she should get a degree in business management. When she chose to major in art, he wasn't happy about it. Said it wasn't a good way to make a living. They had a big fight, and she left home."

"I see. Were you aware if she did drugs? Any illegal substances?" Jason asked.

"She had a boyfriend when she left San Antonio, but they split up years ago. As far as drugs…" Tami shook her head. "Jenny was a health nut. A vegetarian, did yoga, preferred natural and holistic methods of healing. I seriously doubt she would have poisoned her system with illegal substances."

"The coroner will do a tox screen, but from what you say, it's unlikely drugs were involved," Matt said.

Jason shrugged and shifted in his chair. "People change. Get involved with the wrong crowd. Do you know the name of the person she lived with?"

"I can't remember. It was a long time ago. Mom or Thomas probably know. I can ask them when I… How do you tell someone their long-lost daughter is dead?" Tami wiped away tears.

Darla pulled a tissue from her purse, handed it to Tami, then put an arm around the sobbing woman's shoulders. "It will be okay, honey. You don't have to go through this alone."

After a few minutes, Tami composed herself and managed a weak smile. "Thank you."

"One more question," Jason said. "Do you know if your stepsister tried to contact you after she came to town?"

Tami shook her head. "Not that I'm aware of. Don't even know if she knew I lived here. I'd like to think she did and wanted to mend fences. Maybe it was her first step in getting back with the family. What else would have brought her to Driscoll Lake?"

~

"Okay, I'll do it… Next week is fine. See you first thing Monday." Vince hung up the phone. Trailing a suspected cheating wife wasn't exactly the type of investigation he enjoyed. But when Mike Gregory called to offer him the job, he found it hard to say no.

Mike was a successful attorney and long-time family friend. He and Vince attended high school together. Mike had been there for him on more than one occasion and didn't expect anything in return, but Vince felt like he owed him a favor or two.

It wasn't like he had any pressing business in Driscoll Lake. He could be away for several days, and no one would miss him. Least of all, Christine.

They hadn't talked since he phoned her Monday night. She acted like she was glad to hear from him but had to cut the call short. "Someone is at the door. We'll talk soon." That was three days ago.

Maybe Christine wasn't interested in a relationship—friends or more. They wouldn't have even been talking if it hadn't been for the incident Saturday night in the park. Shrugging, Vince turned to his computer. Mike had promised to send him some preliminary information about the case.

After a few minutes, the email notification appeared. He opened the secured file, then began to read. It might prove to be an interesting assignment. The woman was in her late thirties and had been married almost ten years to Eric Taylor, a wealthy business owner. The May-December marriage was her first, his third. The company was family-owned, and he was the last remaining heir. No children from any of his marriages.

She'd signed a prenup agreement stating if the marriage lasted longer than a decade, she would inherit the business upon his death. As of now, the company had a value of at least twenty million.

If they divorced before ten years, she would receive a half-million-dollar divorce settlement.

Not a paltry sum. Unless someone had become accustomed to a particular lifestyle. Vince shook his head. Money was never a significant factor for him. Sure, he liked living comfortably and had been fortunate enough to make a good living over the years. But if he had to choose between money or happiness and a clean conscience, he'd take the latter any day.

Angela Taylor had been the dutiful wife, serving as hostess for parties, attending social functions with her husband. She was indeed a looker. A trophy wife.

Other than local events and occasional lunches with other wives at the country club, she didn't seem to have a life of her own. Kept to herself most of the time.

Until recently. Angela had started to get out more often. Made excuses to take overnight trips, all in the name of philanthropic obligations. Told her husband it was time she began to become "more involved in social and charitable functions," and she wanted to "champion a cause."

There had been no evidence she was having an affair, but the husband was highly suspicious. He said they had begun sleeping in separate bedrooms at her suggestion.

What was it with some women and rich older men? Did money mean so much to them that they would sacrifice a life of happiness? When the loneliness became unbearable, they sought companionship elsewhere. Sounded all too familiar.

Vince's cell phone rang. He glanced at the caller ID before answering, surprised to see Christine's number. "Hey."

"Did I catch you at a bad time?"

"Never too busy for you. What's up?"

"You haven't heard?"

"What are you talking about?"

"Tami Sutton paid a visit to Darla's gallery today asking questions about Jenny Allen. It turns out Jenny was her stepsister."

"What?"

"You heard right."

"And Tami didn't know she was here? I find that hard to believe. Driscoll Lake is a small town."

"Tami was away for a month. Left around the time Jenny showed up." Christine relayed everything Darla had told her.

"So, did she show up here to make amends?"

"No one knows. If she did, there wasn't any evidence Jenny tried to contact Tami. Never even mentioned she had a sister."

"Coincidence?"

"I guess stranger things have happened. Darla was with Tami when she talked to Detective Jerk."

Vince chuckled. "Oh, so you have a nickname for him?"

"And you don't?"

"Believe me. It wouldn't be anything that nice."

"I can imagine." Christine laughed.

Vince heard the outside door open and looked up to see a legal assistant from the nearby law office. He motioned the woman inside, then turned back to the phone. "Someone is here, and I need to go." He almost cringed, his words so reminiscent of what Christine had said during their last phone conversation.

"I understand. Didn't mean to bother you."

"You didn't." An idea struck him. "Have any plans for tonight? We could meet somewhere for dinner and talk more."

She was silent for a few seconds. Vince held his breath while waiting for her answer. Maybe it wasn't such a good idea after all. Or, as he thought earlier, she wasn't interested in being anything other than a casual acquaintance.

"Yes," she said. "I'd like that."

"Great. Casey's at six?"

"Sounds good. I'll see you then."

MATT WAITED ALMOST two hours after Tami Sutton left the station before talking to Jason. He needed time to calm down. Had he confronted the detective immediately after Tami's departure, he might have done something he'd live to regret. Once again, Jason had crossed the line, with his subtle insinuations she might be involved in her stepsister's death.

Driscoll Lake wasn't like a lot of larger cities where there was distrust between residents and police officers, and Matt wanted to keep it that way. Jason was on the fast track to making enemies. Tami Sutton may not have lived in Driscoll Lake long, but she had influence. One story in her paper about the "ethics" of the police department wouldn't look good for anyone, especially Matt. It didn't matter how many city council members wanted Jason around.

He picked up the phone and rang the familiar extension. "Montgomery, I need to see you in my office. Now."

Matt expected him to procrastinate, if for no other reason than defiance. He was surprised when Jason appeared a couple of minutes later.

"Come in and close the door."

"What did I do wrong this time?"

"A better question would be what have you done right? I warned you before. I don't like you playing bad cop with people who aren't suspects."

"Fine. I'll refer to them as persons of interest."

Matt scoffed. "Oh, yes, let's see. You have Christine who found the body. What motive would she have for killing a woman she barely knew? Then we have Vince Green. Why would someone with an impeccable record as an FBI agent agree to go along with her plan?"

Jason shrugged. "Similar incidents have happened."

Matt ignored him. "Next you have the victim's employer, Darla Martell. According to her, Jenny was a model employee the short time she worked at the gallery. Where's the motive? Finally, you practically accuse the dead woman's sister of being involved. She wasn't even in town and didn't know her sister had moved here."

"So she says. Who's to say it's true?"

"I'm not saying any of the people you questioned wouldn't be capable of murder under the right circumstances. I've seen some bizarre things. Hell, even one of my best friends withheld information about a murder case. Ended up costing him his life."

"Kyle Lawrence."

"How did you know?"

Jason shrugged. "People talk."

"Yes, and they'll talk about how you've handled this, too. You may have used these methods before, but they won't work here."

"You never played the 'bad cop' role?"

"If the situation warranted it. It doesn't here. I've already warned you. I won't hesitate to pull you from this case and bring in outside help if you can't handle it."

"I could do my job if you didn't keep interfering."

Matt held up his hand. "Stop. I don't want to hear any excuses. What I need to know is where you stand on the investigation."

"Nothing new. Still waiting on the forensic report. Preliminary coroner's report confirmed she died of multiple stab wounds."

"As expected. What about the murder weapon?"

Jason shook his head. "We combed the area several times. Didn't locate anything. Coroner said it was likely some type of kitchen knife."

"According to her sister, the victim once lived in Taos, but you said her driver's license had a Santa Fe address. The towns aren't far apart, so it's possible Tami was mistaken as to where her sister lived. Any leads there?"

"Haven't checked with anyone in Taos."

Matt resisted the urge to roll his eyes. Was this guy totally clueless? "Then I strongly suggest you get your butt in gear. There's a killer out there. The sooner we find the creep, the better for everyone. Now get on with it."

For once, Jason didn't have a comeback. He merely nodded and left the room. Matt hoped he would follow-through on his suggestions. One more screw up, one more botched interview, and Jason was history.

~

CHRISTINE HATED BEING LATE. She was supposed to meet Vince ten minutes ago. Resisting the urge to speed, she drove toward the restaurant. Pressing the blue tooth button, she spoke the command to dial Vince's cell phone. The call went to voicemail.

Well, that's great. Hope he doesn't give up on me.

An unplanned, last-minute parent conference detained her at school. She rushed home to change clothes and was met by her overly-dramatic teenage daughter. Of all days, Emily announced she had an urgent need to find a dress to wear to the prom.

"Mom, we have to go shopping today. You don't expect me to go without a new dress."

"It's weeks away. You have plenty of time to find something. I can't go shopping tonight. It will have to wait until the weekend."

"But what if I can't find anything? All the dresses will be picked over, and I'll get stuck with something stupid. I don't want something that looks like I got it at Walmart."

"How long have you known about this?"

Emily hung her head. "For a few weeks."

"And you suddenly decided you have to shop today. Sorry, but I can't rearrange my schedule on a whim." Part of Christine wanted to drop everything and take her daughter to Brewster. It had been a long time since Emily had wanted the two of them to do anything together.

"I wasn't sure if I was going."

"What made you change your mind?"

"Ty Fuller asked me to go with him."

Christine knew Emily harbored a secret crush on the high-school senior but would never admit it. At least, not to her. She couldn't help a faint smile. "I see. Ty seems like a nice boy, and I'm happy for you, but I already have plans for the evening. I'm sorry. We'll go to Brewster on Saturday morning.

"Come on. Not until Saturday?"

"That's only two days from now. If we can't find anything there, we'll go to Dallas the following weekend. Make a day of it."

Emily's face lit up. "Dallas? You mean it?"

"Yes. We'll do what's necessary to find the perfect dress. But not tonight. Now, I need to get going. I'm late as it is." Christine already knew Brewster wouldn't suffice and they would end up making a trip to the Galleria. On the bright side, that meant two excursions with her daughter, not just one.

She didn't arrive at Casey's until six-fifteen. Vince was seated at a round booth in the back corner. He stood and acknowledged her as she approached.

"Sorry, I'm late. Had to deal with the latest teenage crisis. Sometimes my daughter is a bit dramatic."

"Not a problem. I haven't been here long. Hope you don't mind the location. Thought it would give us more privacy." Vince waited until she took her seat before sliding back into the booth beside her.

"This is fine." Christine knew he'd chosen a more secluded location, so they could talk freely, but couldn't ignore the sudden acceleration of her pulse. Casey's was a bar and grill. Hardly a romantic setting. What would it be like to go on an actual date with him? The idea appealed more than she cared to admit, and she soon found herself lost in thought.

After the server took their order, Vince turned to her. "You seem quiet this evening."

"Thinking about Tami Sutton. Can't imagine what it would be like to discover your long-lost sister has been murdered. Knowing you'll never get another chance to see her. To talk to her."

"Yeah. I'm sure it's rough." Vince's voice was low, and he looked away.

"Something wrong?"

He shook his head. "Tell me about Tami. You said she went into the gallery to get information."

"And got a lot more than she bargained for. Darla phoned about an hour ago to say she was still with her. Didn't want her to be alone, especially when she told her parents."

"Darla must be the nurturing type."

"That's what she'd like everyone to believe."

"So, it's all an act? Why?"

Christine shrugged. "I don't know. She acts like she cares for Emily and me, but I can't forget about the mother who abandoned her young son. She didn't care about Kyle. Otherwise, she never would have left him with someone like Curtis Lawrence."

"Maybe she didn't have a choice. The judge was very persuasive. Not to mention influential. He had connections."

"I know, but back in those days, it wasn't common for a father to be awarded sole custody. Besides, Darla's family had more money and power than Curtis ever dreamed about."

"Yeah?"

Christine nodded. "The Martell money goes back several generations. First in cattle, then they struck it big in the oil business. Darla's father was once a senator with powerful connections in both Austin and Washington. Can't have much more influence than that."

"Wait a minute. Are you telling me Martell is her maiden name? And her father was Senator Joseph Martell?"

Christine nodded. "One and the same."

"No wonder she uses the family name."

"She may have once been a non-conformist, but she always maintained close ties. Her brother still manages the family ranch near Marathon. That's why I was surprised when she decided to move across the state. I could be wrong, but I'm convinced Darla never does anything unless there is something in it for her."

CHAPTER 8

*C*hristine kicked off her shoes before sitting on the sofa in the hotel room suite. Her feet ached after a long day of shopping, but spending time with her daughter made it all worthwhile. She would be hard-pressed to count how many stores the two of them visited. As expected, an earlier shopping excursion to Brewster proved fruitless. Emily couldn't find any dresses she liked. Christine suspected part of the reason was the prospect of a trip to Dallas.

They decided to go during spring break week and spend the night. Christine booked a room at a four-star hotel in North Dallas. They got off to an early start, arriving at their first stop when the store opened.

Emily's first selection was a red two-piece with a halter top that left her midriff bare and showed too much skin. Christine refused to buy it. Emily protested.

Six hours and two shopping malls later, Emily found "the one"—a royal blue cocktail-length dress with spaghetti straps, a sequined waist, and flared skirt.

"Aren't you glad now you didn't take the first dress?" She smiled at her daughter sitting in the chair opposite her.

"I guess so." Emily grinned. "I'm kidding. It's perfect."

"You'll look beautiful. Ty will probably have a hard time keeping other boys away from you."

Emily's cheeks flushed with color. "You're just saying that because I'm your daughter."

"Not true."

"It is. All parents say things like that." She paused for a moment. "I'm glad we did this, Mom."

"Me, too. We'll do it again sometime." Christine hoped they were finally getting their relationship back to where it had been before Kyle died.

"We can?"

"You bet. Now, what about dinner? Want to go out or order room service?"

"Let's go out."

"Sure. Anything particular?"

Emily shrugged.

Christine picked up a book that listed the area's restaurants. "There's an Italian place within walking distance."

"Okay by me."

Thirty minutes later, after freshening up and changing clothes, they entered the elevator. Christine pressed the button for the ground floor.

As they stepped into the corridor, Emily said, "I forgot my purse."

"It will be fine in the room. Besides, you won't need it."

One look from the teenager told her otherwise.

"I suppose you don't have your room key, either."

"In my purse."

She pulled the card from her pocket and handed it to Emily. "I'll wait near the entrance. Don't take too long."

Christine made her way to the lobby. A crowd of people, dressed in semi-formal attire, stood outside one of the conference rooms. She strolled to the front entrance and watched as a silver BMW pulled up to valet parking. As the attendant went to the driver's side, a man got out of the car. He wore slacks, a dark blue sport coat, and a lighter blue button-down shirt.

After handing his keys to the valet, he dashed toward the entrance.

Her eyes widened when she recognized him. Vince. They hadn't seen or spoken to one another in almost two weeks. What was he doing here? As if it were her business.

"Vince?"

He stopped, then turned in her direction. "Christine? I'm surprised to see you here."

"I'm with Emily. We went shopping today and decided to stay the night."

"Having fun, I hope." Vince glanced over her shoulder toward the crowd of people.

"It's been a blast so far. How are things with you?"

"Uh...fine. I'm, uh, doing okay." His eyes continued to dart around the room.

Did he not want to talk to her? "We were about to go out to dinner. Would you like to join us?"

When his eyes narrowed, Christine looked to see if she could see if he might be meeting someone. A tall blonde woman looked in his direction and nodded.

"Vince?"

"Oh, sorry. I can't tonight. Maybe some other time." He hurried toward the elevators and was soon caught up in the crowd.

CHRISTINE TOOK a sip of iced tea and looked at her friend. Rosa's Taqueria was a popular lunch spot and always crowded during the noon hour. Locals often went there to enjoy the carne asada or a variety of quesadillas. And Rosa was also known for having the best guacamole around. All that made it a less-than-ideal place to hold a conversion. But Rachel was convinced something was troubling Christine, so the two friends agreed to meet for lunch.

"You're brooding," Rachel said. "Want to tell me what's going on?"

"Nothing."

"Don't tell me that. Something's up. Trouble with Emily again?"

"No. Matter of fact, things are better than they have been in a long time. We went shopping in Dallas on Tuesday. Stayed the night. Had a wonderful time."

"That's good. I know the strained relationship has been hard on you."

"Things are looking up."

"Okay, if it's not Emily, then what gives? You act like you've lost your best friend."

"I told you I'm fine."

"If you say so. Looks like you need something to cheer you up. Stephanie and I are planning a girl's night out tomorrow."

"On a Friday?"

Rachel nodded. "Brian is playing a gig with the band. Matt has a conference in Dallas and won't be home until late. I know it's short notice, but can you come?"

"I don't know. Maybe the two of you should go without me."

"Come on. We'll have fun. Matt's mother is babysitting Dylan and Abby. Wouldn't be the same without you."

Christine shook her head. "I'm not sure if I can make it."

Rachel grinned. "Oh? Other plans? Like with a certain FBI agent turned PI?"

She wished. Since their one dinner together a couple of weeks earlier, the only time she'd talked to Vince was when she ran into him in Dallas. Obviously, he had been otherwise occupied. But Christine knew Rachel wouldn't back down. "Why would you think I have plans with Vince?"

"Why not? I know you've been out with him at least once."

"How did you know?"

"Brian happened to see you at Casey's when he stopped for a take-out order."

"We met there for dinner. Wasn't even a date. Just decided to get together and talk."

Rachel cocked an eyebrow.

"As friends."

"Friends. That's a start. Brian almost didn't see you since you were sitting at a cozy little corner booth."

Christine shook her head. "Word spreads through this town faster than wildfire. Didn't know my social life held such interest for anyone."

"Relax. I've been the subject of town gossip, and I'm not about to indulge in it. Especially when it involves one of my friends. There's nothing wrong with you having a date with Vince. I think the two of you would be perfect together."

"Rachel, please don't start playing matchmaker. I know you and Stephanie have good intentions, but this isn't a good time."

"And when will be a good time?"

"I don't know. Not now. Not with everything that's happened lately —finding Jenny's body, Darla moving here. Vince is busy establishing his new detective business."

"Do I need to remind you of everything that happened when Brian and I began seeing one another? Clay Abbott tried to destroy every-thing in Brian's life and make it appear he was a serial arsonist. And what about Matt and Stephanie? They might not have ever gotten together if she hadn't decided to stay in Driscoll Lake to search for the truth about her father. It almost got her killed."

"And if it hadn't been for my husband, she wouldn't have been in that situation."

"Sorry. Didn't intend to bring up bad memories. All I'm saying is, life happens. We can't always choose our circumstances, but we can choose how we react to them."

"Point taken. It's not like someone is out to get Vince or me. We just happened to find a dead body."

"Hey, I didn't mean to minimize the situation. It must have been a horrific experience but don't let it stand in your way. First, you used Emily as an excuse, and now this. Life is too short. You know that. If you have a chance for happiness, grab onto it, and let the consequences be damned."

"Okay, you're right, but it doesn't mean Vince is a part of my future. Sure, we went out to dinner one night, but there wasn't—isn't—any romantic involvement. He hasn't called me since then. What does that tell you?"

Rachel shrugged. "Why don't you call him?"

"I couldn't do that."

"Why not? I know you're out of the dating scene, but it's not uncommon for a woman to call a man these days."

"It wasn't uncommon when we were in high school, either. Doesn't mean I'm going to chase after a man."

"Tell you what. If you can honestly tell me you're not the least bit interested in Vince, then I won't say anything else."

Christine didn't want to discuss their relationship, or lack thereof, with anyone. She glanced around the crowded room. "I'm surprised Brian isn't here. Isn't this his favorite lunch spot?"

Rachel was persistent. "Don't try to change the subject. What's going on between you and Vince?"

"Nothing. That's the problem. Did I tell you I happened to run into him in Dallas? He barely said two words to me. I got the feeling he didn't want me around."

"Did you consider he might have been on an investigation?"

"Not really, but as I said earlier, I'm not ready to talk about it. Why don't you tell me the plans for tomorrow night."

"Dinner at La Hacienda in Brewster and then a movie. We'll meet at Stephanie's house around six-thirty."

"I'll be there."

"Good. And Christine, you know I'm here for you when and if you want to talk.

VINCE DRUMMED his finger on the steering wheel. U2's "I Still Haven't Found What I'm Looking For" came through the speakers. After nearly two weeks on the job, he hadn't found a shred of evidence Angela Taylor was cheating on her husband.

He had tailed her to several fund-raising events and watched her comings and goings. Went so far as to convince an old friend to go as his date on one occasion. There was nothing to indicate Angela Taylor had a lover. He started to believe either she was good at covering her tracks or her husband had an over-active imagination.

Vince had been away from Driscoll Lake too long. While this job paid well, it wouldn't look good for any potential local customers if he disappeared from town for long periods.

His hope of leaving Dallas had dwindled when he met with Mike on Friday morning. Eric Taylor was a stubborn man and not easily swayed.

"One more evening," Mike said. "Eric claims he has it on good authority Angela is to meet someone at a country-western dive in Fort Worth tonight."

"If he's so sure, why does he need a PI? He could easily have his source check it out."

"Because Angela knows this person. She wouldn't recognize you."

Vince sighed. "All right. But a country-western club doesn't seem like it would be Angela's style. From what I've seen, she's more into the symphony. If nothing comes from this night, I'm out of here."

Now he sat in the parking lot, waiting for Angela's presumed arrival. Vince admitted she was stunning. Tall, leggy, brown eyes, dark brown hair. She could have been a supermodel. Instead, she married one of the wealthiest men in Dallas.

As attractive as she was, Vince couldn't help but think of a certain strawberry blonde. While Angela's looks were exotic and striking, Christine's were down to earth and wholesome.

He had thought about her a lot over the past couple of weeks, especially after running into her a few days ago. Too bad he'd been tied up on this case. One of the first things he planned to do when he got home was to call and explain his attitude.

If she wasn't interested in being anything other than a friend, he would live with that, though he wanted more.

Ever observant, Vince watched as people began to arrive. One of the first was cowboy driving an extended cab, dual-wheeled pickup. He selected the closest available parking space.

Shortly after the cowboy went inside, Angela Taylor arrived. She wore appropriate attire for the setting—jeans, boots, and a long-sleeved button-down shirt. Different from her usual high-priced wardrobe.

Vince picked up his cell phone, then called Mike "She's here. I'm going inside."

"As suspected. I hate to ask this, but umm… if she's not with another man, our client wants you to make a play for her."

"What?"

"Sorry, man. You heard right. Eric wants to see how she'd react if a man comes on to her."

"You know how I feel about that. Angela Taylor is a married woman."

"I'm not saying you have to do anything or follow through. Merely see what she'll do."

"Mike, your client may be rich, but he's paranoid. I'll follow her inside, see what she's up to, and report back. But I will not be a part of Eric Taylor's crazy schemes. If he doesn't want her to have his estate, he should divorce her now, pay the settlement, and move on with his life. What's left of it."

"Not that simple."

"Look, man, I didn't want to take this case in the first place. Too many bad memories."

"I understand. If you'll do it this one night, I promise I won't ask anything else. No matter what Eric Taylor wants."

"Okay." Vince ended the call, then walked into the club. He decided to sit at the bar where he had a good view of the area and could observe people coming and going.

He ordered a beer, then turned and looked around the room. Didn't take long for him to confirm Eric Taylor's suspicions. Angela sat at a corner table, cozied up with the dually-driving cowboy. It was apparent theirs wasn't a platonic relationship.

Her husband had been right. Angela was cheating on him with a younger man. The situation was so much like…

Nope. Couldn't think about that now. Had a job to do.

Vince snapped a few photos with a hidden camera, then finished his beer and left the club. He was driving back to Driscoll Lake first thing in the morning. Whatever happened between Eric and Angela Taylor was none of his business. He only hoped her actions didn't end up getting her killed.

~

LA HACIENDA WAS one of the more popular restaurants in Brewster. Christine loved the atmosphere—everything from the brightly painted walls and Mexican tile flooring, to the smell of sizzling fajitas and tasty margaritas.

"What do you think, Christine?"

Her eyes widened at Rachel's suggestion. "You want to see *that* movie?

"Why not?"

"I admit I'm curious, but I'm not sure."

"Lots of people are talking about it. I probably won't get another chance." Brian wouldn't be caught dead watching something even remotely labeled as a chick flick."

"Matt's the same way," Stephanie said. "He's more into action and drama films. As for me, I'd rather watch a movie based on a real-life story."

"Something like *American Sniper*?" Christine asked.

"Yes, but I haven't found the time."

"I'm sure it doesn't hurt that Bradley Cooper is the star." Rachel took a sip of her margarita.

Stephanie shrugged. "Who needs Bradley Cooper when I have Matt?"

"To quote my sister, you're married, not dead. But I understand what you mean. I feel the same way about Brian."

Christine smiled at the teasing banter between her two friends. She enjoyed their occasional evenings, but it was times like these when she felt like the odd person out. If she had a man in her life, she might feel differently. Didn't look like that would be happening soon.

Maybe she needed more single friends. But there weren't many single women in their mid-thirties around Driscoll Lake. Well, there was Libby. But the friendship she shared with Stephanie and Rachel went back to their school days. Circumstances separated them for a while, but now that they had re-established the bond, it wasn't likely to break.

"What do you think, Christine?"

It took a few seconds for Rachel's words to register. "I'm sorry. What did you say?"

"I asked which movie you prefer."

"I don't know. Guess I'd be okay seeing either one. Whatever you two decide is fine with me."

She looked up to see her next-door neighbor walking toward their table. Maybe it was time to get to know her better.

"Hi, Christine. Looks like you and I had similar plans."

"Looks that way. These are my friends, Rachel Nichols and Stephanie Bradford." Turning to them, she said, "Libby is Emily's art teacher and also lives next door."

Rachel and Stephanie smiled and extended greetings.

"Are you here alone?" Christine asked.

"Yes. Decided it was time for a night out, and I didn't want to stay in Driscoll Lake. I'd heard about this restaurant and thought I'd try it."

"It's one of my favorites," Rachel said.

"I can understand why. I'll come here again. Well, it was nice meeting both of you." She nodded at Rachel and Stephanie.

Christine sent a questioning glance to her friends. Both nodded, then she turned to Libby. "We're going to the movies. Would you like to join us?"

"I wouldn't want to intrude."

"It wouldn't be an imposition." Stephanie smiled.

"Thanks, but I'm probably going to meet up with a friend later. Maybe some other time."

SUSAN MASON TOOK a deep breath as she pulled into the parking lot next to Fairview Park. She had come off a long, demanding shift at

Memorial Hospital. One nurse went home sick, and an already full patient count meant extra work for everyone.

At least she had the next three days off. A hot bath and a glass of wine were in order, but she was too keyed up to go home. First, she needed a run to clear her mind and work off her frustration and tension.

Susan hesitated before opening her car door. Twilight had settled over the area, blanketing the otherwise tranquil park with a shroud of foreboding. She couldn't help but think about the woman who had been killed in Driscoll Lake. She had also been alone on a jogging trail at dusk.

Shaking off her thoughts, she got out of the car, then did a few stretches. She was familiar with the place where the murder happened. Had run the trail a few times. It was more isolated and not well lit. Fairview Park, on the other hand, usually had an abundance of runners and walkers. Street lights were interspersed throughout the area. She felt safe here.

At any rate, she didn't plan to stay long. A few laps were all she needed to clear her mind. Several runners were still out. After finishing her stretches, she set off along the trail, jogging at a steady pace. But by the time she approached her third circuit, the park was almost deserted.

She should leave, but she really wanted one more lap. She'd do it quickly and head home.

Susan was halfway around the trail when a faint rustling sound caught her attention. Pausing for a moment to listen, she took a few deep breaths and forced herself to relax. It was her imagination working overtime.

She continued then heard the rustle again, this time accompanied by the faint cry of a cat. Never one to resist animals, she stopped and looked in the direction of the sound. Crouched beneath a bush was a tiny black kitten. It shivered as it uttered another faint cry.

"Oh, poor baby. You're too little to be out here alone. Where is your mama?"

Meow.

The kitten didn't act frightened. Susan bent down and spoke to it softly, trying to coax it toward her. "Come on, baby. I won't hurt you. I'll bet you're hungry."

Meow.

She held out her hand, and the kitten began walking toward her.

Then she heard footsteps.

Calm down. It will be all right.

Fearful the person approaching would frighten the kitten away, she kept her eye on the animal and said, "I'm trying to catch a hungry, frightened kitten. Can you hold up a minute? I almost have him."

But the person didn't slow. In fact, the pace of the footsteps quickened.

Susan looked up. The hair on the back of her neck stood on end. This wasn't someone upset over an interrupted run. She had seen malicious looks before, and this was far worse. The malignant stare on the jogger's face was pure evil.

Adrenaline surged through her body. Susan pivoted and ran. She only made it a short distance when the runner grabbed her from behind and twisted her arm with one hand. The other cupped her mouth, preventing her from screaming.

Hot breath wafted against her cheek. The cold blade of a knife pressed against her chest. "Thought you could get away, huh?"

I'm going to die.

The surge of pain was momentary. Then there was nothing at all.

CHAPTER 9

*T*ami Sutton arrived at the office of the *Driscoll Lake Reporter* before any of the other employees. Being back in town felt strange to her. Only two weeks earlier she had returned after an extended stay with her parents. She never dreamed she would be seeing them again so soon.

Both her mother and stepfather had been devastated over the news of Jenny's murder. Thomas Hartsfield blamed himself, believing if he hadn't tried to push his daughter to take over the business, she wouldn't have separated herself from the family.

They'd been surprised to learn Jenny spent the last year in San Antonio. She lived only a few miles from her parents but hadn't made any attempt to contact them.

Even stranger was her move to Driscoll Lake. Had she known Tami lived here? If so, did she want to reconnect? But Tami didn't have any indication Jenny had tried to see her. San Antonio was a large city. Hiding there would be relatively easy. A small town like Driscoll Lake was another matter.

So many unanswered questions. Why did Jenny move to Driscoll Lake? Did she know someone else who lived here? If so, was that person responsible for her death?

Tami made a mental note to call Jason Montgomery and ask if he had any new information on the investigation. He probably wouldn't give her specifics, but for now, it was enough to know whether he was making progress.

She was in the break area when she heard the back door open.

"Hello? Tami?" Madge Sinclair called out.

"In here, Madge."

"How are you, honey?" Madge pulled her into a warm embrace.

"Hanging in there. It isn't easy."

"I know. Looks like you were about to make coffee. Sit down and let me take care of it. I'll bring you a cup."

"Thanks." She left the room.

A few minutes later, Madge walked into Tami's office with two steaming mugs. She handed one to Tami. "Here you go. One cream and two sugars, right?"

Tami took a sip. "Perfect. Have a seat. We still have a few minutes before we have to face the world. Besides, I wanted to ask you something."

Madge hesitated.

"Don't worry. I'm not trying to get you to gossip. While I was with my parents for Dad's surgery, did anyone come to the newspaper looking for me?"

"I gather you're asking about your sister."

"Yes."

Madge shook her head. "I'm sorry honey. I would have told you if she did."

"It's so strange. Jenny breaks off contact with our family, no one hears from her in years, and then she shows up here. Why?"

"Wish I had the answer for you."

"I may never know the reason. Doesn't make sense. And why did someone kill her? I can't believe she would do anything that would warrant someone wanting her dead."

"She could have been a random victim. By the way, did you hear what happened in Brewster?"

"No, what?"

"Someone stabbed a young woman on Friday night. She was jogging in Fairview Park."

~

"GOOD MORNING, SANDRA." Matt greeted the dispatcher as he walked into the police station.

"Hello, Chief. Detective Randy Somers with the Brewster PD wants you to call him. It's about a murder that happened there on Friday night. A young woman was stabbed—"

"Yeah, I heard about it. Figured Randy would call."

"I asked if he wanted to speak to Detective Montgomery, but he said he preferred to talk to you. Can't say that I blame him."

Matt took the slip of paper from Sandra's hand, ignoring her comment about the detective. "I've known Randy since our police academy days. Jason here yet?"

"He's in his office."

"Thanks." Matt started down the hallway when he passed Jason. "Glad you're here. Come with me."

"What did I do this time?"

"Nothing, I hope. Did you hear about the murder in Brewster?"

"No."

"Stabbing victim. Happened Friday night in Fairview Park."

"Another one?"

"Yeah. Could be the same person who killed Jenny Allen. Detective Somers wants me to call. Figured you need to listen in."

Matt waited until Jason closed the office door before making the call. "Chief Bradford from Driscoll Lake calling for Detective Somers... Yes, I'll hold..."

"Can't imagine why he didn't ask to speak to me." Jason's words were almost inaudible.

Matt chose to ignore him. "Randy? Hey man, what's up?"

"Guess you know by now about Friday night's murder. Similar to the one in Driscoll Lake."

"Heard about it but don't know the details. Randy, I have Jason

Montgomery in the office with me. He's heading up the investigation on Jenny Allen's murder. Mind if I put you on speaker?"

"No problem."

Matt pressed the speaker button and placed the receiver back in its cradle. "Go ahead."

"You probably already know she was jogging alone in Fairview Park. She had come off a twelve-hour shift at Brewster Memorial. No signs of assault or robbery."

"Any suspects?" Jason asked.

"Not at this time. Victim was single. Lived alone. The park was almost deserted. No witnesses have come forth. A couple of runners found the body early Saturday morning."

"Sounds like it could be the same perp," Jason said.

"It's possible," Matt said. "What else have you got?"

"We've sent the body for an autopsy and DNA analysis. She fought the killer. Found traces of blood and skin cells beneath her fingernails. We combed the area for clues. Interviewed friends and coworkers. She was well-liked by her peers. No apparent enemies."

"What about the weapon?"

"Judging from the size of the wounds, my guess would be some type of hunting knife."

"Interesting. The coroner said the knife used on our victim was a smaller blade."

"Killer could have used two different knives." Jason offered.

"It's possible." Detective Somers sounded skeptical.

"Sounds like you have doubts," Matt said.

"Too soon to tell. Not going to speculate on anything but the MO is similar."

"Keep us updated. We'll do likewise." Matt glanced at Jason as he spoke.

"I'll be in touch."

"Thanks." Matt ended the call.

"Sound like we have a serial killer," Jason said.

"Jason, do you always look for an easy way out?"

"No, but—"

"If I were you, I wouldn't be so quick to jump to conclusions. Don't think you're off the hook. I expect you to continue looking for leads. But who knows? Maybe you'll get lucky and not have to work so hard at solving this one."

～

VINCE HAD SPENT most of Saturday wrapping up the details of the Taylor case. Intent on getting home, he dropped by Mike's house to leave his final report. They sat on the patio, discussing the investigation.

"I owe you one, buddy," Mike said. "Appreciate your help."

"Do me a favor and don't call me for another one like this anytime soon."

"Don't worry. I won't. Eric Taylor is a bit eccentric, but he was right about his wife."

"He was that."

"Why don't you stay for dinner? Nothing fancy. Planned to grill some burgers. Patti has been looking forward to seeing you."

"Appreciate the invitation, but I'm heading back to Driscoll Lake tonight."

"She'll be home any minute. If you leave without seeing her, I'll never hear the end of it."

Mike's wife chose that moment to walk outside. "Please, stay. We don't see you much these days. Matter of fact, why don't you spend the night and drive home tomorrow morning?"

"It'll give us a chance to catch up," Mike said.

Vince could hardly refuse the offer. Mike and Patti had stood by him in both good and bad times. After staying awake half the night, he was tired. Made sense to stay and get a solid eight hours before driving home. "Okay, you talked me into it."

"Good."

A few minutes later, Mike placed the burgers on the grill. "When was the last time you saw your parents?"

Vince took a sip of his beer. "It's been a while."

"You've been in Dallas for almost two weeks. Have you even called them?"

"You've kept me busy, remember?"

"Not so much that you didn't have time to visit your family. That excuse might work with someone else, but not with me. Bet they don't even know you're here."

"It's not that I don't want to see them."

"What gives?"

"You know how my mother can be. Always asking questions I don't have answers to. Always reading about similar situations, then dreaming up ways of how they could be related. The sad thing is, nothing she comes up with makes any sense."

Mike hesitated a moment. "Is she… I hate to ask, but have you considered the possibility she could have early onset of dementia?"

Vince shook his head. "No. It's not that. She just wants closure and is grasping at straws."

"As would anyone in her position. She needs you, Vince. So, does your father. Call them."

Mike was right. His parents did need him. And he also knew he'd avoided them. He had allowed his own misgivings to keep him away.

Before going to bed, he phoned and decided to have Sunday brunch with them. Both were glad to see him, and he managed to keep the conversation light. When his father asked if he wanted to play a round of golf, he agreed. Afterward, the three of them ate dinner at the country club.

It was evening before he got back to Driscoll Lake. Too late to call Christine.

Shortly after arriving in his office on Monday morning, he received a call from an insurance company asking him to investigate a suspected fraud case. The new attorney also had a couple of investigations for him. He spent most of the day familiarizing himself with the details of each case.

He worked through lunch, not looking up from his desk until early afternoon. It felt good to be doing something other than spying on a cheating spouse.

But he still hadn't phoned Christine. Vince glanced at his watch. She would be in the classroom. No point in calling now. Leaving a voicemail somehow didn't seem adequate. He wanted to talk to her in person. But to show up on her doorstep uninvited probably wasn't a good idea, either.

Turning to his computer, he spent the remainder of the afternoon researching his cases. Tomorrow, he would visit the site of the suspected insurance fraud. Pleased with his progress, he locked the screen, then noticed the time. Almost six.

Mentally cursing himself, he pulled his cell phone from his pocket then scrolled through the recent calls until he found Christine's number.

She didn't answer until the fourth ring.

"Hey," he said. "I was about to grab a bite to eat and wondered if you had plans."

There was silence on the other end.

Great, Vince. Blurt it out without so much as a hello or how are you.

Seconds passed before Christine answered. "Can't. Having a pizza delivered."

"Another time?"

"Maybe."

"How are things with you?"

"Okay."

Apparently, she wasn't in the mood to talk.

"You sound busy, so I won't keep you. Guess I'll talk to you soon." Without waiting for her to reply, Vince ended the call.

He shook his head. What was it with her? Maybe he had been mistaken, but when they ate dinner together a couple of weeks earlier, she acted as if she'd like to see him again. Not only that, she'd invited him to have dinner with her and Emily in Dallas. Something had changed.

CHRISTINE LISTENED as the line went dead. What was up with Vince?

She hadn't seen or spoken to him until that accidental meeting in Dallas then he suddenly calls to ask her out.

Right. Another one of those "let's get together as friends" dinners. That's all they would ever have. After seeing him in Dallas a few nights ago, it was apparent his interest lay elsewhere. Probably with a certain blonde.

Okay, he had occupied her thoughts the past couple of weeks. She'd even driven by his office a few times. The place looked dark and deserted. It would have been nice to know he planned to be away for a while, but he didn't owe her an explanation.

But why had she acted so rude to him on the phone? He probably had his reasons for not calling. And as for the encounter in Dallas, maybe he had been on an investigation. After all, that was his job. The least she could do was to call him back.

She reached for her phone only to be interrupted by the ringing of the doorbell.

"Pizza's here, Mom," Emily called out. "The driver needs money."

"I'm coming."

Any plan of contacting Vince would have to wait until later.

AFTER THE PHONE call to Christine, Vince decided to stop at Casey's for a bite to eat before going home. Somehow, he couldn't muster up any enthusiasm to cook.

The place was crowded when he arrived. When he learned there was a half-hour wait for a table, he opted to sit at the bar. There were two vacant seats, so he chose the one at the end. With luck, no one would sit beside him. He wasn't in the mood for talking.

"What will you have?" the bartender asked.

"Whatever you have on tap."

"Coming right up."

The bartender placed the beer on the counter. "Need a menu?"

"Not necessary. I'll have the jalapeno burger with mayo, all the toppings with a side of seasoned fries."

"Sure thing."

Vince took a sip of his beer and glanced at the big screen TV. The Mavericks and the Spurs were playing. Too bad he wasn't much of a basketball fan.

Looking around the room, he took note of several people. Some came for happy hour, needing to unwind after a long day. Others were there to drown their sorrows as evidenced by slumped shoulders and sagging facial features.

Which category did he fit in? The beer would help him to relax, but he couldn't help but feel disappointed that Christine wasn't available. Or even willing to chat. But he would be damned if he would come across like a member of some lonely-hearts club. He straightened his shoulders and sat up a little higher.

A few minutes later, he glanced toward the door. A dark-haired woman had just entered. When the hostess pointed to the vacant stool next to him, she looked at her watch and nodded.

Great. Like I want someone sitting next to me.

Vince hoped she wouldn't be one of those chatty types, but he was good at tuning people out when necessary. Pulling his cell phone from his pocket, he began reading through his email. If all else failed, he could always pretend interest in the basketball game.

He didn't have to look to know when she slid onto the stool next to him. No doubt the perfume she wore was expensive, but it was over-powering.

What did she do? Marinate in it?

By contrast, he thought of the light, airy scent Christine wore. Fresh. Clean. Like a mix of sunshine and orange blossoms.

He felt the woman's eyes on him, but he took another sip of beer without acknowledging her presence. No reason to encourage familiarity.

"Hello," she said.

Vince smiled and nodded, then fixed his attention on the TV screen.

"Crowded in here tonight."

"It often is." He hoped the clipped response would discourage her.

"Come here often?"

She didn't take hints easily. Looking her in the eye, he said, "Yes, but usually not alone."

"Oh, I see. Someone special?"

Fortunately, the server placed his burger on the counter, saving him from any additional response. The woman was now talking to the man on her left. With luck, he would be the talkative type. But a few minutes later, he left the bar.

Vince resisted the urge to rush through his meal. Instead, he forced himself to look at the television, aware of the woman looking his way on occasion.

"You're not interested, are you?"

Her words took Vince by surprise. "Excuse me?"

She nodded toward the TV. "The game. You keep watching the screen but aren't paying attention. What gives?"

This woman had nerve. He'd give her that. What did she care whether he liked basketball? Why couldn't she leave him alone? He opened his mouth to reply when his cell phone rang, and he turned away to answer. "Hello?"

"Hi, it's Christine. Sorry I acted so rude when you called."

His day suddenly got brighter. "No reason to apologize. Guess my invitation took you by surprise."

"It did, but that's still no excuse."

"Then let me apologize for not calling you in a while."

"Figure you've been busy."

"Yeah, I've been away on an investigation."

"That's what you were doing in Dallas?"

"Yeah. Not the kind of assignment I like, but it helps pay the bills. Should have told you I would be away for a while."

"It's your job. You don't owe me an explanation."

"I know, but maybe I want to explain. Why don't we get together and talk about it?"

"I'd like that, but I'm going with a group of students to a camp outside Austin. We leave tomorrow morning and won't be home until late Friday afternoon."

"How about Friday evening? Unless you'd rather rest after the trip."

"No, I'll be fine. Probably will need to unwind after spending time with a bunch of fifth graders."

"Tell you what. Not to brag, but I'm a pretty good cook. How about coming to my house around seven, and I'll make stir fry?"

"Sounds great."

"Then it's a date. See you Friday." Vince ended the call, then asked for his check. He pulled some bills from his wallet, aware the woman was watching him. No doubt she'd overheard part of his conversation with Christine.

"The 'special' friend?"

Vince ignored her question. "Keep the change," he told the bartender. Without so much as a glance in the woman's direction, he walked away.

Watching, waiting, hoping. All part of life. It took someone with finesse to know how to handle each. One needed patience to see a job through.

Watching. Being observant. Taking notice of a person's surroundings. The interaction between two individuals. People, places, things. It was something that must be done with discretion so as not to attract attention to one's own self. A master at deceit.

Waiting. Timing had to be executed perfectly. Too early and things wouldn't work out as planned. Too late meant an opportunity missed. An opportunity missed was never a good thing.

Hoping. Only fools relied on hope alone. Hope without action was useless. And action without careful planning was futile.

The lone figure slipped away from the restaurant, smiling. Convinced all the right attributes had been mastered. Patience, finesse. The courage to act. Everyone would be shocked to know the identity of Jenny's killer. But not to worry. The likelihood of anyone learning the truth was slim.

CHAPTER 10

*J*ason Montgomery rubbed his forehead as he looked through the file on his desk. Three weeks had passed since the murder of Jenny Allen, and he still wasn't close to finding her killer. Chief Bradford wanted to meet with him this afternoon to discuss the case, and he wasn't looking forward to it. If he had even one new piece of evidence, he might feel differently.

Instead, he mentally prepared himself for Matt's reaction. Jason couldn't understand why the police chief held such animosity toward him. No, he wasn't Carlos Gonzales. The man had almost thirty years of experience in homicide investigations before moving to Driscoll Lake. Hard to compete with a person of his caliber.

Carlos was instrumental in solving a twenty-year-old murder case involving the father of Matt's wife. That probably scored him a few points with the chief.

But Jason was also a good detective. His methods might be a bit unorthodox by some people's standards, but they worked for him. People weren't trustworthy until they proved otherwise. That belief had helped him catch more than one criminal over the years.

Didn't matter this was the type of town where everyone knew

everyone. The world was filled with evil people. Big cities. Small towns. The death of Stephanie Bradford's father proved Driscoll Lake hadn't been immune to crime. The double murder occurred more than twenty years ago by a supposedly upstanding citizen.

None of that seemed to make a difference to Matt. Jason suspected there were other reasons for the chief's apparent dislike of him.

Jason liked women. Nothing wrong with that. The incident with the dispatcher made Matt even more suspicious of him. Sandra Stewart had an outgoing personality, and Jason had mistaken her friendliness for something else.

Flirting with Officer Daniels while on duty hadn't been his brightest idea. From now on, he'd leave his personal life out of the office. Better yet, he wouldn't become involved with anyone on the police force. He'd look elsewhere. Driscoll Lake wasn't short of attractive women.

Tami Sutton was one. Tall, blonde, dark blue eyes. After his encounter with her at the bar a few weeks ago, he knew she wasn't above using her looks to get what she wanted. Not that he hadn't done the same thing.

In spite of what he said to Matt, he didn't believe she had anything to do with her sister's murder. Tami had an iron-clad alibi. Must have been devastating to learn your long-lost sister had shown up only to end up dead in a few short weeks.

Jenny Allen was an enigma. Nothing about her past gave him any clues as to who murdered her. He'd spoken to people who knew Jenny in Taos, Santa Fe, and San Antonio. No one had been able to provide anything that would point him to her killer.

Everyone he'd spoken with said Jenny was quiet and kept to herself. Wasn't one to make enemies. Jason was beginning to believe the killing had been a random act. Same as the murder in Brewster. He'd kept in close contact with detective Somers.

So far, Brewster police hadn't come up with a suspect. That was a good thing. If these murders were the work of a serial killer, which was yet to be determined, Jason wanted to be the one to solve the crime. What better way to get in Matt's good graces and secure his position on the force? And that was only the stepping stone to bigger and better things.

As he looked at the file, another issue came to mind. How was Jenny's killer able to escape unnoticed? No one who had been jogging that evening reported seeing anything suspicious. Vince Green and Christine Lawrence approached the crime scene from opposite directions. Neither of them saw anyone along the path.

The coroner estimated the victim had only been dead a short time before they found the body. There were no footsteps in the soft earth alongside the path, which meant the murderer had either walked or run at least a short distance along the paved trail.

Christine or Vince might have seen something or someone and had blotted it from their memory. Jason knew of instances where it had happened. The shock of witnessing a brutal crime or being the first on the scene was overwhelming for some people.

If that were the case, he'd be willing to bet Christine was the one who had forgotten. Vince Green was a former law enforcement officer. Trained to be observant. He would notice things most people would overlook.

It was time to have another talk with Ms. Lawrence.

DARLA SMILED at the two smartly-dressed women as they entered the gallery. She recognized Evelyn Martin, who had purchased the Saldana painting. Her instincts had been correct. Evelyn had visited the gallery a couple of times since, looking at new inventory. She had also sent a few potential customers Darla's way.

"Good afternoon, ladies."

"This is my new neighbor, Sonya Ramsey. She and her husband recently moved to Driscoll Lake from San Antonio. Sonya, this is Darla Martell, the gallery owner."

"Nice to meet you." She extended her hand in greeting.

"Likewise." Sonya Ramsey returned the handshake and flipped a strand of long brown hair over her shoulder.

"Sonya fell in love with my new painting," Evelyn said. "We wondered if you might have others by the same artist."

Darla shook her head. "I'm afraid that's the only Saldana I had in stock, but I know a gallery that has several pieces of his art. If you would like to step into my office, I can show you some digital images. Then, if you see anything you like, I can arrange to have the painting shipped here."

"A digital image? I'm not sure."

"You wouldn't be obligated to buy. I realize looking at a photo isn't the same as seeing the original artwork."

"If that's the case, then yes, I'll take a look."

Within an hour, Sonya selected two paintings she was interested in possibly purchasing. "How soon do you think you'll have them?"

"Shouldn't be any problem with getting them here by next week. The gallery owner is a friend. I'll phone her and arrange expedited shipping. Once they arrive, I'll give you a call."

"You want to do what?" Matt looked at the man sitting in front of his desk, not believing what he had heard. He thought Jason was finally doing something right regarding the investigation into Jenny Allen's murder. Now, he wasn't so sure. A quick look through the open blinds told him several in the department overheard. People stopped what they were doing and looked his way.

He lowered his voice. "Tell me I didn't hear what I think I heard."

Jason was calm. "I want to interview Christine Lawrence again. But not as a suspect. I think there is a possibility she saw someone or something and doesn't remember. The killer had to escape somehow, and we couldn't find any footprints leading away from the crime scene. Whoever this person is, he or she had to have walked or run at least a short distance along the trail."

"You have a point, but why Christine? What about Vince? The killer could have gone in his direction."

"It's possible, but I think he would be more apt to notice anything out of the ordinary."

"Because of his training. I agree, but I'm not sure how Christine will react when she learns you want to talk to her. You're not exactly her favorite person."

"Yeah, I blew it." Jason shifted in his chair. "I was wrong."

Matt tilted his head. He found it hard to believe the arrogant detective would admit to being wrong about anything. Maybe there was hope for him, after all. "You want me to call and explain?"

"Would you?"

"If it will help to solve the crime, yes."

SEATS on the chartered coach were more comfortable than a school bus, but Christine felt relieved as they neared Austin. Making a five-hour trip with thirty fifth and sixth graders was enough to try the patience of a saint.

To make matters worse, the woman sitting next to Christine was the talkative type. Hannah McDade was one of the parental chaperones. She chatted almost non-stop the first hour before Christine pulled out her phone. Putting in her earbuds, she opened the music app, leaned back, and closed her eyes.

She would have preferred to read, but trying to concentrate on a book would be useless. At least she wouldn't be in the same hotel room with the woman.

They had almost reached their destination when her phone rang. Surprised to see Matt's number, she hurried to answer. It was unusual for him to call. Her first thought was of Emily.

"Matt? Is something wrong?"

"Everything is fine. Just needed to run something by you. Jason Montgomery wants to speak to you again about the night of the murder."

"I think he said enough. He certainly made it clear he considered me to be a suspect."

"Well, he's changed his mind. Realizes he was wrong about you and Vince. He thinks there may be a chance you could provide more information."

"I don't see how. I told him everything I know."

"Is it possible you've forgotten something? Maybe saw someone along the path before you discovered the body and blotted it from your mind? Traumatic events sometimes cause us to obliterate things we don't want to remember."

Christine lowered her voice. "I'm sure it happens, but I'm equally confident I remember everything I saw."

"You're probably right but give it some thought. Could have been in the surrounding woods. Nothing more than a brief glimpse of something or someone."

"I doubt it, but I'll think on it. I'm in Austin for a few days, but tell Detective Montgomery I'll phone him when I return on Friday." Christine ended the call as the bus pulled into the hotel's parking lot.

"Is something wrong?" Hannah asked.

"Police are still trying to solve Jenny Allen's murder. Wanted to know if I might have forgotten a few details that could help lead them to the killer's identity."

"Do you think you did miss something?"

Christine shook her head. "Doubtful. It was an ordinary day. Not many people were still in the park. I had seen and talked to Vince a few minutes earlier."

"Vince? Who is that?"

"He's the man—the friend—who came along right after I discovered Jenny's body. He was running the trail in the opposite direction, and we had met up on the other side of the lake."

"Think he might have seen someone?"

"No. And if he had, he would have remembered. He was with the FBI. Doesn't miss much."

"Sounds to me like the police are grasping at straws."

Christine shrugged. "They're doing what they have to do. The murder affected a lot of lives. I haven't gone running since then. Don't want to be out alone. Wish I could remember something. I'm sure everyone will feel safer once they catch the murderer."

CHRISTINE LOOKED across Vince's dining room table and smiled. The trip to Austin, along with her afternoon meeting with Jason, had left her exhausted to the point she almost canceled their plans. She was glad now she didn't. He'd put a lot of effort into this evening. Soft music. Candlelight. A home-cooked dinner.

"Delicious meal," she said. "I had no idea you were such a good cook."

Vince shrugged. "I have a few surprises up my sleeve."

"Oh, really?"

"Seriously, when you live alone, you learn. Got tired of eating out all the time and decided to do something about it."

"Self-taught, huh?"

"For the most part. How about dessert? It's cheesecake with strawberries."

"You made cheesecake?"

He shook his head. "Dessert is one thing I don't do. Stopped by that new bakery in Cameron Place. It's close to your mother-in-law's gallery."

"Darla says their desserts are great."

After they finished eating, Christine offered to help clean up the kitchen, but Vince declined. "Have a seat in the living room, and I'll join you shortly."

A cold front had moved through that afternoon, reminding everyone that even though spring had teased, winter wasn't ready to quit. The forecast called for lows in the upper twenties with a chance for light snow.

Vince had built a fire earlier, and the logs crackled softly. The flames cast a soft glow as Christine sat down on the overstuffed leather sofa. The coziness of the room made her grateful for the cold weather.

"Penny for your thoughts," Vince said as sat beside her.

She smiled. "Not sure they're worth that much. I saw a few snow flurries on the drive over."

"You like snow?"

She nodded. "It's almost magical. So silent and peaceful when it falls. Seems like the whole world has stopped to listen. Makes me realize I need to slow down more often and not take for granted what's around me."

"Yeah. I know what you mean."

"I spoke to Jason Montgomery this afternoon. Matt called me when I was in Austin to say he had a few more questions."

Vince frowned. "Like what?"

"He realized he had misjudged me—us. They don't have any suspects or leads. Jason seems to think I might have forgotten something. Maybe I saw someone and blotted it from my memory."

"It happens. I've interviewed witnesses who don't remember things until weeks or even months later."

"I'm thinking about undergoing hypnosis. Probably won't make a difference, but I'm willing to try.

"Did Jason suggest it?"

She shook her head. "I mentioned it to him. Wasn't sure if any information obtained would be allowed in court."

"Texas has allowed it for a long time. But many don't agree with the reliability of forensic hypnosis."

"What do you think?"

"I believe it can be useful in some cases."

"So, you're not convinced it works."

"Not everyone can be hypnotized. Some people want to be but subconsciously fight it."

"Didn't know that. Guess I won't know unless I try."

"True. How about we change the subject? It occurred to me that I don't know a lot about you."

"Not much to tell. I grew up in Driscoll Lake, went away to college, married my high school sweetheart, and returned here. You already know I teach fifth grade and have a teenage daughter. My parents retired and moved to Arizona a few years ago. I have an older brother who is career Navy and currently stationed in San Diego."

"Are you close to your family?"

"You could say we have a good relationship. I don't see them often. What about you?"

"I probably visit my parents once or twice a year."

"They live far away?"

Vince shook his head. "Dallas."

"Then why—Sorry, none of my business."

"They're on the go a lot. I'm busy. I did see them last weekend."

Christine sensed there was more to the story. "Any siblings?"

His eyes were fixed on some object across the room. She wondered if he had even heard the question.

"Vince?"

He jerked his head toward her. "I'm sorry. You were saying?"

"I asked if you had any siblings."

"A brother. He lives in Naples, Florida. Haven't seen him since… It's been a couple of years."

Definitely a story there, but Christine didn't want to push for information. She didn't know him well enough to ask. Maybe in time, if they continued to see one another, he would confide in her.

They sat in silence for a while, watching the flames dance in the fireplace. Even with the awkward moment earlier, Christine felt safe. Content. She could get used to this.

"Think you'll ever marry again?" His voice was so low she almost didn't hear him. Even so, she wasn't sure she'd understood.

"What did you say?"

"Probably shouldn't have been so blunt. I tend to say what's on my mind."

"I don't have a problem with someone being frank, but your question caught me off guard."

"Why? You're an attractive woman. It's been a while since Kyle's death."

"Guess I haven't thought a lot about it. I've only been out on a few dates."

"Easily changed. I'd like to make sure it does."

She offered a tentative smile. "You don't mince words, do you?"

"Everything that has happened the last few weeks has made me realize how short life can be. If someone has a chance at happiness, they should grab onto it and not let go."

"Someone recently reminded me of that."

"So, what do you think? Interested?"

Christine smiled. "I'm more than interested."

CHAPTER 11

There was a time when Matt Bradford's life revolved around his job. He made himself available twenty-four seven, never took vacations, and didn't socialize except to attend public events related to his position as police chief.

All that changed when he married Stephanie. He kept weekends open to spend time with his family. His staff knew not to bother him unless something major came up. When the phone call came from Jason Montgomery on Saturday morning, Matt knew it was important.

"Chief, this is Jason. Got a call from Detective Somers this morning. There's been another murder in Brewster."

Matt pinched the bridge of his nose, a habit he'd developed when faced with stressful situations. "Same MO?"

"Yes. Young female. Multiple stab wounds. Found alongside a quiet street two blocks from her apartment. Last seen alive by her roommate around eight when she went out for a run."

"Alone? At night? Despite two recent murders?"

"Yeah. Victim told her friend she needed to clear her head and that she planned to run the track at the high school practice field. When she hadn't returned two hours later, the roommate became concerned and phoned the police."

"Anything suspicious with the roommate?"

"Not according to Somers. They believe it's the same perp who killed the nurse a couple of weeks ago."

"Serial killer?"

"Looks that way."

"People will start to panic when word gets out."

"Yeah. Somers thinks it might be a good idea if both departments conduct a joint press conference at ten. I planned to drive over there this morning. Thought you might want to come along."

"Yeah, guess I'd better. Give me half an hour. I'll meet you at the station."

Matt ended the call, then went into the bedroom. Stephanie had morning sickness earlier and was back in bed.

"Who was on the phone?" she asked.

"Jason. There's been another stabbing in Brewster. Looks like the work of a serial killer."

"Think the same person killed Jenny Allen?"

"Possibly. Whatever the case, once the public gets hold of the information, rumors will start flying. Jason and I need to meet with the police at Brewster. There's a press conference later this morning. Sorry I have to leave you, honey."

"I understand."

"Want me to see if Mom will watch Abby?"

Stephanie shook her head. "It's okay. I'm feeling better now. I'll call her if I need anything."

Matt bent down and kissed her. "I'll be home as soon as I can."

THE CLOUDS MOVED out during the night, and their departure eliminated any chances of snow. Even with the bright sunshine, Christine couldn't help but feel a twinge of disappointment when she awoke the following morning.

Silly. Her happiness didn't depend on the weather. But being with Vince last night--watching the firelight glow while intermittent snow fell to the ground—brought a sense of contentment. One she hadn't felt in years. Something she didn't want to slip away.

She had stayed until almost midnight. Vince walked her to the car, promising to call today. Stretching languidly, she smiled as she remembered the kiss they shared.

Even though they both agreed they wanted to see one another more often, Christine couldn't help but believe Vince was holding something back. He was reluctant to talk about leaving the FBI. Other than brief comments about his family, he wouldn't discuss them.

Something had happened to make him give up the career he'd strived for. She'd be willing to bet whatever it was had put a strain on the relationship with his family.

Sighing, she got out of bed. Emily had spent the night with Darla. This would be a good day to run some much-needed errands.

Two hours later, having finished her to do list, Christine found herself driving aimlessly around town. She kept replaying yesterday's events in her mind—the conversation with Jason, her evening with Vince. Without conscious thought, she ended up at Stephanie's house. Matt's pickup wasn't in the driveway, so she decided to stop.

She walked to the door but hesitated before ringing the bell.

Maybe coming here wasn't such a good idea. Stephanie was a good friend, but Christine wasn't sure she was ready to talk. At least not yet. Still, she pressed the button.

"Christine. This is a surprise," Stephanie said when she opened the door.

"Sorry for dropping by unannounced."

"It's okay. Come in."

Christine followed her into the living room, then sat on the sofa.

"Care for some coffee?"

She shook her head. "I can't stay long. I was in the neighborhood, and I…"

"What's on your mind?"

"It's about Jenny Allen's murder." Okay, it wasn't exactly a lie. She had given considerable thought to her conversation with Jason.

"Finding the body couldn't have been easy for you."

"It wasn't, but I'm dealing with it."

"Everyone is shaken up over the whole thing. Especially since two similar murders were committed in Brewster."

"Two?"

"Another one last night. Matt and Jason are there now."

"Montgomery had some more questions for me yesterday."

Stephanie rolled her eyes. "I can imagine what that was like. He isn't exactly Matt's favorite person."

"Actually, it went okay." She told Stephanie about Jason's idea that she may have forgotten some things related to the murder.

"I did some research into suppressed memory a few years ago for a book I wrote. It happens more often than you realize."

"So I've been told. I'm thinking of undergoing hypnosis to see if it will help me remember. I talked to Vince about it. He's not sure. Said it had helped in some cases, but he's skeptical."

"Vince, huh?"

"Yeah, I was at his place last night and—"

Stephanie grinned. "His place? Last night?"

"Not what you're thinking. He invited me for dinner. That's it."

"That's a start. I think the two of you would be great together."

Christine looked away and glanced around the room. She loved the open look of the log home, the high ceilings, and loft. "Can't believe you and Matt are selling this place."

"We love it here. But with the new baby coming, three bedrooms aren't enough. More importantly though, you're changing the subject. Tell me more about you and Vince."

Christine hesitated. "Stephanie, I'm afraid. Vince seems like a great guy, and honestly, I've wanted to get to know him a long time, but…"

"Think you're betraying Kyle's memory?"

"In a way."

"Let me ask you something. What if you had been the one to die? If Kyle found a chance at happiness, would you want him to take it?"

"Of course, I would."

"Don't you think he'd want the same for you?"

"Probably, but it's not that simple. I have Emily to consider. Not sure how she'll feel about me becoming involved with someone."

"You've been using Emily as an excuse for a while now. And it's not like Vince is the first man you've dated since Kyle died. Why do I get the feeling there's another reason behind your hesitation?"

"Maybe because Vince is the first man I've considered having a long-term relationship with."

"And that's a problem?"

"I think he's holding back some things. He doesn't want to talk about his past. Won't say why he left the FBI. Relationships are supposed to be built on trust. If he can't trust me enough to tell me, then it could be over before it begins."

"I see." Stephanie steepled her fingers and rested her chin on them.

"Guess I'm being over-sensitive. But knowing Kyle kept secrets all those years…" Christine shook her head.

"That was a different situation. The biggest mistake you can make is to compare Vince to Kyle."

"I know that. I'm not trying to compare the two of them."

"Let me tell you something. When I first came back to Driscoll Lake, it wasn't all roses between Matt and me. Matter of fact, I think he resented me being here. Our first meeting was, shall I say, less than cordial."

"You're kidding?"

"Wish I was, but that's a story for another time. My point is, I wasn't sure I could trust him. When those anonymous notes began showing up, I couldn't help but wonder if he was responsible."

"No way!"

"It's true. Then rumors started about him being responsible for his first wife's death. Eventually, he felt comfortable enough to confide in me. It took a while, but we both had to build up trust between one another."

"I'm surprised. Especially given how you felt about him in high school. And I'm pretty sure he felt the same way about you."

Stephanie shrugged. "Who's to say what might have happened if I hadn't moved away. But the important thing is, Matt and I found our way back to one another. Give Vince a chance. You've been out on what —two, three dates?"

"Guess I am trying to rush things."

"If Vince cares about you, and I'm sure he does, he'll come around."

"Thanks. I needed to hear that."

"You're welcome. By the way, don't worry about Emily. I was once in her position. It was hard for me when Mom first began dating David, but I couldn't ask for a better stepfather. Emily will be okay."

WHEN TAMI SUTTON received a call from a colleague in Brewster about a second murder that happened, she decided to attend the press conference. A month had passed since her sister's death, and police were still not close to finding the person responsible.

Now it appeared a serial killer was on the loose. Had Jenny been an arbitrary victim? Was the killer a psychopath who singled out young women? Or had someone deliberately targeted her?

If so, what was the connection to the other victims in Brewster? Jenny hadn't lived in Driscoll Lake long enough to know a lot of people. As far as Tami could tell, she had nothing in common with the other women.

Susan Mason was a nurse. The latest victim, Lori Huff, worked as a paralegal in a local law firm. Both professionals. Jenny had been a would-be artist who worked in an art gallery. All three women were single and in their late twenties.

The two women from Brewster were runners. Jenny's body was found alongside a jogging trail, but Tami had never known her to be a runner. Then again, almost six years had passed since they'd last seen one another. As Jason Montgomery once pointed out, people change.

Tami sat in the conference room of Brewster City Hall, content to listen while other reporters directed questions to Brewster's lead investigator. Officials must think Jenny's murder was related. Otherwise, Matt Bradford and Jason Montgomery wouldn't be present.

"Do you believe the same person is responsible for the murders of Susan Mason and Lori Huff?"

"Were the victims specifically chosen?"

"Did the victims know one another?"

Any other time, she would have had a few questions of her own, but something troubled her. Police often withheld information, things only the killer would know, to catch a potential suspect during interrogation. Were they withholding something? If so, what?

Her interest piqued when a reporter from a local TV station mentioned her sister. "Detective Montgomery, do you believe the murder of Jenny Allen is related to these killings?"

Jason exchanged a quick look with Matt, then spoke into the microphone. "At this point, we're not going to rule out anything."

What were they not saying?

"You think another person is responsible for the Driscoll Lake killing?"

Matt answered this time. "We won't rule out any possibilities until we complete our investigation."

"Detective Montgomery, do you have any suspects in the Driscoll Lake murder?"

"Like Chief Bradford said, our investigation is still ongoing. We're cooperating fully with Brewster officials. Everyone wants a swift solution to these murders."

Tami chewed on her lower lip and tried to concentrate on what else was being said. The Brewster Police chief was speaking now, but his words barely registered. On the one hand, learning Jenny had been a random victim would be devastating.

Knowing she had been in the wrong place at the wrong time would be a bitter pill to swallow. But if someone had deliberately targeted her... Tami wasn't sure which would be worse.

When the press conference broke up, she caught Matt Bradford's eye. He nodded briefly. They may have had their differences in the past, but Tami knew he wanted justice served. Yet she couldn't shake the feeling he and Jason were hiding something.

∼

MATT WAS quiet during the drive back to Driscoll Lake. He had hoped the visit with officials in Brewster would provide new information, but the meeting left him with more questions than answers.

Jason looked straight ahead as he drove and kept the conversation to a minimum. Something had changed with him in the last couple of weeks. He'd been more cooperative, hadn't caused any disruptions in the office, and had been putting in long hours on the case.

The change in Jason's attitude made Matt's job a lot easier. He wasn't about to question why. Better to leave well enough alone. He had enough to handle without dealing with an insubordinate employee.

They were on the outskirts of Driscoll Lake when Matt finally spoke. "Something doesn't add up."

"What makes you say that?"

"Not sure. Just a feeling."

Jason scoffed. "Feeling? I would have thought you of all people wouldn't try to solve a case on feelings."

"I'm not. Thinking out loud."

"Each victim was stabbed more than once. All were out jogging, or at least on a running trail. All close to the same age."

"That's true."

"What more do you want?"

Matt glanced at Jason. "Proof. The autopsy report on Jenny Allen indicated seventeen separate wounds. Someone stabbed her repeatedly and likely in rapid succession. I believe it was a crime of passion."

"You don't think the others were?"

"Not sure. Neither of them was stabbed that many times."

"Okay. Let's assume you're right. Who hated Jenny enough to kill her?" Jason pulled the car into the parking lot of the police station.

"I think we can rule one thing out. She didn't live in Driscoll Lake long enough to make an enemy like that."

"You believe someone knew she was here, came to town, killed her, and moved on?"

"It's possible."

"I haven't found anything in her background that would warrant someone hating her that much."

"We're missing something. Here's another thing. Jenny wore street clothes. Not running attire. Probably went to the park immediately after leaving the gallery."

"So that proves her murder is unrelated to the others?"

"No, but she could have gone to the park to meet someone."

"If that was the case, she didn't agree to meet them by phone. Records indicate she made an early morning call to her job. Nothing else for the rest of the day."

"Someone could have phoned her at work. Maybe even visited her."

"Okay, it's possible. Darla Martell stated she was at the gallery until four when she went to pick up her granddaughter. I'll talk to her again."

"My guess is she doesn't have surveillance video in the store."

"Even if she did, most of those only record for a certain amount of time. Would probably be recorded over by now." Jason shook his head. "Guess I blew an opportunity."

Matt narrowed his gaze. This was the second time Jason had admitted he'd screwed up. "Not unless the killer made an appearance at the gallery while Darla was there. Maybe she can help. Talk to her. Ask if someone visited Jenny that day or phoned her at the gallery's number. Customers, a friend, anyone."

"Okay, I'll pay her another visit."

IT WAS after two before Christine arrived home. Stephanie had insisted she stay for lunch. Since Emily was spending the day with Darla at the gallery, there was no reason to refuse the invitation.

Libby was outside and waved as Christine pulled into the driveway.

When she looked in the rearview mirror, she saw her next-door neighbor walking toward her. She pressed the button to unlock the tailgate of the SUV, then got out and walked to the back.

"Hi, Christine. Recovered from the trip yet?"

"Getting there. Love going with those kids, but ten-year-olds have lots of bundled up energy."

"I'll say. Probably why I don't teach that age."

"Yeah, but you have to deal with moody teenagers like my daughter."

"True, but Emily is a good student. Never gives me any trouble."

No, she saves that for me. "That's good."

"Need any help?"

"Thanks. If you could grab those two packages, it will save me an extra trip."

Libby did so, then followed Christine into the kitchen. "Where do you want these?"

"Put them on the counter, and I'll deal with them later. Want a bottle of water? I'd offer iced tea, but I haven't made any recently."

"Water's fine."

Christine pulled two bottles from the refrigerator, then handed one to Libby. They both sat at the counter. Christine couldn't help but stifle a yawn.

"You're tired. I should go."

"No, I'm fine. I just need to unwind. Didn't get home until late last night. On top of that, I had to meet with Jason Montgomery when I got back from Austin."

"He's still questioning you?"

"Just trying to find answers. He thinks there's a chance I may have seen something or someone and don't remember."

Libby's eyes grew wide. "Do you think so?"

"Not really. The park was almost deserted. I'm almost sure I didn't see anything out of the ordinary."

"But you aren't positive?"

"Guess there's no way to be certain. Have you heard of people suppressing memories? It sometimes happens when they've encountered a traumatic event, and their mind blocks out certain things."

"Do you think it might have happened to you?"

Christine shrugged. "I guess it's possible. There are cases where people undergo hypnosis to remember such things. Vince doesn't think much of it."

"Who is Vince?"

Christine hesitated before answering. To say he was her significant other didn't seem right since they hadn't been in a long-term relationship. Boyfriend seemed too juvenile. Best to keep the explanation simple. "He's a friend. He was also running that evening and came along right after I found the body."

Libby took a sip of water. "Then maybe he could have forgotten something too."

"Doubt it. FBI agents are trained to be observant."

"You're telling me an FBI agent was with you when you found the body?"

"Former FBI agent. He's a private investigator now. If Vince saw something out of the ordinary, he would have remembered."

"Is he involved in the investigation?"

"No. Wouldn't be even if he was still with the FBI. His part in this is strictly as a witness."

"I wasn't sure how that worked. The idea of hypnosis is fascinating. Did you talk to the police about it?"

Christine shrugged. "I made an off-hand comment. Not sure they would even want me to do it."

"But if you have forgotten something—"

"Then maybe it will come to mind." She stood, walked to the pantry, then pulled out a box of brownie mix. Right now, she didn't want to talk about the murder.

"My mother-in-law invited me for dinner tonight. I promised to bring dessert. Sorry, Libby, but I need to get busy."

CHAPTER 12

*D*arla ran her hands over the clay bowl, taking note of the smooth, symmetrical sides and the rich colors of the glaze. She smiled at the young artist. "You're very talented. How long have you been making pottery?"

Kristen Monroe's face lit up. "Since high school. I love working with my hands and recently received my BFA. I'm taking off this spring and summer and plan to start studying for my masters in the fall."

"Wonderful! As you can see, most of what I have in the gallery are paintings, but I've wanted to expand to include some other forms of art. If you're agreeable, I'd love to display some of your work."

The young woman's eyes grew wide with excitement. "That would be awesome."

One of the things Darla liked about having an art gallery was the opportunity to work with new and unknown artists. Many of them needed help in getting started. "I gather you have other items."

"Yes, I have a variety, including pitchers, bottle vases, and urns in with an assortment of glazes. I've begun experimenting with Raku firing, but nothing is ready for sale."

"Why don't we start with a few of your completed pieces to see how they sell, and we'll go from there. Can you bring them early next week?"

After agreeing to the terms of the consignment, Kristen turned to leave, almost bumping into Jason Montgomery at the door.

"I'm sorry."

Jason flashed her a smile, then winked. "It's okay. Not often I bump into someone as pretty as you."

Kristen's face grew red as she rushed out the door.

Darla rolled her eyes. The man would flirt with anyone. Since her encounters with Jason had been less than favorable, she wasn't over-joyed to see him. Squaring her shoulders, she said, "What can I do for you?"

"I was hoping to ask you a few questions." His gaze scanned the room.

"I gather you're not here to look at art, so I can only assume it's in regards to Jenny's murder. I've already told you everything I can. Isn't that enough?"

Jason appeared unfazed. "You may already know there have been two similar murders in Brewster."

Darla gasped. "Two?"

"Another one last night. Matt—Chief Bradford and I—are working with Brewster officials in hopes to bring about a quick resolution."

"Go on."

"We have reason to believe the suspect may have lured Jenny to Cameron Park. Her phone records didn't reveal calls from any unknown numbers. It's possible the killer visited the gallery that day. Do you have security cameras?"

Darla shook her head. "Sorry. Have a first-rate alarm system, but no video surveillance. I probably should have some installed."

"It was worth a try. What about customers that day? Anything out of the ordinary? Phone calls? Visitor"

"Nothing I can remember. I left for a few minutes during lunch, then again at four when I went to pick up my granddaughter."

"What about Jenny's behavior? Did she act nervous or upset?"

"No. She was cheerful. If something happened to upset her, it was after I left."

"I see. I won't take up any more of your time. If you do think of anything—"

"I'll call you. Detective, believe me, I'd like to see Jenny's murderer caught and punished. And if there's a serial killer out there targeting young women, a lot of people aren't safe. Rest assured, you have my full cooperation."

"I would hope so." Jason strolled out of the gallery.

Darla watched him leave. What was it about that man? He acted almost amiable today until his last comment. She despised his arrogance. Oh well. At least today he didn't insinuate any of her family was responsible for Jenny's death.

THE NEW COFFEE shop in Cameron Place had become a favorite hangout. It was an excellent place to indulge in the pastime of people watching. A person could easily blend into the background and still observe patrons coming and going, not only in the coffee shop but in various other stores in the area—including the art gallery.

If anyone watched long enough, they would know when someone was there alone. Even though there was a service entrance, Darla Martell always entered and left through the front door. As had Jenny.

Pre-occupation with the gallery had diminished now that Jenny was dead. But sometimes the desire to sit and observe was strong. Today was one of those times. And as it turned out, Darla Martell had an unexpected visitor. Detective Jason Montgomery.

Luck. Chance. Fate. Being in the right place at the right time. What business did Jason have with Darla? He was up to something. Why else would he visit the gallery? Doubtful he went there to purchase any artwork.

The latest scuttlebutt said he was asking more questions about the murder. He was a little unorthodox with his methods, but maybe he wasn't a pushover. After all, the city council didn't hire him for his good looks.

What was Jason suspicious of? How did it tie to the gallery? Couldn't afford to have him get too close to the truth. But there was little to worry about. Jenny Allen's life was a mystery. Except for her estranged sister, it wouldn't be easy to trace her to anyone in Driscoll Lake.

All was safe.

At least for now.

DARLA GLANCED at her granddaughter sitting in the passenger seat. She had been quiet most of the afternoon. Hard to tell what was on the teenager's mind. Wild horses couldn't drag information from her if she didn't want to talk.

"I have to make a quick stop at the grocery store before we go home. How about hamburgers for dinner?"

Emily shrugged.

"Would you rather have something else?"

"Doesn't matter."

Darla knew not to push. She turned the Escalade into the super-market parking lot then found a space near the entrance. Want to come inside?"

Emily shook her head.

A few minutes later, Darla returned with her purchases.

"You don't like him, do you, Gigi?" Emily asked as Darla pulled onto the street.

"Who are you talking about?"

"The detective. Montgomery or whatever his name is."

"Why would you think I dislike him?"

"I overheard Mom talking about him to her friend. She doesn't like him, either."

"Doesn't matter how anyone feels. He has a job to do."

Emily shrugged. "Guess so. He upset Mom, and now she's gotten all friendly with that man."

Darla frowned. Did she detect a hint of jealousy in her granddaughter? Could be good or bad. Good in the sense that Emily was beginning to show she cared about her mother. Bad if Christine allowed Emily's feelings to dictate her life. Darla was sure Emily was talking about Vince, but she decided to act innocent.

"What man?"

"The one who used to be with the FBI."

"Vince?"

"Yeah. They were together when she found that woman's body. Now she's always on the phone with him."

Darla suspected her granddaughter was exaggerating. Typical dramatic teen. "All the time?"

"She couldn't even take me shopping to buy a formal for the prom because she had to meet him."

Aha! Emily was jealous. "I thought you found a dress."

"Yeah. A few days later. After all the pretty ones were taken."

"Emily, she took you to Dallas. As many stores as there are, I'm sure you didn't have to settle for something you didn't want. You were excited about it."

"That's not the point."

"Then what is?"

"She... I don't know."

"Let me guess. Since your father died, it's been you and your mom. You're afraid someone else is going to take your place in her life. That she won't be available when you need her."

Emily shrugged.

"Have you been there for your mom? Supported her through the pain and the grief?"

"Yeah, I guess."

"Then why do you often treat her like dirt?"

Emily jerked her head, and her eyes widened. "I don't do that."

"Yes, you do. I've seen it. Times when she reached out to you, wanting to do something special, but you were too busy with friends. Or said you'd rather spend time with me. Don't get me wrong. I cherish the time we spend together. You didn't have to let me into your life, but I'm grateful you did."

"I'm glad you're here, Gigi."

"Me, too." Darla squeezed Emily's hand. "Sweetie, having friends is important. But remember this. A mother is the one person who will always be there for you. She'll stick with you when others won't."

"You didn't. You abandoned my father."

Darla's eyes misted. What Emily said was true. She'd left her son to be raised by his overbearing father. Something she would never forgive herself for doing.

"You're right. I did. The reasons don't really matter now. But your mom isn't like me. No matter what happens, she won't leave you. She loves you very much."

Emily took a deep breath and exhaled slowly. "I guess you're right. But now that… She was with him last night. I heard her talking to him before she left for Austin. She was gone three days and couldn't spend her first night back with me."

"You had already planned to spend the night with Bethany. And today, you could have gone home. Instead, you wanted to be at the gallery. Did you stop to think that maybe your mom made plans because she knew you'd rather be with your friends?"

"Guess not."

"Honey, not having your father around is hard for both of you. You have a social life, but your mother is lonely. At her age, there's a difference between friends and a partner. Don't begrudge her a second chance at happiness."

TAMI SAT at Jason's desk and stared at the autopsy report in her hands. She swallowed hard. "The killer stabbed my sister seventeen times? Who would do such a thing?"

"That's what we're trying to find out. Your sister didn't leave many clues about her life—before and after Driscoll Lake."

"Doesn't make sense. Jenny moves here, and in less than a month, someone kills her."

"You probably don't want to hear this, but it could be a case of simply being—"

"In the wrong place at the wrong time. Yeah, yeah. I've heard it all before. Was that what happened to the women in Brewster? Random victims? Were they stabbed as many times as Jenny?"

Jason's gaze shifted to the papers on his desk. "Both had multiple stab wounds. The coroner's report on the latest victim isn't complete. Those investigations are under Brewster Police jurisdiction."

"You are cooperating with them?"

"We share information."

"Did you see the report on Susan Mason?"

Jason ignored her question. A nagging suspicion was growing in the back of his mind, but he didn't want to share it with anyone just yet. After his conversation with Matt, he suspected the police chief thought the same thing.

"Look, I want this case solved as much as anyone. So far, all the leads we've had haven't panned out. Doesn't mean we won't keep trying. And if—when—we have something, you'll be the first one outside the department to know."

"Guess that's all I can hope for. What was the reason for—never mind."

Jason frowned. "What?"

"Nothing. Just keep me updated."

Tami hurriedly left the police station. Got into her car, then drove back to the newspaper office. She parked behind the building and sat for a few minutes without going inside.

The more she thought about it, the more convinced she became Jason was hiding something. Maybe if she spoke with Matt. No, that wouldn't work either. Tami felt sure Matt knew whatever it was Jason wasn't telling, but he wouldn't talk.

Was it the work of a serial killer? Since the perp had struck twice in Brewster, Jason would probably leave it up to them to solve the case.

No way was she ready to accept it as fact. Too many unanswered questions. Why was Jenny at Cameron Park dressed in street clothes? Had she merely gone there to unwind? Or was there another reason? To meet someone? If so, who and why?

Whatever the case, Tami didn't expect to get any answers from Jason. An idea formed in her head. She got out of her car, then hurried inside the building.

"Madge, I'm going to be busy this afternoon. Don't let anyone disturb me unless it's an emergency. If someone calls take a message."

Once inside her office, she closed the door. Time to do a little research. Two hours later, she had the information she wanted. If the police didn't do their job, she would take matters into her own hands.

She needed someone who would investigate her sister's death discretely. Someone honest and fair. Money wouldn't be an issue. No doubt her stepfather would pay anything to learn who was responsible for his daughter's death. Tami picked up the phone, then dialed the familiar number.

When her mother answered, she asked her to put Thomas on the phone, then quickly explained the situation.

"Do what you have to do," Thomas said. "Don't worry about money. I'll take care of all expenses."

Tami took a deep breath, then exhaled slowly. Exactly what she'd hoped for. "Thanks, Tom. I want to know who's responsible."

"Your mother and I want the same thing. We're behind you on this. Let me know what you need."

Tami ended the call, grateful to have her stepfather's support. Finding someone to do the job wasn't an issue. The ideal person was right here in Driscoll Lake.

LIKE MANY DRISCOLL LAKE RESIDENTS, Matt often went to Casey's when he wanted a drink or quick bite to eat after work. It was a place where friends gather around the bar to watch the latest sporting event on one of several large-screened TV sets. But most of the time, he preferred the quieter, laid-back atmosphere of Hank's Tavern.

The food was good, the service friendly, and the owner kept a variety of craft beers on tap. There were no televisions, only a couple of pool tables, and a few booths in addition to the bar.

Matt didn't frequent the place often these days, usually going home to his wife and daughter. But Stephanie had called earlier to say his mother was watching Abby and she planned to spend most of the evening finishing the last few chapters of her latest manuscript.

He knew better than to disturb her when she was writing, so he decided to stop at Hank's for a quick dinner. It had been a tough week at work. Despite Jason's new and improved attitude and his sudden dedication to solving Jenny Allen's murder, he admitted to being at a dead-end. Lead after lead had failed.

Of course, as was the case in many of these types of events, several people came forward with useless information. Some meant well, while others only wanted their five minutes of fame. Determining what was useful as opposed to mere speculation was often a job within itself.

Matt decided to sit at the bar. He considered calling Brian to see if he'd like to join him. Sometimes it was nice to share a drink or two with a friend. But Brian wisely avoided alcohol, so no point in tempting him. Decided to call Vince, instead. He was unavailable.

"I gather you're here to unwind. The tavern owner respected his customers' privacy but was always willing to engage in conversation with the regulars.

Matt took a sip of his beer. "Yeah. Rough week. And it's only Tuesday."

Hank sat a plate of fajita nachos in front of him. "I'd say a rough few weeks with that murder investigation."

"You're right. Glad we don't have crimes like this very often."

"Especially with the other murders in Brewster."

"Yeah, having three so close together is unusual for this area."

"I phoned that detective a few times. He never returned my calls."

"The one from Brewster? That's surprising. I've known Randy for years, and he's usually prompt."

"No. Jason Montgomery."

"What business would you have with him?"

"She came in here a few times, you know."

"Who? The victim?"

"Yeah. Didn't realize it was her until I saw the picture on the news last week."

"Was she alone?"

"Always came by herself, but she would usually strike up a conversation with other patrons. Guess I should say with men. One fella in particular."

"Go on."

"I didn't think anything about it at the time. After all, this is a bar."

"Is he a regular?"

Hank shook his head. "Never saw him until a couple of months ago. Haven't seen him since she was killed."

"Could you describe him? Remember anything specific? Maybe saw what kind of car he drove?"

"Around thirty. Average height. Light brown hair. Always wore jeans and a leather jacket. Overheard her call him Sean. Wish I could tell you more."

"That's okay. What you've told me is important."

"If he does show up, want me to say anything?"

"No. Don't confront him. Call the station but do it discreetly. He's a person of interest. Would you be willing to stop at the station tomorrow? Jason might have more questions for you."

"Not a problem."

"Do you remember if there were any others she may have met here?"

Hank frowned and pursed his lips. "Not that I recall... Wait a minute. I remember now. She was here one night, and this Sean character wasn't around. The detective was here. The two of them struck up a conversation."

"You mean Jason?"

"Yep."

"They didn't come in together?"

"No. I don't remember who was here first, but they sat over there. Real cozy like." Hank pointed to a booth in the corner.

"Thanks. You've been very helpful. I'll be in touch." Matt pulled his wallet out, paid his tab, then left. So much for a relaxing evening. It was time to confront Jason Montgomery.

~

MATT PACED HIS OFFICE, willing himself to calm down as he waited for Jason. Hank's revelation had deepened his distrust of the detective. Sure, it could have been a chance meeting between two people at a bar, but if so, why keep it a secret?

Now he was faced with a dilemma. Allow Jason to continue working the case, assuming he had a reasonable explanation, or call in outside authorities. It wasn't a decision to make lightly. Sure, he'd threatened to remove Jason before, but this was different. Unorthodox investigation methods and poor treatment of witnesses was one thing, but withholding information about a relationship with the victim was another. He turned at the sound of someone knocking.

"You wanted to see me?" Jason asked.

"Come in and close the door." He sat down, then nodded for Jason to do likewise.

"Something wrong?"

"I'll say. Why didn't you tell me you knew her?"

Jason frowned. "Who are you talking about?"

"Who else? Jenny Allen. Had a little visit with Hank Norton this evening. He told me he'd seen the two of you together."

There was a long pause before Jason spoke. "I didn't really know her. Saw her one time at the tavern when I went there for a drink. She came in shortly afterward. We started talking, and I suggested we sit at one of the booths. We were there an hour. Two, tops."

"Couple of hours, huh? And just what did you talk about?"

"This and that. Said she was new in town. Pretty much small talk."

"You expect me to believe that?"

"Why not? It's true."

Matt slammed his hands on the desk. "Damn it. You still should have said something. Were you only pretending you didn't know her name the night she was killed? I seem to recall I was the one to point you in the direction of Darla Martell."

"I wasn't pretending. She only told me her first name. Didn't tell me she worked at the gallery. Matter of fact, she was reluctant to discuss anything about herself."

"Then answer this. If you weren't trying to hide anything, why haven't you returned Hank's calls? He's phoned you several times."

"In case you haven't noticed, I've been busy trying to solve a murder. Figured he was like everyone else. Just calling with useless information."

Matt's eyes narrowed. "Hank owns a tavern. One where Jenny frequented. Didn't it occur to you he might know something? What he told me today might be relevant to the case."

"Do you know how many calls I've fielded from people who had 'relevant' information?"

"Hank's info is for real. But as it stands now, you may have compromised this entire case."

"Because I had a drink with the victim one time? I swear I never saw her again."

"It would be much easier to believe you if you'd come forward earlier."

"Want to know why I didn't say anything?"

"Yeah, I do."

"Because of the way you're acting. You never give me the benefit of the doubt."

Matt scoffed. "With good reason."

Jason stood, then began to pace. "Maybe I didn't use good judgment, but I swear I had nothing to do with her death. If I knew something—anything—that would benefit the investigation, I wouldn't withhold it."

"Yeah, well tell it to someone who might trust you."

"And you don't?"

"At this point, I don't believe a word you say."

Jason stood up. "Okay, I deserve that. What are you going to do?"

"I don't know yet."

"No matter what you think, I want to see her killer caught and brought to justice. What can I do to persuade you?"

"I'm not sure you can."

CHAPTER 13

$\mathcal{D}$arla smiled at the delivery driver as she signed for the package. She had been almost as eager as her customers for the Saldana paintings to arrive.

Once she was alone, she opened the box carefully, then pulled out the first painting. Sonya Ramsey had good taste. This landscape was even better than the one she'd sold Evelyn Martin. She quickly recognized the setting as the Chisos Mountains near Terlingua. The artist had captured the vivid oranges and deep blue hues of a West Texas sunrise.

The second painting was probably somewhere in the high desert of New Mexico. Its colors were more subdued but equally stunning. She would be hard pressed to choose between the two if she were buying. Maybe Sonya Ramsey would purchase both.

Darla placed both canvases on easels, then picked up the packing crate, intending to put it in the storage room. Surprised to find the box wasn't empty, she looked inside to see an unframed portrait of a woman.

The bold initials in the lower right-hand corner confirmed the same artist had done all three paintings. Strange, because Darla had never known him to do anything but landscapes.

She studied the image. Set against a backdrop of muted teal, the portrait was a side view, but the woman's head was turned toward the artist. Light brown hair cascaded over her bare shoulders. Her lips were slightly parted, and one hand rested lightly at the base of her throat.

Darla recognized her right away. Why had Sue included this painting in the shipment?

She picked up the phone, then dialed a familiar number.

"Jensen Galleries, Sue speaking."

"It's Darla."

"I hoped to hear from you today. Did the paintings arrive?"

"Got them a few minutes ago. I believe my customer will be pleased."

"That's good to know. In my opinion, they are two of his best works."

"I agree. However, I'm a little confused as to why you included a third painting in the shipment."

"A third painting? What is it, and who is the artist?"

"It's another Saldana—a woman's portrait."

There was a pause on the other end. "I'm sorry. Rafael packed them for me. He must have included that one by mistake. I gather you recognize her."

"Of course, I do."

"I've had the painting stored away for months. I would have offered it to her husband, but under the circumstances, I didn't think he would want it."

"I'd say that's a safe bet. From what I've heard, he would probably rip it to shreds. What do you want me to do with it?"

"It's a shame to keep the portrait hidden. It's good and shows Saldana's versatility. I hate to see it packed away and forgotten."

Darla looked at the canvas. "I agree. Why won't you display it?"

"Do you have to ask? I made a promise to the Saldana family to try to sell all his paintings. They know about the portrait."

"I assume they didn't want it, either."

"I don't think it's a matter of them not wanting it, but—"

"More like trying to forget what happened. Why not send it somewhere else? Surely you know of a gallery that would take it."

"Good idea. You could display it there. I doubt anyone in Driscoll Lake would know the circumstances. If your customers like his other paintings, maybe they'll be interested in this one."

"I'm not sure. We may be over six-hundred miles away, but the world can be a small place."

"Think it over. If you decide to send it back, I'll pay the shipping costs."

Darla took a deep breath, then exhaled slowly. "Okay, I'll keep the painting for now. As far as putting it on display, I'll have to think about it."

MATT LAY ON HIS BACK, hands clasped behind his neck, and stared at the bedroom ceiling. After confronting Jason last night, he hadn't spoken to him all day. Both men spent most of their time in their offices with the doors closed.

The tension was thick throughout the station, but no one dared say anything. Even the dispatcher, who was usually cheerful and outgoing, acted as if she walked on eggshells. Matt was glad when five came so he could leave. His somber mood had continued through dinner and up until bedtime. He was unaware of Stephanie's presence in the room until he felt the bed shift.

"Want to tell me what's bothering you?" She lay down beside him.

"What makes you think something is wrong?

"Because I know you. This morning you hardly had anything to say, and you kept brooding during dinner. Is it the murder investigation?"

Matt turned his head to look at her. "Sort of. Problems with Jason again."

"What did he do this time?"

"When I went out last night, Hank told me he'd seen Jenny Allen there with Jason."

"You're kidding? Jason knew her and didn't say anything?"

"Okay, maybe 'know' isn't the right word. Hank saw them together one time. They didn't arrive or leave together, but Jason should have told me."

Stephanie turned on her side and propped herself on an elbow. "Yes, he should have said something, but meeting someone in a bar doesn't constitute a relationship. Do you have any reason to believe he was involved in her murder?"

"No. He swears he only saw her once. Said Jenny didn't say anything that would give him any clues about her background. Didn't tell him any more than she did Darla."

"Then what's the problem? I know you don't like him, but everyone makes mistakes."

"I don't necessarily dislike him. Don't care for his methods and his attitude, but he has potential."

"Then let him do his job. Maybe he needs a little encouragement."

"Think so?"

"It's possible."

Matt grinned. "You're good for me, you know."

Stephanie quirked an eyebrow. "Oh, yeah?"

"Yeah. In more ways than one." He drew her into his arms.

TAMI SUTTON WAS confident she'd selected the right man to investigate her sister's background. Not only did he have the knowledge and experience, but he also had the tenacity to learn the truth. But given the circumstances, convincing him to take the job was another matter.

She'd learned enough about Vince Green to know he was a man not easily swayed. If he didn't want to take on this case, no amount of pleading on her part would make him change his mind. Nevertheless, she had to try.

On Thursday morning, she walked the two blocks from the newspaper to his office. "Good morning, Agent Green."

His eyes narrowed. "Tami Sutton. What brings you here today?"

"Came to see you, of course."

"It's been a while since anyone referred to me as Agent Green."

She cast a glance around the office. "Nice place you have here. Small but efficient. Good location."

"Suits my purpose. But I gather you're not here to discuss my place of business." Vince sat on the corner of his desk.

He was straightforward and to the point. Tami liked that. "You're right. I want you to do a job for me. Money's good."

"What kind of job?"

Tami sat in a chair facing Vince. "I want you to locate my sister's killer."

He shook his head. "Afraid I can't help you. That's police business. They're conducting the investigation."

"Yeah, right. Jason Montgomery couldn't find—" Tami cleared her throat. "He's...inexperienced. I need someone who knows the ropes. Anyway, what I have in mind won't interfere with whatever it is he may or may not be doing."

"And what would that be?"

"Find out everything about Jenny from the time she left home five years ago to when she showed up in Driscoll Lake. My family recently learned she lived in both Taos and Santa Fe for a few years, and then she moved back to San Antonio. There are some gaps, but I'm confident you'll fit the pieces together. And when you do, I believe we'll have the killer."

"Why not hire someone who lives in New Mexico? Or even San Antonio?"

"Because I believe you're the best suited for the job. I've checked your background, so I know about a certain incident in Alpine. It turns out, we have something in common."

Vince's jaw tightened. "That isn't a subject up for discussion."

"No? Then I won't mention it again. But I think you'll agree we have the same goal."

"How's that?"

"Like me, you want answers and are willing to take risks to get them. So much it cost you a promising career."

"Leaving the FBI was my choice."

"That's not what I heard."

"Yeah, well, someone told you wrong. You should verify the information before jumping to conclusions."

His reaction told Tami she was at least partially right, but she knew she needed to tread lightly. "Okay, I made a mistake. Does this mean you won't take the job?"

"I didn't say that." Vince stood then walked to the window. There was a long pause before he spoke. "You're right about one thing. The truth is important to me."

"You'll do the job?"

"I'll consider it. That's all I can promise you now."

"Then I'll hold on to that promise." She stood to leave. Upon reaching the door, she stopped. "One more thing. I'd like you to keep quiet about this. If you do take the job, I wouldn't want anyone to know."

"I can assure you I treat every case with confidentiality. But if you didn't want anyone to suspect something, you weren't wise to come to my office. This town has eyes and ears."

"I'm aware of that. Who's to say why I came? I'll contact you by phone from here on."

MATT PARKED HIS PICKUP, then walked toward the police station. When he reached the front entrance, he was surprised to see Hank Norton on his way out the door.

"Didn't expect to see you here today, Hank."

"I got a call from Detective Montgomery early this morning. I came in to tell him what I know about the murder victim."

"He called you? Let me guess. He demanded you come to the station rather than him coming to you."

"My idea. He said there was someone who could sketch the man I saw if I could describe him. Thought it was best to do it here rather than for them to show up at the tavern where there would be interruptions and curious onlookers."

"Probably right. I hope he treated you okay."

Hank frowned. "He did. Why wouldn't he?"

"Jason has a bad habit—Never mind. I'd better get in there and see what he has."

The older man started to step aside, then paused and rubbed a hand over his jaw. "Chief. About what I said the other night. Didn't mean to give you the wrong impression. I don't think there was anything between your detective and that woman. Just two people who met one time in a bar."

"Did Jason put you up to saying that?"

"No. Something I've been thinking about since you left. I've seen a lot of interaction between people over the years. I'd be willing to bet it was nothing more than a one-time meeting between strangers."

"Thanks, Hank. We'll be in touch if we have more questions."

When Matt went inside, yesterday's frosty atmosphere was still present. And he'd played a role in creating the hostile environment. Time to remedy the situation. It wasn't good for work or morale.

"Morning, Sandra," he said to the dispatcher. "Jason in his office?"

Her eyes shifted downward before she answered. "Yes."

Matt grimaced. Jason wasn't Sandra's favorite person, but the dispute seemed to have affected even her. "Don't worry. I'm not going to bite his head off today."

A slow smile crept across her face. "That's good to know."

Matt grinned, then proceeded to Jason's office. He tapped lightly on the door frame before entering.

Jason's shoulders slumped when he saw Matt. "I gather you saw Hank leaving."

"Yes, I did."

"And you're wondering why I had him come here."

"He told me. It was a good idea."

"You're kidding me? You agree?" Jason's eyes grew wide.

"He mentioned something about a sketch."

"Uh, yeah. Martin Brooks with the Brewster PD offered to do a composite. He left a few minutes ago."

"He's good at what he does. Do you have the drawing?"

Jason pointed to the charcoal sketch on the corner of his desk.

Matt studied the drawing. "Interesting. What did Hank think?"

"Said it was a good likeness."

"Then go with it."

"What?"

"Get the sketch out to the media as someone who is a person of interest in the death of Jenny Allen."

"Does that mean you want me to continue with the investigation?"

"Yes. Just keep me informed. No more withholding information. Fair enough?"

Jason's smile seemed genuine. "You got it."

VINCE WAS unable to concentrate after Tami's visit. A few of her comments struck a nerve. What's more, she knew things about his background that he didn't want to discuss with anyone. At least not now. But what did he expect? She was a reporter. Good at digging up stuff.

It was almost five when his phone rang. He smiled when he recognized Christine's number. "Hey, there. What's up with you?"

"Getting ready to leave the school. Emily has plans for the evening, and I wondered if you wanted to grab dinner somewhere. We could meet at Casey's."

"I have a better idea. Let's drive into Brewster. I need to get away. Clear my mind."

"Bad day?"

"Let's say it was an interesting one."

"Which you probably can't talk about."

"Not really. What do you think about going to Brewster?"

"Sounds good to me."

"Dress casual. Can you be ready in an hour?

"You bet."

"Great. I'll pick you up around six."

Two hours later, they sat at a popular restaurant chain. Vince nursed a beer while Christine sipped a glass of wine. Like many restaurants these days, TVs had been placed in various locations around the room. The volume was low, and no one could hear the words. He guessed some people had nothing better to do than to stare at a silent screen.

A glance around the room revealed several people glued to their smartphones, ignoring their companions. Whatever happened to one-on-one communication? He shook his head.

"What are you thinking about?" Christine asked.

"Just wondering why they have TV sets in noisy restaurants when no one can hear what's being said." Vince nodded toward the nearest screen.

"I've often wondered the same thing. Maybe to keep some people from having to indulge in conversation. Guess some people are just too shallow and self-centered to have meaningful relationships."

"Spoken like someone with the voice of experience. Was your husband—"

Christine shook her head. "No, it wasn't Kyle."

"Sorry. Didn't mean to pry."

"It's okay. Sometimes we were on different wavelengths, but Kyle always took time to listen. Last year, I dated a guy a few times. He always picked restaurants that had televisions. After a few dates, I realized he was more interested in whatever sporting event was on the air than in me. I broke it off with him. Guess it made me a little gun shy about becoming involved with someone."

Vince reached across the table to grasp her hand. "You don't have to worry about that with me."

"I know." She met his gaze, then lowered her eyes.

He couldn't help but smile, remembering when they met on the jogging trail. Christine tried to come across as strong and independent. In many ways she was, but she was also cautious. Maybe a bit bashful. He couldn't rush her into a relationship.

"Heard anything new about the investigation?"

"No, but I'm not exactly in the loop. Not that I want to be."

"I keep thinking of her family. Can you imagine never knowing who was responsible for your sister's death?"

He shrugged. "Why don't we change the subject."

Christine furrowed her brow. "Sure. I just thought you cared."

"I do care, but I don't want every discussion we have to revolve around the subject of Jenny's death. I think our relationship is worth more. At least, I hope it is."

"You mean that, don't you?"

"Yes, I do."

The server arrived to take their order. They spent the remainder of the evening in pleasant conversation—mentioning neither Jenny nor anything about Driscoll Lake. When Vince signaled for the check, Christine excused herself from the table.

As he signed the credit card receipt, he had the distinct feeling someone was watching him. A likely possibility in a crowded restaurant and often an innocent gesture. But he sensed this was something different. Cunning. Calculated. Even sinister. He'd had that same feeling the night he met Brian at the diner.

He didn't want to alert anyone of his suspicion, so he forced himself not to look around.

When Christine returned to the table, he smiled, not wanting to alarm her. "Ready to go?"

She nodded.

Vince stood, then put his arm around her waist as they left the restaurant.

HE WAS HERE. Sitting at a table. Alone. No. A closer look at the table not only revealed his empty beer mug but a wine glass. Who was his companion?

Have patience. Time will tell.

It wasn't long before a young strawberry blonde woman returned to the table.

Well, that's interesting. It looks like Mrs. Lawrence is no longer the grieving widow.

Of course, it could be a platonic relationship. A simple meal shared with a friend.

But the arm he placed around her waist as they walked out the door said otherwise.

CHAPTER 14

*D*amn! She overslept. Not surprising since she was up half the night. Christine rushed to dress, then dashed to the kitchen. Emily sat at the table, eating a bowl of cereal, eyes glued to the television across the room.

"What's up with you? Not like you to watch TV so early in the morning."

"If you'd *bothered* to ask me last night, the local station has a story about the upcoming art exhibit. Ms. Gordon thinks my drawings are good enough to show."

"That's great, honey. I didn't know you wanted to participate. Last time we talked, you didn't think you were ready."

"Yeah, well, there are lots of things you don't know about me."

Christine poured a cup of coffee, then took a sip. "Where's this coming from?"

"As if you didn't know."

"I don't. Want to tell me?"

"Not really." Emily stomped out of the room.

What had she done to push the wrong buttons this morning? Didn't take much these days. Every time their relationship took a step forward, she'd do something to cause a backslide. Worst part was, she rarely knew what. Shaking her head, she reached into the freezer for a breakfast taco, then placed it in the microwave.

Maybe it was a phase common to all teenagers. Had she ever been this way? Talking to someone with experience would be nice. But who? Darla sadly lacked skills in the parental category. Nell Bradford was a possibility. She'd raised both a son and a daughter. But from what Christine remembered about Matt's older sister, she hadn't been the rebellious type.

At any rate, Nell was busy being grandmother to Abby as well as a surrogate grandmother to Rachel and Brian's son.

Calling her own mother wasn't an option. When Kyle died, Lillian Starnes tried to convince Christine to move to Arizona. "You should be close to your family. Raising a teenager is hard enough when both parents are around. You're a single mother now, and you'll need all the help you can get."

Christine had refused. Except for her years away at college, Driscoll Lake was the only home she'd known. She didn't want to leave. The decision to stay became a sore spot between her and her mother. No, she wouldn't call and ask for advice about raising a teenager. To do so would be admitting failure.

She down at the counter with her taco and reached for the remote to turn off the TV when Jason Montgomery's face filled the screen. The camera had cut back to the reporter by the time Christine turned up the volume.

"Driscoll Lake Police have a person of interest wanted for questioning in the murder of Jenny Allen. A source confirmed the unidentified male shown in this composite drawing was seen several times with the victim at a local bar. It is unknown if the same person is a suspect in Brewster, where two similar murders occurred. Tune in tonight for more updates on Channel Ten, your number one source for local news."

They had a lead. At least someone who might provide information. She picked up her phone to call Vince when she remembered his words from last night—

I don't want every discussion we have to revolve around the subject of Jenny's death.

She quickly put the phone away, then jumped when Emily's voice cut into her thoughts.

"Planning to call him, I suppose." Emily was standing near the door leading to the garage. She crossed her arms and frowned at her mother.

It wasn't hard to figure out who she meant. "You mean Vince?"

"Who else?"

"Why should that bother you?

"Because. Because… I don't know." She turned, slamming the door behind her.

Christine shook her head. She had to talk to someone. Emily's hot and cold attitude was becoming too much to handle.

Tami scrutinized the sketch for the third time that morning. Jason delivered a copy to her yesterday, telling her it would be broadcast over the media. Since then, she'd searched her memory for someone connected to Jenny's past. Each time she came up blank. If the man in the drawing played a significant role in her sister's life, it was after she left home.

She emailed a copy to her parents, but neither could identify him. Now she could only hope someone would see the drawing and come forward. At least the police weren't sitting idle, although she still had a few doubts about Jason's crime-solving skills.

The sound of footsteps announced his presence at her office door.

"Detective. I didn't expect to see you. Wasn't Madge at her desk?"

"No. Is there a problem with me stopping by?"

Tami shook her head. "I'm just surprised you're here this early in the day."

"Why is that?"

"Somehow, I don't picture you as an early riser. I see you more as the night owl type."

Jason smiled, lowered his voice, then moved closer to her desk.

"Maybe I am. But best to save personal discussions for another time. That is if you're interested."

Was he flirting with her? Despite his arrogance, he was attractive. Problem was he knew it. Tami cleared her throat, ignoring his statement. "Okay, so what's going on?"

"Came to check on you. Any luck with the drawing?"

She shook her head. "Nothing. I sent a copy to my parents. They haven't come up with anything, either."

"Well, it was worth a try. Does the name Sean mean anything to you?"

"Should it?"

"Thought your sister might have mentioned someone by that name. We didn't release the information to the media, but Hank is almost certain it's the name your sister called him."

"I'll ask Mom or Thomas and let you know."

Jason stood. "Appreciate it. This is the first real break we've had on the case. Hope it leads us somewhere."

"Me, too."

Tami watched him leave. She couldn't figure him out. He'd had the gall to flirt with her but still showed interest in the investigation. Too bad he didn't have the experience of someone like Carlos Gonzales. If so, she'd feel more confident. As it stood now, she still needed Vince Green. He'd promised to let her know his decision. Maybe it wouldn't hurt to nudge things along.

VINCE DECIDED NOT to go into the office until late morning. He sat at the kitchen table with a cup of coffee and a copy of the *Brewster Times*, but he couldn't concentrate on reading. The events of last night occupied his mind. After they left Brewster, he'd driven Christine home. They talked until almost midnight.

It was after one before he climbed into his own bed, then spent much of the night tossing and turning. Between Tami Sutton's request and the eerie feeling he had at the restaurant, sleep was a long time in coming. Some people would accuse him of being paranoid, but he wasn't. Call it gut instinct—someone had been watching him. And he couldn't shake the feeling it was related to Jenny Allen's murder.

With a yawn, he opened the paper. The composite sketch was a surprise. He read the accompanying article with interest. Maybe this was the lead police had hoped for. If so, Tami wouldn't need his services. Still, it could take weeks or months to identify the person, especially if they weren't from the area. Everything he'd heard about Jenny Allen indicated she'd lived a mysterious life. He still found it odd she had broken all ties with her family only to move to a small Texas town where her sister happened to be the newspaper editor.

But why hadn't she tried to contact Tami? Was she aware of her sister's absence and awaiting her return? Why the big secret about her identity? And if Jenny didn't come to Driscoll Lake because of Tami, then why? The more he thought about it, the more interested he became about looking into her past. Then there were the similarities…

No, he wasn't going there. The circumstances of Jenny's death were only a coincidence. Had to be. Fate couldn't be that cruel.

Vince studied the photo. What if there was a connection? Could the man in the drawing be the link? There was only one way to find out. He picked up his phone, then punched in Tami Sutton's number.

She answered on the first ring. "Vince? I was about to call you. Hope you have the answer I'm looking for."

"You still want me for the job, given the police have a new lead."

"Yes."

"Okay. I'll need everything you can give me about Jenny's background."

"You know there are gaps."

"Doesn't matter. I want it all. Who her friends were. Past relationships. Her address when she lived in New Mexico. Even if something seems insignificant, it might not be. I need to know everything you know."

"I can do that. I'll check with my parents. My stepfather probably has some information. He hired someone to find her a year or so back. I'll call him right away."

"Good. I have a secured email where you can send everything. You have my office and cell numbers." Vince gave her the email address before ending the call.

He finished the last of his now lukewarm coffee, then walked to the kitchen sink. Despite his initial reservation, he felt confident in his decision. Maybe this could be the key to burying the past and destroying the ghosts that still haunted him.

DARLA FLIPPED the sign on the front door to closed, turned the key in the lock, then retreated to her office. She glanced at the portrait sitting on an easel in the corner. All things considered, she'd had a successful day. After receiving the Saldana canvases the day before, she'd placed a call to the prospective buyer.

Sonya Ramsey was out of town and hadn't been available to view the paintings until late in the afternoon. She took her time deciding but, in the end, purchased the West Texas landscape, stating the colors were better suited to the interior of her home. Sonya also looked at the new pottery exhibit and expressed interest in possibly purchasing some pieces in the future.

She dialed Sue Jensen's number. "Good news. I sold the landscape of the Chisos Mountains."

"Wonderful! I think it's one of his finest pieces."

"I'd hoped the buyer would take both. She seemed interested enough."

"Don't be disappointed. You've sold two of his paintings already. That's two more than me. Want to hold on to the other one for a while? Another interested buyer could come along."

"It's possible. Both purchasers are influential people with active social circles."

"Then keep it." There was a pause before Sue spoke again. "Have you decided about the portrait?"

Darla looked at the painting in question, took a deep breath, then exhaled. She couldn't bring herself to keep it in a storage room, but neither was she ready to display it to the public. "Not yet."

"I understand. No rush."

"Thanks, Sue. I'll let you know something soon." She hung up the phone, then busied herself with dimming the lights, taking care to make sure everything was secure. After Jason Montgomery's visit a few days earlier, she'd considered having cameras installed. The cost would be minimal and would give her an added layer of security. She made a mental note to contact someone on Monday.

She frowned when someone tapped lightly at the front. Who would stop by this late in the day? Surprised to see her daughter-in-law, she hurried to unlock the door. "Christine, what brings you here?"

"Can we talk?"

"Of course, dear. Is something wrong?"

"No. Yes. It's about Emily."

"Let me guess. Her attitude."

"How did you know?"

"I've noticed how she's been acting."

Tears formed in Christine's eyes. "I'm not sure how much more I can take."

"Oh, honey. Come into my office so we can talk."

"Okay." Christine sniffed.

Darla led the way, then waited until they were both seated before speaking. "She's jealous, isn't she?"

"Jealous? Why would you think that?"

"She said as much the other day. I had a long talk with her, hoping it would help."

"You talked to Emily about me?"

Darla nodded. "I told her she shouldn't resent you for having a chance at happiness. I noticed the interaction between you and Vince when he was at your house the day after Jenny died."

Christine stood up, then paced the room, stopping in front of the painting. "There wasn't anything between us then. We hadn't even been on a date at that time."

"Didn't matter. I could tell there was something between you. For the record, I think it's wonderful."

"You do? I mean, Kyle was your son."

"Yes, he was, but that doesn't mean I don't want you to find love again. If Vince is the one who makes you happy, go for it."

"But what about Emily?" She turned to face Darla.

"What about her? I know it's been pretty much the two of you since Kyle's death, but she'll get over her anger. If necessary, I'll have another talk with her."

"I don't know."

"Don't worry. I won't tell her I discussed it with you." Darla shifted in her chair, then looked at the ceiling before turning to face Christine. "I wasn't much of a mother to your husband. I'll have to live with my regrets for the rest of my life because of a bad decision."

"I always thought—"

"I gave up Kyle of my own accord? That's what Curtis wanted everyone to believe. I was foolish to let him have his way. It's no excuse, but he was a manipulative bastard. But let's not talk about it now. What's done is done. Someday I may have the courage to tell you the entire story."

"Only if you want to."

"Yeah, I think I do, but not today. Right now, I want to do whatever I can to help you and my granddaughter."

"Thanks. I really appreciate it."

Darla grabbed a couple of tissues from her desk and handed one to Christine. "Look at us. We're both ruining our makeup. Do you have plans for tonight?"

"No. Emily is spending the night with Bethany. I planned to grab a burger or something before going home."

"I have a better idea. You like seafood?"

Christine nodded.

"Why don't we go to that seafood restaurant on Lake Brewster? My treat."

"I'd like that."

"Give me a couple of minutes." Darla paused for a moment. "By the way, I've been meaning to give you a set of keys to the gallery."

"Me? Why?"

"I want someone to have a set in case… You're my closest relative here, and I want you to have them. Never know what might happen."

"Is there something you're not telling me?"

"No. But Jenny's death made me realize the unexpected can and does happen.

"You're right about that."

Darla handed the keys to her daughter-in-law. "Now, let me grab my purse then we'll leave. I don't know about you, but I'm ready for dinner."

Christine turned to look at the canvas while Darla gathered her things. "Nice painting. Why do you have it in your office and not on display?"

"Long story."

"She's beautiful. Do you know who she is?"

"I… knew the artist." She noted the slight frown on Christine's face as she studied the painting. "Something wrong?"

"No. She looks familiar, but there's no way I could know her." Shrugging, Christine left the room.

TAMI TYPED the last few sentences of the article, then hit the save button. "Finally."

Six o'clock on a Friday evening and she was still at the office. Worse, she had never taken this long to write her weekly editor's column. Most of the time she had the article ready to go by Wednesday. This had been an unusual week. Then again, when was her last normal one?

She took a deep breath and rubbed the back of her neck. A visit to the spa was in order, complete with a massage, manicure, and pedicure. She pulled out her phone, then called the familiar number to make an appointment for Saturday afternoon. After confirming the time, she ended the call, then leaned back in her chair. Relaxing at the spa was one thing, but for now, she needed to unwind. Do something to work off pent-up stress. If she were a runner, she'd go for a long jog in the park. But she wasn't. And it wasn't a good idea, anyway Not with the deaths of three women in the past month and a murderer still on the loose.

A long time had passed since she'd been dancing. Maybe she would drive to Pinnacle in Brewster. They always had live entertainment on Friday nights. Trouble was, she didn't want to go alone. She had a quick thought about giving Vince Green a call but nixed the notion. Rumor had it he and Christine Lawrence were an item. At any rate, going out on a date with someone she'd hired for a job probably wasn't the wisest plan. Best to keep their relationship professional.

The ringing of the phone jarred her back to the present. She was surprised to see Jason's number. "I hope you're calling with some good news."

"Wish I was. Wanted to keep you up to date. Had a few calls today regarding the drawing but none of them proved useful. We've put it on our Facebook page and other social media sites. Brewster Police did the same. Might get something there."

"I knew better than to expect anything so soon. Still, I can't help but be disappointed."

"Hang in there. Someone will eventually come forward."

"Let's hope."

"Don't want to keep you. You're probably busy."

"Actually, I'm still at the office. Wrapping it up for the evening."

"Me, too."

An idea struck her. Crazy, given his chilly reception to her a few weeks ago, but he had flirted a bit this morning. "Do you like to dance?"

"Yeah, why?"

"Ever been to Pinnacle? I was thinking about going tonight and wondered—"

"What time?"

"Seven-thirty?"

"Give me your address, and I'll pick you up."

She smiled as she ended the call. A date with Jason Montgomery. Was she insane?

Maybe she was. Then again, perhaps not.

CHAPTER 15

*V*ince straightened his seat to an upright position as the plane began its descent into Albuquerque International Sunport. A glance at his watch indicated the flight was on time, a rarity these days. He had plenty of time to pick up a rental car, make the trip to Taos, then visit the art gallery where Jenny Allen once worked before closing time.

He'd considered driving, as northern New Mexico was a favorite destination. But this wasn't a sight-seeing trip. Traveling by car would have taken almost twelve hours. He wanted to wrap things up as soon as possible and return home. Leaving now, just as he was beginning a relationship with Christine, wasn't ideal. When he told her on Saturday night, she said she understood. He hated not being able to tell her the reason for his trip, but Tami had sworn him to secrecy.

The plane taxied to a stop at the terminal. Vince remained in his seat while passengers pushed and shoved their way to the front. Once the aisle was almost clear, he made his way inside the terminal. In less than an hour, he was on the road.

His route took him near Santa Fe, and he thought of making it his first stop. But from all accounts Jenny had spent more time in Taos, so he hoped he would find most of the information he needed there.

Two hours later, he entered the outskirts of town. Checking the GPS, he drove past the adobe structures of the downtown historic district. Planters and hanging baskets with brightly colored pansies adorned the sidewalks and overhangs. Sunshine abounded, but the late March day was chilly, and a low in the upper twenties was forecasted for tonight.

Vince turned onto the street where Gallery 221 was located. The town had an abundance of art galleries and museums, so he felt fortunate Tami had been able to provide a name. Jenny worked there five years ago. Hopefully, he would meet someone who knew her and could give some information.

He parked the car, then grabbed his leather jacket before getting out. After feeding the parking meter, he strolled through the doors of the gallery. Soft music played over an intercom. Various paintings in eclectic styles filled the walls. Amid the landscapes of the nearby mountains, Taos Pueblo, and spectacular sunsets, one brightly-colored abstract caught his attention.

Titled "Summertime," the psychedelic tones were reminiscent of the sixties. It looked as if the artist had taken cans of paint and splashed them on the canvas without giving any thought to the design. Vince inwardly cringed when he saw the price tag. He obviously didn't understand modern art.

A middle-aged man approached him. "Can I help you, sir?"

"I hope so. Vince Green."

"Anthony Sullivan. I'm the owner."

Bingo. This could be the connection he needed. "Pleasure."

"Are you interested in a certain type of art? As you can see, we have a variety of styles. Something to fit most tastes."

"I'm not here to buy. I'm a private investigator and wondered if you could provide some information." Vince whipped out his ID.

The man's eyes narrowed, and he shifted his feet. "That so? What kind of information?"

"It's about a former employee by the name of Jenny Allen. I understand she worked here a few years ago."

"You working with that police officer? If so, I have nothing more to say. I don't appreciate his accusations."

Vince knew he was speaking about Montgomery. Anthony Sullivan wouldn't be the first one Jason had alienated during his investigation. A young woman of Native American descent entered the room from an interior door near the back. "I'm working as an independent investigator on behalf of the victim's family."

"I already told him everything I know about her. She worked here a couple of years before moving away. Don't know anything about her personal life or who might have killed her."

"I'm only trying to find answers for Jenny's family. She was estranged from them, and they would like to put the pieces of her life together. You must realize her death came as quite a shock."

"I'm sure it did, but I can't help you."

"Can't tell me anything about her friends or acquaintances? The family understood she had a boyfriend or perhaps a husband since her last name had changed." Vince exchanged looks with the woman who now stood behind a counter. She knew something. Apparently, she wouldn't, or couldn't, talk in front of Sullivan.

"I didn't know her, outside our working relationship."

Vince moved toward the back of the room, then reached in his pocket. "I understand. Sorry to have taken up your time. If you do remember anything, here's my business card." He placed the card on the counter and looked directly into the woman's eyes.

She nodded, ever so slightly, before he turned to leave.

Once inside the car, he gave a satisfied smile, confident he would hear from her soon. Time to check into a hotel for the night and wait.

JASON SAT AT HIS DESK, rubbing his forehead. For the past three days, he'd fielded calls regarding the composite sketch. So far, none proved useful.

One caller stated he saw the man and Jenny Allen together in Cameron Park shortly before her murder. A few well-placed questions proved the statement false.

He hoped someone—anyone—would come forward with something concrete. It seemed as if the man known as Sean was as much an enigma as Jenny Allen herself. With no new evidence and no additional clues, the investigation was growing stale. The last thing Jason wanted was for it to end up in an archive of cold cases. Jenny's family, as well as the public, deserved to know the identity of her murderer.

Likewise, Brewster police had no new leads. When he spoke with Randy Somers earlier, the detective expressed relief no repeat murder occurred over the weekend. But he, too, was frustrated over the lack of progress.

Jason took a deep breath, then slowly exhaled. He was at a loss as to what to do next. Would he ever catch a break? When the phone rang, he was surprised to see the number for the Brewster PD.

He pressed the speaker button. "Montgomery."

"This is Randy. Just had an interesting conversation with the sister of Lori Huff. Seems an heirloom necklace is missing from her personal effects. It's a Celtic knot pendant with a large diamond in the center. According to Lori's roommate, she was wearing it the night she was murdered."

"And you're just now discovering this?" Looks like he wasn't the only imperfect detective.

"First time anyone has mentioned it. We had no way of knowing it existed until now."

"Sorry." Jason could have easily been in the same position. "Strange that someone would wear an expensive necklace while jogging."

"I agree. Both her sister and the roommate said she rarely took it off."

"You think robbery was the motive?"

"Could be. I reviewed the autopsy photos, and there's no sign anyone ripped the chain from her neck. If so, she would have had marks or bruising in the area."

"How does this fit with the other victim?"

"Susan Mason wasn't known to wear a lot of jewelry at work—only an inexpensive watch. She had just come off her shift at the hospital, and the watch was still on her wrist when the body was discovered. We found her wallet and cell phone locked in her car. Had about fifty dollars cash."

"One would almost assume there were two killers."

"Yeah. If not for the DNA match. It could be the murderer only thought Mason had something worth stealing. Once he discovered she didn't, he killed her to avoid being to be identified."

"We already know robbery wasn't a motive in Jenny Allen's death."

"Every time we find another piece of the puzzle, it seems it takes us backward."

"Same here. Maybe we'll get a solid lead from the composite sketch."

"Hope so."

"Yeah. Me, too." Jason hung up the phone, wishing he could believe it would happen.

VINCE PULLED ON HIS BOOTS, then reached for the set of keys on the nightstand. After checking through a list of nearby restaurants, he decided on local cuisine. The Mexican food found in this part of the country was a nice change from the usual Tex-Mex he often enjoyed. Now it was a matter of deciding where to eat.

He glanced at his watch. Six o'clock and still no word from the woman at the gallery. But he wasn't ready to give up. He was confident he would hear from her soon. His phone rang. Perfect timing.

"Vince Green."

"This is Sarah Grant from Gallery 221. If you need information on Jenny, I think I can help you." Her voice was low, and Vince got the impression she didn't want anyone to overhear the conversation.

"Go on."

"Can we meet somewhere?"

"Sure. My hotel is near the plaza. I was about to go out for dinner. Thought I'd try some of the local fare. Care to join me?"

"There's a cantina a couple of blocks away that's famous for their local cuisine. I could meet you there in about thirty minutes."

"Sounds good."

After giving Vince directions to the café, she hung up the phone.

Vince reached for his jacket, then pocketed his set of keys, deciding to walk the short distance. A half-hour later, he was seated at the restaurant, sipping a beer and waiting for Sarah Grant. He liked the looks of the place with its stucco walls, colorful Mexican tile tables, and straight-backed chairs. A distinct smell of piñon came from the corner fireplace.

It was another ten minutes before Sarah arrived. She smiled as she sat opposite Vince. "Sorry. We had a last-minute customer, and Anthony asked if I would stay."

"Not a problem." He signaled for the waiter.

"Something to drink, ma'am?"

"Just water, thanks."

Vince waited until drinks were served, and they placed their order before asking questions. "I gather you knew Jenny Allen?"

Sarah nodded. "I met Jenny when she first moved to Taos. We worked together for almost two years."

"What can you tell me about her?"

"She was a private person. Took a while before she would talk about anything personal, but we eventually became friends. She'd had a falling out with her family but didn't talk a lot about them."

"Did she go by the name Hartsfield when she first arrived?

"Yes. About six months later, she married a local artist named Jeremy Allen. The marriage lasted almost a year."

"Is he still around?"

Sarah nodded. "Jeremy remarried. He and his wife have two children. They live north of town."

"Any reason for him to harm Jenny?"

"No. Their divorce was amicable. Both realized they had made a mistake. I guess keeping his name was Jenny's way of making a complete break with her past."

"Do you recall her ever mentioning someone named Sean?"

"No, the name doesn't ring a bell."

The waiter returned to their table. "Your dinner will be out shortly. Do either of you need refills on your drinks?"

Sarah shook her head. "I'm good for now."

"Another beer for me."

"Coming right up."

Vince waited until the waiter departed. "Tell me about Anthony Sullivan. Why is he reluctant to talk?"

"Anthony is harmless. Doesn't like to get involved in things. I can assure you he has nothing to hide."

The waiter returned with their food. Vince took a bite of a chile relleno before continuing. "You said you worked with Jenny for a couple of years? Did she quit? Go to work at another gallery?"

"She moved to Santa Fe to work at a gallery there. We stayed in touch. A few months later, she met someone. He was an artist who had also lived in Texas."

"Did she know him before moving to Santa Fe?"

"No. Jenny told me he'd had some sort of tragedy in his life and needed a clean break from the past. They had just moved in together when he died in an accident. His car skidded off the road on a mountain pass. We lost touch after that, but I heard she returned to Texas. People said she took his death hard."

"From all accounts, she moved back to San Antonio but never contacted her family."

Sarah tucked a strand of long black hair behind her ear. "That's too bad. She could have used their support. But I can understand why she didn't stay in Santa Fe."

"Why is that?"

"Some people speculated Jesse's death wasn't an accident and that he killed himself. Said he'd never gotten over his past love. Who knows?"

"Did you know him?"

"I met him a couple of times. Nice guy. Jesse had a lot of talent. I don't believe he took his own life."

Vince frowned. "His name was Jesse?

"Yes. Jesse Saldana."

SOMEHOW, Vince made it through dinner without showing too much emotion. Jesse Saldana was the last name he expected to hear. He only saw the man once but knew about his background and reputation.

If Sarah sensed something was wrong, she didn't say. She promised to contact him if she thought of anything else that might be useful.

After paying for the meal, Vince left the restaurant and strolled to his hotel. He wasn't in a hurry. The night air was cold, but he hoped the walk would help clear his head. He needed to collect his thoughts before calling Tami.

I've checked your background.

Had she known? Was that the reason she chose him for the job? He should have realized the similarities were too great to be mere chance.

We have something in common.

Tami must have known something. But if she knew about Jesse, why go to the expense of hiring an investigator?

Knowing Jenny had been romantically involved with Jesse Saldana was surprising, but it didn't bring him any closer to discover the identity of her killer. Vince needed to visit Santa Fe. Talk with her former coworkers and neighbors. He hoped she hadn't been so secretive when she lived there.

At this point, he saw no need to involve Jenny's ex-husband. According to Sarah, he had been devastated to learn of her death. He also had an iron-clad alibi—he was a participant in a city-wide art exhibition the weekend of her death.

Once back at the hotel, he took the elevator to the third floor. In his room, he sat on the bed, then dug out his cell.

Tami must have been expecting his call because she answered on the first ring. "Got anything?"

Not so much as a hello. Well, two could play that game. "Does the name Jesse Saldana mean anything to you?"

"Should it?"

"Just answer the question."

"No. I have no idea who you're talking about. Want to fill me in?"

"He's the man your sister lived with before she returned to Texas."

There was a long pause before Tami spoke in a low voice. "I see. Do you think he killed her?"

"Hardly. He died in a traffic accident a few weeks before Jenny left Santa Fe."

"Is he the reason she left there?"

"Not sure. I'm in Taos now. Spoke with someone she once worked with. Jenny was married briefly, but there's nothing to indicate her ex-husband was involved. According to her friend, they agreed on the divorce."

He filled Tami in on the things Sarah shared, except for the possibility of Jesse's death being a suicide. It was only speculation and likely irrelevant to Jenny's murder.

"So, what's next?"

"I'll drive to Santa Fe tomorrow. See what I can find there. After that, the next stop is San Antonio. Doubtful there's anything to be gained from that trip. From all accounts, your sister was extremely secretive about her life by the time she moved there."

"Do what you can. That's all I ask."

"Oh, I'll do the job. Regardless of the reasons why you hired me."

"What's that supposed to mean?"

"I want to know if there is anything you haven't told me."

"Why do I get the feeling I'm being interrogated?"

Vince rubbed the bridge of his nose. "Forget it. We'll talk when I get back. In the meantime, I'll let you know if I learn anything important."

He ended the call, then lay back on the bed. What he wouldn't give to be home tonight. To see Christine. Hear her voice. Time to come clean. No more secrets.

You lived in Marfa?

Vince recalled his question to Darla. Jenny Allen knew Jesse Saldana. She moved to Driscoll Lake and went to work in Darla's art gallery. Made no effort to contact her sister.

There had to be a connection between Jenny Allen's murder and what happened in Marfa. Until he figured out what the link was, it was best to keep silent about his past.

CHAPTER 16

*V*ince looked out the window to see the familiar sight of Reunion Tower. The plane would land in a few minutes. Traffic on Stemmons Freeway was steady, but the worst of the rush hour was yet to come. Afternoon sun reflected on the glass and steel skyscrapers of downtown Dallas.

His decision to fly into Love Field was two-fold. Baggage claim took less time than at DFW, and access to parking was easier. Not only that, but the smaller airport was closer to Driscoll Lake. In two hours, he would be home and hopefully be able to spend most of the weekend with Christine.

They phoned each other several times while he was away. He hated not being able to tell her his whereabouts or discuss the case with her.

During one of their phone calls, she talked about Darla and how she might have misjudged her mother-in-law.

"I was wrong to question her motives for moving here. She realizes she made mistakes with Kyle but wants to have a close relationship with Emily and me. Never thought it would happen. In some ways, she understands me better than my own mother."

Vince hoped she wouldn't be in for a rude awakening.

She and Darla were becoming closer—something Christine said she never expected to happen. But until Vince learned more about Darla, it was best to keep silent.

At any rate, Tami had sworn him to secrecy. To tell Christine he was in New Mexico or San Antonio might tip her off.

Vince couldn't help but feel the trip was a waste of time. Except for the information he obtained from Sarah Grant, he'd come up short-handed. No one in Santa Fe or San Antonio was able to provide anything useful.

People he spoke with in Santa Fe agreed Jesse Saldana's death was an accident. Everyone said the rumors of suicide were just that. Rumors. Once again, no one knew of Jenny's association with anyone named Sean.

When Jenny moved to San Antonio, she distanced herself from any art communities and took a job as an administrative assistant in a large accounting firm.

Her coworkers were surprised to learn Jenny's parents lived nearby. Why then would she move to a small town if she knew her sister lived there? Didn't make sense.

Tami denied knowing anything about Jesse, but Vince felt sure she had lied.

He couldn't shake the feeling this man was the common thread. But how? He didn't kill Jenny. A trip to Marfa or Alpine might give him some answers. But he wasn't ready to go back. Not now. Maybe not ever.

CHRISTINE GOT out of her SUV, then stretched. It was a beautiful early April afternoon. Temps in the low eighties, clear with brilliant sunshine. A great day to be outdoors.

Six weeks had passed since the murder in Cameron Park. Six weeks since Christine last ran there. She had jogged through her neighborhood. Even used the track at the football stadium a few times. But for her, nothing compared with being outdoors surrounded by nature.

The days were getting longer, and with Daylight Saving Time in effect, she still had a few hours before dark. Many women were hesitant about running in the park since the murder, but with no repeat incidents, some had started to go back, careful to ensure there were other people around.

Christine had little doubt runners would fill the trails today. She hurried inside her house to change into her running clothes. A good run would help ease some of the tension she'd felt this week, as well as give her something to do on a Friday evening.

Funny thing, she was supposed to be in a relationship. But since she and Vince decided to start dating, he had been out of town more than he was home. He'd called several times during the week. She had no idea where he was or what kind of case he was on but understood he had to maintain client confidentiality.

The last time he called, he said he hoped to be home for the weekend, but she hadn't heard from him today.

An hour later, she paused to do a few stretches before starting on one of the jogging trails at Cameron Park. She decided to avoid the lakeside path—the place where she found Jenny's body. Too many bad memories. One day, she would put them behind her. But not now. Not without Vince around.

As she guessed, she didn't have to worry about being alone. A lot of people were taking advantage of the warm weather. She ran a couple of miles through a wooded trail before turning back. The sun was already low in the sky. To remain here after dark was foolish. No matter how independent she wanted to be, she'd learned her lesson.

Almost halfway back to the start of the trail, she felt a prickling on the back of her neck. Strange. Was someone watching her? A quick look revealed a few other runners, none of whom seemed to be paying attention.

Probably nothing. Just the idea of being out here again. She patted her pocket, confirming she had both her cell phone and pepper spray. Christine had to smile when she remembered the time she'd told Vince she could take care of herself. What she wouldn't give to have him here now.

She increased her pace, thankful when she met a couple of joggers running toward her. They nodded a greeting before continuing along the path, and she relaxed a bit.

When she neared the parking area, the eerie feeling returned. It was still daylight, and there were several cars in the lot, but she couldn't shake the thought that someone was watching her. She didn't see anything or anyone out of the ordinary.

Still… Something was wrong. Her racing pulse had nothing to do with the fact she'd run two miles. Danger lurked nearby. Forget a cooldown. She was going straight for her SUV and locking the doors. The sooner she left here, the better.

Upon reaching the lot, she saw a familiar car pull into a parking space. Vince. How had he known she was here? She raced toward him.

Vince got out of his car. "Christine? What's wrong?"

"I…I don't know. Decided to come here to run. Figured I had plenty of daylight. Everything was fine at first. Then I had the strangest sensation someone was watching me." Christine sniffed, trying not to cry. She wasn't usually this emotional, but the entire ordeal had her on edge.

Vince frowned. "Watching you? Did you see anything?"

"No. That's just it. The only people around were runners. Intent on enjoying the day. I guess… Maybe I'm crazy." This time she didn't fight her emotions.

"No, you're not, babe." Vince pulled her into his arms.

After a few minutes, her tears subsided. Maybe it was the pressure of the last few weeks. The murdered woman, Emily's behavior, starting a new relationship, trying to figure out her mother-in-law.

But Christine knew the facade had lasted much longer. She had tried to put on a brave front since Kyle died. It was time to let go.

"I'm sorry. Don't know what came over me."

"Don't apologize. I'm glad I was here for you. Come on. Let's get you home."

~

ANGER WAS OFTEN the driving force behind many actions. The motivation to keep going, to finish the task. But patience was equally important. Timing had to be right. It was never good to rush a job or force an issue.

Seeing Christine Lawrence and Vince Green together was confirmation. There was something more than friendship between them. An undeniable attraction. The way he embraced her. The way she willingly went into his arms.

Following them had been relatively easy. Not hard to remain unnoticed if one used caution. It wasn't surprising Vince was now at Christine's house. Would he stay the night? There wasn't any point in waiting around to see. Didn't matter.

Take a few deep breaths. Calm down. Now isn't the time. You must endure a little longer.

When the time was right, another person was going to die.

CHRISTINE STOOD BENEATH THE SHOWER, allowing the warm water to cascade over her body. After assuring Vince she was okay to drive, he insisted on following her home.

She invited him to stay. After not knowing when he would return home, his presence was a welcome surprise. The timing perfect.

Something happened between them at the park. Although unspoken, she sensed a change in their relationship. Vince was someone she could trust. Someone who would be there for her. She hadn't felt this way since Kyle…

Maybe I've never felt this way.

Smiling, she reached to turn off the water, stepped from the shower, then wrapped a towel around herself.

A few minutes later, dressed in jeans and a pull-over shirt, she walked into the living room.

Vince looked up from the sofa and offered a smile.

"Hope you don't mind, I ordered pizza. Figured you wouldn't want to go out."

"You're right about that. You okay with us staying home?"

"As long as I'm spending time with you, it doesn't matter." Vince glanced around the room. "Where's your daughter?"

"Where else? At her grandmother's house."

"She spends a lot of time there?"

Christine shrugged. "They're getting to know one another. Darla says she has a lot of time to make up for."

"Yeah, about seventeen years."

"Vince, I was wrong about Darla."

"That's what you said a few days ago. What made you change your mind?"

"I don't know what caused her to leave Kyle with his father, but I got the feeling Curtis threatened her in some way. She did what she thought was best for her son. Told me she would regret it for the rest of her life."

"That's quite a turn-around for you. A few weeks ago, you thought she had ulterior motives for moving here."

"People make mistakes. She seems to be trying. The other day she even—" The doorbell rang, interrupting her words.

"Pizza's here." Vince walked to the door.

"I'll get our drinks."

Later, after they finished eating, they returned to the sofa in the living room. "How did you know I would be at the park?" Christine asked.

"A hunch, I guess. I came here first because I wanted to surprise you. When you weren't home, I planned to go to my house and call you from there. Passed by the park and saw your SUV."

"I'm glad you found me. Today was the first time I've been back there. The weather was nice, and I'm tired of having to run along busy streets. I decided enough people would be around and figured I would be safe."

"I don't want you taking any unnecessary chances."

"Don't worry, I won't. I couldn't bring myself to run the lakeside trail. I'm not sure if I ever will. Is that silly of me?"

Vince put his arm around her and drew her close. "No. What

happened that day was traumatic. It takes time to get over some things. You'll know when and if you're ready. Don't force it."

"When that time comes, will you be there with me?"

"Yes." His voice was low and husky, and he pulled her into his arms.

"Thank you."

They sat for a few minutes in silence, content to be with one another.

"Vince, is it silly for me to think someone was watching me? I didn't see anyone. It was more of a—"

"Feeling?"

"Yeah."

"It's not silly. Sometimes relying on our instincts is best. But I want you to be careful. A killer is still out there somewhere."

"Do you think I'm in danger?"

"Who's to say? Anyone could be a target. But I know one thing."

"What's that?"

"I don't want to lose you."

Their lips met in a searing kiss.

Officer Steve Woods stifled a yawn and glanced at his partner sitting in the passenger seat. Tessa Hill had joined the Brewster Police Force only two weeks earlier. Tonight was their first patrol together.

"Is it always this quiet on a Friday night?" she asked.

Steve shook his head. "With everything that's gone down the past few weeks, I'm glad for a boring shift."

"You mean the murders?"

"Yeah. I was one of the first officers on the scene of the second one."

"Let's hope another one doesn't happen tonight."

"I agree. It's—"

Steve's response was cut short by the dispatcher's voice on the radio. "Unit 118, we have a 10-16 at 242 Elm Street."

"10-4, we're on it." Steve started the engine, then drove toward the outskirts of town. "Looks like Charlie is at it again."

"Who's Charlie?"

"Charlie Nelson is a Vietnam vet. He still carries a lot of emotional scars from the war. Occasionally, they surface."

"Does he become abusive?"

Steve shook his head. "Just hits the bottle and cranks up the music. He's been arrested for public intoxication a couple of times, but he's harmless. Wasn't easy for those guys."

"What can we expect?"

"He'll calm down, apologize, and lower the music to an acceptable level. We'll be in and out of there in no time."

A few minutes later, Steve pulled into the driveway. "Ready?"

"Sure."

The two officers got out of the car, walked to the front door, then knocked. Steve took the lead. "Charlie? Come to the door. Music's too loud. Neighbors are complaining."

Receiving no response, he pounded again. "Come on. Open up."

Still no response.

Steve looked at his partner and shrugged. He tried the doorknob and found it unlocked.

"Should we go in?" Tessa asked.

Steve nodded, then opened the door.

The smell of stale cigarettes and whiskey permeated the room. Creedence Clearwater Revival belted out the words of "Fortunate Son" on the stereo.

Charlie was passed out on the couch with his right arm flung over the side, and the left across his chest with something clutched in his hand.

Tessa crossed the room to lower the volume on the stereo while Steve went to Charlie. After confirming he had a pulse, Steve shook him on the shoulder, "Come on, wake up. You're disturbing the neighbors. Charlie!"

"Huh? What's going on?" The older man rushed to stand. At the same time, he unclenched his hand.

The two officers looked at one another in surprise as a Celtic knot pendant fell to the floor.

CHAPTER 17

$\mathcal{A}$n intermittent ring pierced the foggy edges of his sleep. Jason rolled over in bed, trying to determine the source of the noise. Still drowsy, he looked to see his cell phone flashing. Someone calling at four in the morning usually meant bad news.

Please, God, don't let it be another murder.

He picked up the phone, then glanced at the caller ID. If Detective Randy Somers was calling, it was important. "Montgomery."

"Sorry to bother you this early in the morning."

"Hope you're not about to tell me there's been another stabbing."

"No. Two of our officers answered a disturbance call around midnight. They brought in a man named Charlie Nelson for questioning."

"I gather there's a connection to the murders."

"Charlie had a pendant in his possession matching the description of the one belonging to Lori Huff."

"Think he killed her?"

"Don't know, but I plan to question him about her death."

"I assume you'll ask about the other killings."

"Yeah. Thought you'd want to be here. Maybe this is the break we've been needing."

"I can be there in half an hour." Jason ended the call. In the bathroom, he splashed cold water on his face. No time to shave. He kept an electric razor in the console of his car for situations like this. It would have to suffice. Five minutes later he was dressed, in his Camaro, and on the road to Brewster.

He considered calling Matt but didn't see any reason to disturb him. The interrogation could go on for hours. He would call later and fill him in on the details. Hopefully, he would have some vital information relative to Jenny's murder.

His thoughts then drifted to Tami. After their "date" last weekend, he'd begun to understand how deeply the ordeal had affected her. Even though she hadn't seen her sister in five years, the pain was still present. From what little she'd told him, the two of them were once close.

Time and circumstance caused them to drift apart. First Tami left home for college, then Jenny had a falling out with her father. Sad when misunderstandings led to family separations. Jason hadn't experienced it first hand, but he'd seen similar situations far too many times.

In cases like Jenny's, the surviving family members often felt guilt. Some wondered if they could have done something that may have prevented their loved one's death. Others expressed remorse at having never reconciled. Tami hadn't indicated any such feelings, but Jason sensed she was keeping some things hidden.

Whatever the case, she deserved the truth. To have closure. He wondered how he could have misjudged her when she approached him for information shortly after the murder. Neither of them knew at the time the victim was her sister. He hated giving information to an inquisitive newspaper editor. Had he known about her relationship to the victim, he would have acted differently.

He hoped today would provide answers. Not only for Tami but also the families of the other women.

JASON HAD BEEN INSIDE several interrogation rooms during his career. Whether large or small, bright or poorly lit, most looked much the same. All contained a table and uncomfortable chairs. Many had glass on one wall that allowed others to observe without being seen.

This one had a coffee maker sitting on a small table in the corner. The stench of the burnt brew infiltrated the air. Someone forgot to flip a switch, and the pot had boiled dry. Probably happened often since Randy brought a fresh cup into the room.

These rooms were essential to conducting investigations, but they were depressing even to Jason. How much more for the person being questioned? Especially if they were innocent.

He entered the room with Detective Somers to see a man of around seventy years of age sitting at one end of the table. A uniformed officer stood guard in the corner.

The suspect had hollow cheekbones and a jaundiced complexion. His hands trembled slightly and his clothes, though clean, were threadbare. But it was his eyes that caught Jason's attention. Troubled eyes. Eyes that had seen the face of death too many times. This man's problems ran long and deep.

Yet he also held a keen sense of awareness. Alert to everything around him. Probably went back to his military training.

At first glance, he appeared to be incapable of harming a fly, but according to Randy, Charlie Nelson was once a Recon Marine. Served two tours in Vietnam and was trained in hand-to-hand combat. How many times had he been forced to use that training?

But killing the enemy during wartime was one thing. The senseless death of innocent victims another.

Randy took the chair opposite the suspect. "Charlie, we need to ask you a few questions. Want some coffee?"

The older man shook his head.

Randy ignored his refusal and shoved a steaming cup across the table. "This might take a while, so I brought you one anyway."

Jason knew what Randy had in mind.

"Okay, let's get started. This is Detective Jason Montgomery with Driscoll Lake Police. He's going to be sitting in and may also have a few questions for you. Before we get started, I want to point out you're not under arrest. We're just looking for information."

The older man briefly nodded as Jason sat down next to him.

"Can you tell us where you were on the night of March 20? Say around nine?"

"I don't know. Home, I guess."

"But you can't be sure?"

"Don't get out much, you know. I think I was home."

"Alone?"

"Yeah."

"What about March 13? Where were you that night?"

"I don't know."

"Let's talk about Fairview Park. Ever go there?"

"Not in a long time."

"So, you weren't in the park on the evening of March 13?

"Told you I haven't been to that place in a while."

Randy opened the file folder, pulled out photos of Lori Huff and Susan Mason, then slid them across the table. "Do you know either of these women?"

Charlie hesitated, then rubbed the back of his neck. "No."

"You've never seen them?"

"Of course, I've seen them on TV. They're the ones who were killed."

"Aside from that, you've never been in contact with either of them?"

"No." Charlie's hands shook as he took a sip of the hot beverage.

Randy paused for a moment before nodding at Jason. "Okay, I'm sure Detective Montgomery has a few questions for you."

Jason was surprised Randy hadn't asked about the pendant but figured there was a good reason. He cleared his throat and looked at the notepad in front of him. "Going to tax your memory a bit more. Can you tell me where you were on February 21 in the late afternoon or early evening?"

"Can barely remember last week, but I will tell you I wasn't in Driscoll Lake."

"I didn't say anything about Driscoll Lake. I asked where you were."

"Where else would you be talking about? I didn't kill that woman. That's why you're here. Trying to pin her murder on me. Just like he's trying to do with those other women." Charlie pointed toward Randy.

Jason guessed right about the man. He was more alert than most people would give him credit for. "So, you're positive you weren't in Driscoll Lake they day she was killed?"

"Yeah, I'm sure. I was in the VA hospital in Dallas. Stayed there over a week. If you don't believe me, you can check it out."

Jason narrowed his gaze. "We'll do that."

"Tell us about the necklace," Randy said.

"What necklace?"

"The one you had clutched in your hand when the two officers showed up at your house."

"Found it."

"Where?"

"Don't remember."

"Come on. You expect us to believe that? Think again."

"Told you I don't remember."

"Is that why you killed her?"

"Who?"

"We know the pendant belonged to Lori Huff. Now tell me."

Charlie shifted in his chair but didn't say anything.

"Here's what I think. You went out that night. Probably looking for something to drink. You spotted Lori, saw the necklace, decided it would buy a lot of booze. So you killed her, then took it."

"No. That's not what happened."

Randy's eyebrows shot up. "Then why don't you tell me what did."

Charlie began to sob. "She… she was already dead. I swear I didn't kill her."

VINCE RARELY WENT to his office on Saturdays, but since he'd been out of town most of the week, he decided it would be a good time to finish his report. He could have easily done it from his laptop at home. Probably should have. He wasn't ready to talk with Tami, and although she was tenacious, the chances of her coming to his house were less than at the office.

He phoned her from San Antonio early Friday morning to say he was close to wrapping things up. Didn't tell her he planned to fly home late that afternoon, but he was surprised she hadn't called to check.

Damn the woman for getting him involved in this. Yes, he had a choice. Or did he? The more he thought about it, there was only one right decision. Help Tami learn who killed her sister. If only she hadn't sworn him to secrecy.

After last night, it would be harder to conceal things from Christine. He wanted—no needed—to come clean with her. Relationships needed to be built on trust. They were bound to fail when one or both partners kept secrets. He didn't want that with her.

But until he learned if Darla was connected in any way, he needed to keep silent. He didn't believe Darla was a killer, but he had a lot of questions. She lived in Marfa for years. Suddenly decided to move to Driscoll Lake to be near her daughter-in-law and granddaughter. Was it guilt over not being a mother to her son? Or something else?

Did she know Jesse Saldana? Marfa wasn't a big town. If Darla was involved in the art community, it was almost a given that they'd met. And if she knew Jesse, how much did she know about his lover's murder?

Vince didn't want to see Christine get hurt. He hoped Darla was sincere in her intentions. Her being here could be happenstance.

Yeah, right.

He took a deep breath, his decision made. He needed to pay a visit to Darla's art gallery.

IT WAS ALMOST noon before Jason arrived back in Driscoll Lake. When he left home that morning, he hoped to be able to provide Tami with the answer as to who killed her sister. It wasn't to be.

There was a possibility Charlie killed Lori Huff. He'd admitted to being on the scene of her murder. His involvement with Susan Mason's death was uncertain. Even if the former marine killed both women, there wasn't any way he could have been responsible for Jenny's murder. His story about being in the hospital checked out.

Jason wasn't convinced Charlie killed anyone. He readily agreed to have a DNA test performed. A guilty person wasn't likely to do that. The more Jason studied the details of each case, the more he believed Jenny's murder was unrelated. He suspected Matt thought the same thing, although the two of them hadn't discussed the matter.

Instead of going back home, Jason drove to the police station. Of all people, Sandra was the dispatcher on duty today. Since the incident with her shortly after he arrived in Driscoll Lake, she treated him coldly. Not that he blamed her. He'd tried apologizing several times, but she wouldn't have any of it. They still had to work together, so he decided to be cordial.

"Hey, Sandra. Chief hasn't been in today, has he?"

"He doesn't work on Saturdays. You should know that." Her tone was icy.

"I do, but I need to talk to him. Guess I'll try him at home."

"You shouldn't bother him unless it's an emergency."

When did Sandra become Matt's self-appointed keeper? "I wouldn't call it an emergency, but it's something he needs to know."

"Whatever. It's your skin, not mine."

And you'd love to see me in trouble.

Jason bit back the retort. He shook his head as he went into his office. Closing the door behind him, he sat down at his desk, then reached for the phone.

"Bradford." Matt's voice came over the line.

"It's Jason. Just got back from Brewster." He quickly relayed the events of the morning, including his theory about Jenny's killing being unrelated to the Brewster murders.

"Beginning to sound that way."

"Something else has been on my mind. Both victims in Brewster tried to fight off their killers. Jenny didn't have any DNA cells beneath her fingernails. To me, that indicates she knew the killer and was taken by surprise."

"Never thought I'd say this, but for once we agree on something. The killer was probably someone she was comfortable with. She didn't have time to react."

"Jenny didn't know many people in Driscoll Lake. The person in the composite sketch could be our man. Maybe he's someone who passed through town or came here intending to find her. If not—

Matt finished Jason's thought. "It could be someone we know."

CHAPTER 18

*C*hristine smiled as she pulled into her garage, having finished her Saturday morning errands. The weather was perfect for early April. Clear. Sunshine. Warm but not hot. Hard to be in a bad mood on a day like this. Of course, after the previous evening with Vince, she would have been just as happy if it had been cold and pouring rain.

For the first time in years, she felt alive. Now she understood the looks she saw on Rachel's face when she began dating Brian. Stephanie acted similarly when she became involved with Matt. Christine supposed during the early days of her marriage to Kyle, she'd had the same look. But they were young, high school sweethearts, so it was hard to remember what the freshness of a new relationship was like.

At least, it used to be. Now, just thinking about Vince made her smile. And when he kissed her…

The word smitten came to mind. It seemed so old-fashioned. Wasn't it another word for being in love? Only a few weeks ago, she hesitated to become involved with anyone for fear of betraying her late husband's memory.

Not any longer. She and Kyle had a good marriage, even with its ups and downs, but he had been gone over three years. Christine was confident he would want her to move on with life.

While opening the hatch of her SUV, she spotted Libby kneeling beside the front walk, a garden spade in hand, surrounded by several flats of colorful flowers, bags of potting mixture, and mulch.

"Hey, Libby. It looks like you have your work cut out for you today."

"It's too nice a day to be inside. I decided to plant some annuals to give the place color. If I owned the house, I'd dig up the shrubs and plant azaleas. I grew up in Arizona. About the only things that grew there were cactus and succulents."

Christine thought of her own yard. Gardening wasn't something she enjoyed. Low maintenance shrubbery suited her fine. "I'm sure it will look nice when you're finished. I admire you undertaking such a task."

"When it's something I enjoy, I don't look upon it as work. I gather you don't like to be outdoors?"

"I do, but I'd rather be running or taking a walk along a nature trail. I finally went back to Cameron Park yesterday."

"Is that wise since the killer is still at large?"

"I made sure it was daylight, and there were plenty of people around." Christine didn't mention her moment of fear or her impression someone had been watching.

"You of all people shouldn't take any chances."

"I'm no different than any other woman. Everyone should be careful."

"You're right. Guess I was just thinking about you being the one to find the body. Have you given any more thought to trying hypnosis?"

"Not really. Don't think it would be beneficial. Honestly, I'm ready to put the entire thing behind me. Vince and I talked a little about it last night."

"Sounds like the two of you are becoming close."

"You might say that."

"Must be nice to have someone like him."

Christine thought she detected a hint of sadness in Libby's voice. "What about you? Anyone special in your life?"

Libby shook her head. "There was someone once. He... it didn't work out."

VINCE WASN'T SURPRISED to hear someone pounding at his office door. He didn't have to look to know it was Tami. He'd managed to ignore a couple of her calls, but eventually, he needed to talk to her. No sense in putting it off any longer.

Still, he took his time getting to the door. Tami stood with her arms crossed, tapping one foot on the sidewalk. "Well, it's about time."

"I was in the middle of something."

"I hope it has to do with my sister." Tami pushed past Vince, then planted herself in front of his desk.

"Not much more to add. I pretty much told you everything on the phone."

"What about San Antonio? Did you learn anything new?"

Vince shook his head. "Jenny was even more secretive once she moved there. I showed everyone the composite sketch. No one recognized him."

"Damn. I was hoping—You're sure her ex-husband wasn't involved?"

"Positive."

"What about this man she lived with?"

"Yeah, let's talk about Saldana. Tell me what you know about him."

"Me? What makes you think I know anything? If I did, there would be no reason to involve you."

"I think Jesse Saldana is the reason you hired me."

"That's ridiculous. I didn't know my sister moved to Santa Fe until after she died. How would I know who she was living with?"

"Don't play innocent with me. I don't mean his connection to your sister. I'm talking about his earlier life."

Tami squared her shoulders. "I never met the man."

"Didn't say you did. But there were things you said to convince me to take this case. Things like us having something in common. You checked into my background. Come on. Spill it."

"Okay. I know what happened in Alpine. You're right. It's the reason I chose you."

"Why didn't you say anything up front?"

"Because I was afraid you wouldn't take the job."

"Maybe I wouldn't have, but I don't like it when people are dishonest."

"I didn't lie."

"No? You conveniently omitted a few things. That's the same as being untruthful."

"Oh, and you're always up front and honest? How many people know about your connection to Alyssa Weber? I'm sure Christine would understand."

"Do. Not. Go. There."

"I promise not to say anything. But why keep it a secret? Guilt?"

Vince slammed his fist on the desk. "That's enough. I'll have the final report to you by Monday, along with an itemized expense list. Now I think it's best you leave."

DARLA SMILED as she handed the envelope to the young woman sitting on the opposite side of her desk. "Your first commission. A lot of customers commented on your pottery. Several expressed interest in seeing more of your work."

Kristen Monroe's eyes widened when she looked at the check. "Wow! I didn't expect this amount in such a short time."

"Doesn't surprise me at all. You have a gift, Kristen. People with an eye for art recognize that."

"Thank you. The money will go a long way into purchasing supplies."

"I hope that means you'll be bringing more pieces. As you can see, only a couple of vases haven't sold." Darla nodded to the display near the front window.

"I have a few items in the car. I'll have more time to work with clay now that I'm no longer employed."

"Oh?"

"I had a part-time job before moving here. Haven't found anything yet. Every place I've applied wants someone full-time. The ones who have part-time positions need people who are committed long term."

"You recently moved here? Tell me a little more about yourself."

"I grew up in Alpine and attended Sul Ross."

"Interesting. My family is from Marathon. My sister and one of my brothers attended Sul Ross."

"You didn't?"

Darla shook her head. "UT Austin."

"I've been accepted there for the fall semester. I'm going for my master's degree."

"What brought you to the Driscoll Lake area?"

"My parents moved here last summer when Dad took a faculty position at Brewster Community College. After I finished Ross, I moved in with them. Trying to save money before I leave for Austin."

"Is your dad an art teacher?"

Kristen scoffed. "Hardly. He teaches political science. Says he doesn't understand much about art. I got all my creative genes from Mom's side of the family."

"He sounds a lot like my father. So, are you interested in working a few hours a week?"

"That would be ideal. A part-time job would still allow me time to make pottery."

Darla laced her fingers together. She considered herself a good judge of character. "Tell you what. I need someone to assist customers, tag and catalog inventory as it arrives, and keep accurate sales records. I prefer to hire a person who knows about art. Are you interested?"

"A job in the gallery? Sounds perfect." Kristen's face lit up.

"Wonderful! Can you begin work Monday morning at ten?"

"I'll be here."

"Great. Now, let's get those pieces of pottery inside."

Kristen stood, then turned to leave the room when she spotted the woman's portrait in the corner. "She's beautiful. Is the painting not for sale?"

Darla shook her head. "It's a long story."

Moving closer to the painting, Kristen said, "I thought Jesse Saldana only did landscapes."

"Did you know him?"

"Not personally, but it's hard for anyone living in Alpine not to know about him. Especially anyone interested in art."

"DAMN STUBBORN SPOT!" Tami picked up a scouring pad, then began to scrub the cooked-on stain. She wasn't sure what her efforts would accomplish. She'd tried scouring pads, vinegar, and a mixture of baking soda and dish soap. So far, nothing worked.

It would be easier to buy new drip pans, but she needed to do something to work out her frustrations. What better way than to attack the kitchen stove? At least she wasn't hitting something or someone. When she met with Vince earlier, her mood changed from one of optimism to disappointment. Not only that, she wasn't exactly happy with him right now.

She didn't have any problems with the way he conducted his investigation. It came as no surprise he was unable to learn much about Jenny. She'd done a good job in keeping details about her private life a secret. What Tami didn't like was Vince's accusation that she knew about Jesse Saldana.

Yes, she had heard the name and knew about the similarities between her sister's death and that of Alyssa Weber three years earlier. But she was honest about not knowing Jenny had become involved with the artist.

If Jesse hadn't died first, Tami would have suspected he killed her sister. How many men had been involved with not only one woman, but two women, who were later stabbed to death?

There had to be a connection. But what? Whoever first said dead men tell no tales spoke volumes. Other than their association with Jesse, Alyssa and Jenny had nothing in common. What was the link? Had Jenny left Santa Fe in fear? Was that the reason she became even more secretive in San Antonio, cutting herself off from the art community? If so, why did she move to a small town and take a job in an art gallery?

Would she ever know who killed her sister? More than two years had passed since Alyssa Weber's death, and authorities still didn't have any suspects.

Maybe she could persuade Vince to make a trip to Alpine.

Like that's going to happen now. You screwed that up.

She tried to put herself in his position. How would she feel?

Maybe I should have been more upfront with him.

Tami blew a strand of stray hair from her forehead, then rinsed the drip pan in the sink. Her efforts paid off in part. At least the stain was smaller. It would have to suffice.

After putting the burner back together, she pulled off her rubber gloves. She threw them in the trash on her way to the sink. That was enough spring cleaning for today. What she wanted now was a long hot soak in the bathtub and a glass of wine, not necessarily in that order.

She started toward her bedroom when the doorbell rang. *Who would drop by uninvited on a Saturday afternoon?*

Better not be someone trying to sell something. With the mood I'm in, I'll be more than happy to set them straight.

Back in the entryway, she looked through the peephole. When she saw who was standing on the other side, she hurried to open the door.

"Jason. What are you doing here?"

"Can I come in?"

"You have news about Jenny?"

Jason cleared his throat. "Yes and no."

Tami motioned him inside and pointed to the sofa. "Have a seat."

"Thanks."

She sat beside him. "Have you found the killer?"

"Wish I could say we have. Last night, Brewster police brought in a man named Charlie Nelson for questioning regarding the murder of Lori Huff. He had something in his possession that belonged to her."

"Is he the killer?"

"He denies it. Readily agreed to DNA testing. I have my doubts about his guilt."

"You have doubts? If so, he must be innocent. You're the one who's always so quick to blame someone."

Jason winced. "I deserved that."

"Sorry, I call it as I see it."

"You're right. I have been quick to judge. At first, I didn't put as much effort into the investigation as I should have. I made a lot of mistakes, but believe me, I've changed."

She paused to consider his words. There was something different about him. A sincerity that hadn't been there before. "I believe you."

"That means a lot to me." Jason smiled. "Now, about the investigation. Even if Charlie killed Lori Huff and Susan Mason, there's no way he could have killed your sister. He has an iron-clad alibi."

"Are you sure he doesn't have someone just claiming to vouch for him?"

"No, this one checks out. He was in a hospital in Dallas at the time of her death."

"Okay, so you have the wrong man. You keep searching, right? A killer is still at large."

"Or killers."

Tami gasped. "What?"

"For a few weeks, I've had doubts the Brewster murders were related to Jenny's. Talked to Matt this morning, and he agrees. I probably shouldn't tell you this, but I think Jenny's killer was someone she knew."

"The man she met at Hank's Tavern?"

"Possibly. Could be someone else."

"Then who?"

Jason took her hand. "That's what I intend to find out. Don't worry, Tami. I'll find the person responsible."

CHAPTER 19

"*Y*ou look beautiful, honey." Christine fought to hold back tears. Her little girl was growing up. Wasn't it only yesterday when she and Kyle brought their little bundle of joy home from the hospital? But almost seventeen years had passed, and now Emily was getting ready to attend her first prom.

Christine still recalled the excitement and nervousness of being new parents. Kyle had been especially anxious. He didn't have the ideal father figure, and his absentee mother was busy with her own life. But he stepped up to the plate and became a loving and supporting dad—the antithesis of Curtis Lawrence.

Kyle had doted on his daughter. He would be proud of her. Probably a little overprotective now that boys were a part of her life. Since his death, Emily wavered between grief and anger, but it was because she missed her father.

Even with all her rebellious actions, sometimes the vulnerable little girl would surface. The one who would like nothing more than to curl up in her daddy's lap when she needed comfort.

But it wasn't a day for sadness. Emily's face shone with excitement as she looked in the mirror. Christine had treated her to a morning at the spa—complete with a manicure, pedicure, hairstyle, and make-up.

"I hope Ty likes my dress," Emily said.

"Believe me, he will, but that's not all he'll like."

Emily blushed. "Mom!" A few seconds of silence passed before she spoke again, this time her voice softer. "Did you and Dad go to the prom together?"

"When we were seniors. We didn't start dating until that year."

"So, you went out with other boys?"

"A few. I didn't even like your father at first."

"You didn't? Why?"

"It had more to do with your grandfather, but that doesn't matter now. Once I got to know your dad, I realized he was the only one for me."

"If that's the case, then why, how…"

"Can I have feelings for someone else?"

"Yeah."

Christine chose her words carefully. "Honey, no one can ever take your father's place. But he's gone now. Vince is someone I enjoy being with."

"Are you going to marry him?"

"It's a little premature to think along those lines. We haven't been dating that long, but lots of people marry a second time. Stephanie's mom remarried after her father died. It doesn't mean she didn't love her first husband. She just got a second chance at happiness. Can you understand that?"

"Yeah, I guess." Emily sniffed. "It's just that I miss Dad so much."

Christine wrapped her arms around her daughter. "I know, honey. I miss him, too. But hey, don't cry now. You don't want to ruin your make-up."

Emily pulled away, then looked in the mirror as the doorbell rang. "Oh, no. My eyes are red, and Ty is here."

"Too early for him. It's probably your grandmother. She wanted to come by and take some photos. Go freshen up. I'll get the door." She started to leave the room when Emily spoke.

"Mom?"

"Yeah?"

"Sorry I've acted like a jerk about Vince."

Christine exhaled a sigh of relief. Maybe her daughter was finally coming around. "Apology accepted."

"Are you going to see him tonight?"

"Yes. We're going out."

Emily smiled. "Good."

VINCE WAS surprised when he saw Darla's SUV parked in Christine's driveway. According to her, Darla rarely visited. Of course, that probably changed since the two of them were becoming closer.

He couldn't help but feel annoyed. Darla's presence could interfere with his plans to take Christine out for a nice, quiet dinner in Brewster. But her being here could also work to his advantage, especially since he wanted to learn more about any connection she might have to Jesse Saldana.

After parking his car, he got out, then hurried up the sidewalk. He was surprised when Darla opened the door.

"Hello, Vince."

"Ms. Martell. Nice to see you."

"Oh, please. Call me Darla. I'm not big on formalities."

He smiled. "Okay. Darla it is."

"Christine is running behind. Had to spend a little more time with Emily than anticipated. Have a seat. She'll be out in a few minutes." She nodded toward the sofa.

Vince sat in what was becoming a familiar spot, taking note of the expensive DSLR camera on the coffee table.

Darla took a seat in a chair near the window. "I won't be staying long. Just came by to take some snapshots of my granddaughter."

"Nice camera. Are you a professional?"

"No. I took a couple of photography classes when I was at UT, but I only take photos for pleasure."

"I would guess you majored in art since you own a gallery."

"I have a fine arts degree, but it's in creative writing. My late husband, Andrew, was an artist. He was fairly well known in Marfa."

Vince nodded. This could be the open door he needed. Maybe he could pry more information from her.

"I remember you saying you once lived in that area. Guess in a small town like Marfa, you pretty much knew everyone."

"Not everyone, but most people you at least recognize by name. Most of Andrew's friends were involved in the art community."

Vince wanted to ask her point blank about Jesse, but he didn't want to arouse suspicion. It was best to ease the name into the conversation. "I'm sure you knew a lot of the local artists."

Christine entered the room. She looked stunning in an above-the-knee black dress. A simple diamond necklace and bracelet were her only jewelry. She had taken off her wedding rings.

"When did you become interested in art?" S leaned down to kiss him.

"Just making small talk."

"I'm afraid not everyone shares my passion," Darla said.

"Apparently some people do. Your gallery is becoming quite successful." Christine smiled at her mother-in-law.

"True. Speaking of which, I hired someone to work there. She brought in a few pieces of pottery a few weeks ago to sell on consignment. When she came for her check today, she mentioned needing a part-time job. Perfect arrangement for both of us."

"That's great," Christine said.

"Ironically, she recently moved to this area from Alpine. Got her BFA from Sul Ross."

The mention of the West Texas town caught Vince's attention. "What brought her to this area?"

"Her father teaches at the college in Brewster. She'll only be here through the summer because she has plans to attend UT this fall." Darla stood, then picked up her camera. "I'd better go and let you two get on with your plans. Didn't intend to stay this long. I enjoyed visiting with you, Vince."

He smiled. "Likewise."

"I'll walk you to the door." Christine followed her mother-in-law to the front entry.

Vince contemplated Darla's words while waiting for Christine to return. Jesse Saldana lived in Alpine. The town was less than thirty miles from Marfa by car. If Darla and her husband had been heavily involved in the art community, they likely knew Jesse Saldana.

Saldana had been romantically involved with Jenny. Darla hired her to work in the gallery. Was she lying when she said Jenny didn't talk about her background? Had Darla known Alyssa? Unless they lived under a rock, anyone residing in Marfa had to know about her murder and the fact she had a lover.

Just how much did Darla know? Somehow, he had to learn whether there was a connection between the deaths of Jenny and Alyssa.

THREE DAYS HAD PASSED since Tami's confrontation with Vince. As promised, she received a copy of his report, along with an itemized list of expenses on Monday. She emailed the statement to her stepfather, asking him to expedite payment. After their disagreement, Tami was sure Vince was ready to sever all ties with both her and the investigation.

She sat in her office, studying his report. Her parents shared her disappointment at not being able to learn anything that might lead to the identity of Jenny's murderer. What Tami didn't tell them was Jesse Saldana's connection to Alyssa Weber and her similar death.

Nor did she tell Jason. She was walking a fine line by withholding possible evidence, but saying anything would break her promise to Vince. She owed him that much.

Why was Vince reluctant to talk about Alyssa? He wasn't responsible for her death. Couldn't he see the similarities between her murder and Jenny's? After all, the man was trained in law enforcement and investigations.

He has to suspect something. I need to talk to him.

Tami picked up the phone to dial his number, then quickly put it down. Vince would recognize both her cell phone and the number of the newspaper office. He wouldn't answer. She needed to see him in person.

Glancing at her watch, she saw it was almost eleven. Her decision made, she grabbed her purse, then walked to the front lobby, pausing a moment at Madge's desk.

"I'm going to take an early lunch," she told the older woman. "I should be back in an hour or two."

"Not taking your car?" Madge asked as Tami neared the front door.

Tami shook her head. "It's a nice day. A walk will do me good. I might try that new deli. Either that or Rosa's"

"Can't go wrong with her place. I'll see you later."

Vince's office was only two short blocks away. Tami hoped he would be there and not away on another investigation. She was in luck. Taking a deep breath, she opened the door.

Vince looked up from his desk when she entered the room. "What are you doing here? I've given you my report, so we have nothing more to say to one another."

"I know you're angry with me, but please hear me out. If you don't agree with what I have to say, I won't bother you again."

Vince folded his hands and leaned back in his chair.

"First of all, I owe you an apology. I've done a lot of thinking the past couple of days. If I'd been in your position, I would have expected to know everything. I'm sorry for not being upfront with you."

"Go on."

"I also have an idea—"

"Why did I guess you had another reason for coming here? I hope you're not going to try to convince me to reopen your sister's case."

"I wish I could. A trip to Alpine could provide us with the information we need. But I won't ask that of you."

"Good thing because I would refuse to go."

"I figured as much. Mind if sit down?"

"Be my guest."

Tami waited until she was seated before continuing. "I've read over your report several times the past few days. There's one thing that stands out in my mind, especially knowing about Alyssa's death."

"Don't start."

"I'm not. I promised you I wouldn't tell anyone what I know. It's because of that promise I'm here today."

"Why the sudden turn-around?"

"In spite of what you might think of me, if I make someone a promise, I don't go back on it. However, I'd like to see my sister's killer caught and punished, and I'm sure you'd like that, too."

He nodded for her to continue.

"Don't you think it's strange that Jesse Saldana was involved with two women who were murdered? Not only that, both were stabbed to death."

Vince closed his eyes for a moment before answering in a low voice. "No, I don't believe it was a coincidence. But it's obvious he didn't kill your sister, and officials cleared him of any involvement in Alyssa's death."

"How much do you know about him?"

"He was well-liked among his peers. Left Alpine after Alyssa's murder and the ensuing scandal. I didn't put this in my report, but there was talk of him committing suicide. Some said he still pined for his lost love."

Tami bristled at his words. "Are you saying my sister was just a substitute?"

"No. According to everyone I spoke with in Santa Fe, the two of them were close. All his friends and colleagues discounted the suicide theory. Most people I spoke with said he seemed like a different person after he met Jenny. From all accounts, they were happy together."

"That's good to know. I hate the thought of any man using her."

"I can understand that. But let's get back to the task at hand. We've already agreed me going to Alpine is out of the question. So, what do you propose?"

"I think we need to tell Jason about Jesse and Alyssa. He could contact authorities in Alpine. Maybe between the two police forces, they can find the killer."

Vince rubbed his forehead. "Let's say you're right about Alyssa and Jenny. You're discounting the two women from Brewster."

"You have to keep this to yourself, but Jason told me he doesn't believe those murders are connected to Jenny's. He thinks she was killed by someone she knew."

"Authorities believed the same thing about Alyssa. Her own husband was brought in for questioning."

"So, you agree we should talk to Jason?"

"I don't think we should withhold any potential evidence. But can I ask you a favor? I know of a potential link—"

"What? Who?"

Vince held up his hand. "Don't ask. It's only a theory, and if I'm wrong, several people will be hurt. Give me twenty-four hours to check it out. If I don't find what I'm looking for, we'll go together and tell the police what we know."

"Okay, I'll wait twenty-four hours. But if I don't hear from you by then, I'm talking to Jason."

CHAPTER 20

*V*ince rubbed his forehead. Since Tami left, he'd been fighting a headache while trying to figure out the best way to approach Darla. Maybe he was too close to the situation, allowing his feelings for Christine to cloud his judgment.

He didn't want her to get hurt, and if Darla was involved in some way, it would affect both Christine and Emily.

Okay. Think.

He didn't believe Darla killed Jenny. But did she know someone who might be connected? Had she known about Alyssa's death and her involvement with Jesse Saldana? Did she know Jenny also had an association with him?

The best way to find out would be to ask her outright. Maybe if he explained… No, he couldn't do that. Not yet. Not until he talked to Christine first. He owed her that much.

There had to be another way.

Of course. Wyatt Blake. Why didn't I think of him earlier?

Vince first met Wyatt when the two of them served together in the Dallas FBI field office. Later, Vince transferred to the resident agency in Brewster. Wyatt went to Alpine.

Throughout the years, they remained friends. When Vince decided to leave the force, Wyatt tried to convince him to stay. But Vince wanted a clean break after Alyssa's murder. He also carried a lot of self-imposed guilt.

Local authorities had enlisted the FBI to assist in the investigation of Alyssa's death, and Wyatt had been assigned the case. He kept Vince informed if there were any new details or leads, no matter how small or insignificant. He was trustworthy, a straight shooter, and one who didn't mince words.

It was time to make a phone call. Vince locked the exterior door before going into his office. He didn't want to take a chance on anyone walking in and overhearing the conversation. He dialed the familiar number, identified himself, then asked to speak to Agent Blake, drumming his fingers on the desk while waiting for an answer.

"Vince. How are you, buddy? Haven't heard from you in a while."

"Yeah, I've been busy. Getting my new PI business established."

"I gather it's going well?"

"Pretty much as expected. I wanted to talk to you about the investigation into Alyssa's murder."

"Wish I could give you good news, but there are no new leads. I would have called if I had anything."

"I know. I may have something for you. A similar murder occurred here in February. Victim's name was Jenny Allen. It turns out she once lived with Jesse Saldana after he moved to New Mexico. I believe there's a connection to Alyssa's death."

"Saldana is dead. Killed in an auto accident near Santa Fe a year ago. He couldn't have murdered this woman. You already know authorities cleared him of any suspicion in Alyssa's murder."

"Yeah."

"Are you working with authorities on the case?"

"No. The victim's sister hired me to look into her background. She had distanced herself from her family several years earlier, and they wanted to learn everything I could find out about her. That's how I knew she lived with Saldana."

"You tell this to the police?"

"Not yet. There's a couple of things I want to check first."

"Such as?"

"Rumor mill said Alyssa's husband had a lover, and she might have been the one who killed Alyssa. Anything to substantiate that?"

"Nothing we could find. Travis has become somewhat of a recluse these days. Rarely ventures off the ranch."

"According to Alyssa, he was that way a few years ago. Part of the reason she turned to Saldana. Grew weary of the loneliness. But if Travis had a lover, could she have visited him there?"

"It's possible, but somehow I doubt it. From what I hear, the man has never gotten over losing Alyssa. He may be a little strange, but everyone believes he loved her."

"Tell me what you know about Darla Martell."

"Senator Martell's daughter? She was married to a local artist. He died a couple of years ago. Left this area. Not sure where she went."

"She lives in Driscoll Lake. Owns an art gallery. Jenny Allen worked there at the time of her death."

"Do you think Martell had something to do with the murder?"

"I don't believe she killed Jenny, but I wonder if she knows something. You don't think she was having an affair with Travis?"

"No way. They didn't run in the same circles. Travis wasn't known to associate with anyone in the art community. And from what I've heard, his father and the senator were political rivals. There was a lot of bad blood, so to speak. Darla Martell was loyal to her father. I seriously doubt she would have become involved with Travis Weber."

"That's a relief to know."

"Why are you so interested in her?"

He waited a beat before answering. "I'm dating her daughter-in-law. Darla's son died a few years back. She claims she moved here to be close to Christine and her daughter."

"You believe her?"

Vince paused again to consider the question. "Yeah, I do. She made a lot of mistakes when she was younger, but she seems to have her family's best interest in mind. Christine and Emily have been through a lot in the last few years, and I'd hate for them to know Darla is mixed up in a murder."

"Since her husband was part of the art community, it's likely Darla knew Saldana, but I don't think you have to worry about her."

"Appreciate your help. I'll talk to the local investigator and have him contact you. But do me a favor, okay?"

"What is it?"

"Don't mention I was asking about Darla."

"Can't see any reason I need to tell anyone."

"Thanks, man. Maybe this time we'll finally have some answers."

"I hope so."

Vince breathed a sigh of relief when he ended the call. Someday he needed to tell Christine everything, but it could wait.

IT WENT against Tami's better judgment to put off talking with Jason, but she promised to give Vince a little leeway. Not that it was any of her business, but she wondered why he was still reluctant to talk about what happened in Alpine. He'd done nothing wrong. Whatever the reason, he would have to deal with it sooner or later.

Tami was so engrossed with her thoughts she failed to notice the man walking down the sidewalk. She was almost past him when he called her name.

"Tami?"

"Oh! Hi Jason. I had a million things on my mind. Sorry, I wasn't paying attention."

"Were you coming from Vince Green's office?"

"Yes, why?"

"Just curious as to what business you would have with him."

"I thought I might do a series of stories on new businesses in town. Wanted to ask if he would be interested in an interview."

Jason frowned. "Oh, okay. I was on my way to grab a bite of lunch. Can you join me?"

"I'd love to. If you don't already have something in mind, I was going to try that new deli. Interested?"

"Sure. Maybe the owner would consider being interviewed."

"What?"

"It's also a new business. I'm sure they'd love the publicity."

"Oh, right."

They walked in silence to the deli. Tami hated lying to him, but a promise was a promise. Betraying a confidence was not something she would do.

She managed to keep the conversation light during lunch. She didn't mention her sister. Jason didn't bring up the subject of interviewing the owner. He was friendly, with an edge. He clearly suspected something.

They had almost finished their meal when her cell phone rang. Recognizing Vince's number, she excused herself to take the call. "Sorry, but this is important. I'll be right back."

"No problem," Jason said. "I need to go anyway.

She waited until she was out of earshot before answering. "Got anything?"

"Negative," Vince said. "My theory didn't pan out."

"So, we talk to Jason?"

"Yeah. How about first thing tomorrow morning?"

"Sounds good to me. I'll swing by your office, and then we can go to the station together."

JASON TOOK A SIP OF COFFEE, trying to clear the cobwebs from his mind. In spite of what he once implied to Tami, he wasn't a morning person. In fact, he hated early mornings. It usually took him a couple of cups of strong brew to feel functional.

Not to mention he'd stayed up half the night watching a baseball game that went into extra innings. Wouldn't have been so bad if the game hadn't been played on the west coast.

When his intercom buzzed, he prayed it wasn't a call from another "helpful" person. Since they released the composite sketch a few weeks ago, he had been inundated with calls, all of which proved useless.

He picked up the phone. "Montgomery."

"Detective, you have a couple of visitors who say they have information related to the murder investigation."

Jason rolled his eyes. In addition to fielding calls, several people had dropped by the station offering "pertinent" information. Like the phone calls, none of them had been helpful. But he couldn't afford to turn anyone away. Who was to say when someone would share something important?

"Did they give their names?"

"Yes. Vince Green and Tami Sutton."

Jason was glad he didn't have coffee in his mouth. Otherwise, he would have choked or spit it across the room. While he suspected Tami hadn't been telling the truth yesterday, he didn't expect the two of them to show up here.

"Thanks, Hawkins. Send them back." He rose from his chair, then walked to the door to wait. Tami looked nervous, something out of character for her. It was hard to read Vince Green, but the man was former FBI. Jason knew some agents who were almost as good as the secret service at hiding their emotions.

He motioned them inside. After they were seated, he closed the door then returned to his own chair. "Hawkins tells me you two have information about Jenny's murder."

Tami glanced at Vince, and he nodded for her to begin. "Yes. I hired Vince to look into my sister's background, hoping he would discover something that might lead us to her killer."

Jason narrowed his eyes. It was within her rights, but he wished she would have come to him first. Did she doubt his ability to solve the case? Probably. He'd given her, as well as others, plenty of reason to think he was incapable of doing his job.

Most of the time, he didn't care what people thought of the way he conducted investigations. He'd proven them wrong several times, but for some reason, Tami's apparent distrust bothered him.

"I see."

Vince spoke this time. "Tami asked me to check out where she lived before moving here. I visited Taos and Santa Fe, as well as San Antonio."

"Yeah, I spoke to people in all three places. Didn't get much information. I gather you did."

"Not a lot, but I did discover something that might be important."

"Go ahead."

"First of all, I should tell you a similar murder happened almost three years earlier near Alpine. A young woman was stabbed to death. Like Jenny, she had multiple wounds. To date, the killer hasn't been caught."

"Were you the investigator?"

Vince shook his head. "I know the agent in charge."

"Okay, so the murder was similar. How does it tie into Jenny's death?"

"Alyssa, the victim, was having an affair with a man named Jesse Saldana. He was an artist and resident of Alpine. After Alyssa's murder, Jesse moved to Santa Fe. He and Jenny met and later lived together."

Okay, this was important. Jason reached for a legal pad to make notes. "Do you think there is a possibility he killed them both?"

"Impossible. Jesse died in an auto accident a year ago. But I do think the similarities are too great to ignore."

"How long have you known about this?"

"I got back into town Friday night. Needed a couple of days to verify some information. I told Agent Blake to expect your call. Here's his contact information." Vince pulled a card from his pocket, handed it to Jason, then stood to leave.

Jason also stood to extend his hand to Vince. "Appreciate you coming by. I'll be in touch if I have questions."

Vince nodded, then left the room.

Tami remained seated. "Jason, I—"

"Sorry, Tami. Can't talk now. Need to get to work on solving your sister's murder."

CHAPTER 21

*T*ami never missed a day in the office unless she was out of town. But after her meeting with Jason and Vince, she couldn't muster up any enthusiasm for work. Her weekly column was already done, and if something urgent came up, she had staff that were more than capable of handling it.

She supposed she should feel some enthusiasm. The Saldana connection was the first real lead authorities had that could point them to her sister's killer. Jason had agreed to contact the FBI agent in Alpine. He must have thought the idea had merit.

So why did she feel so sad? As she drove out of the police station parking lot, she pressed the Bluetooth button to call the office. Madge answered.

"Hey, it's me. I'm not feeling well today and won't be in. If it's an emergency, you can reach me on my cell phone. Otherwise. I'll see everyone tomorrow."

"Of course, dear. We'll take care of everything. Is there anything you need?"

"No, thanks. Nothing a day of rest won't cure."

Liar.

"Okay, but if you change your mind, I'm a phone call away."

"Thanks, Madge." Tami ended the call. She started to drive home, but the warm spring day beckoned. She needed to be outside. Breathe some fresh air. Take in the sights of spring.

Cameron Park, even in broad daylight, wasn't an option. Tami doubted she would ever be able to go there again, especially to the place where Jenny died. City Park, on the other hand, would be perfect for what she had in mind.

Although smaller, it was beautifully landscaped. The dogwood trees were in full bloom, as were the azaleas and a variety of spring flowers.

"City Park it is." She turned in that direction. A few minutes later, she parked near the front entrance, then got out of the car. She strolled along one of the paths until she found herself near a small pond.

Tami sat on a bench facing the water. Even with the near-perfect weather, the sadness wouldn't leave her.

What is wrong with me?

Do you have to ask yourself that question?

She knew the answer. Jason. Hard to forget the look in his eyes when he learned she'd hired Vince to check Jenny's background. Why should that matter? She hadn't done anything that would interfere with his involvement in the case. She had every right to hire a PI. The fact that she had shouldn't concern him.

Or was that the reason he seemed upset? Could it be because she lied to him? And if so, why did it bother her? A few weeks earlier, they couldn't stand one another. But now…

Okay, Jason was a fun date. She enjoyed being with him the night they went dancing. Get him away from the office, and he was relaxed and outgoing. It didn't take long for her to realize beneath the smooth exterior and cocky attitude was a warm and caring individual. A man who, for some reason, chose to conceal his true personality.

She suspected he was someone who, deep down, was dedicated to learning the truth. And for that, she hated herself for lying to him. Would she ever be able to make him understand?

JASON SAT IN HIS OFFICE, reviewing the file on Jenny Allen, hoping to see something he'd missed. A week had passed since Tami and Vince came to him with the information about Jesse Saldana. He contacted Agent Blake, and the two of them agreed there was a strong possibility the murders were connected.

Learning how and why was another matter. Jenny never lived in the Alpine area. She never met Alyssa. Likewise, Alyssa never lived in New Mexico. No one knew of any enemies Jesse may have had, save Travis Weber, but he was cleared of any suspicion. At any rate, there was no indication he ever knew Jenny, let alone murdered her.

Jason contacted the Brewster police to share that information as well as his theory that the murders of Susan Mason and Lori Huff were unrelated to Jenny's.

Randy Somers didn't discount the possibility, but he wasn't ready to give up on the idea of one killer. "Guess a lot depends on what we learn about Charlie."

"We already know he couldn't have killed Jenny."

"I know. I'm not convinced he killed anyone."

Jason shook his head as he recalled the conversation. It seemed the only thing they could agree on was that there hadn't been any more murders. Yet. He'd leave it up to Randy to sort out the situation with Charlie Nelson. Right now, he thought it was more important to work with Wyatt Blake to learn any possible connection involving Jesse Saldana.

Matt was supportive in the matter, but Jason wondered if he would have been so quick to agree had Vince not been involved in the discovery. He quickly squelched that thought. Matt cared about learning the truth. It didn't matter how and where they obtained leads.

When the phone rang, he closed the folder, then picked up the receiver. "Montgomery."

"It's Randy. We got the DNA results back on Charlie."

"So soon?"

"I asked for expedited testing. Miracles sometimes happen. It looks like he told the truth. He's not a match."

"Another dead end."

"Yeah. Although I am happy to know Charlie wasn't involved. He has a lot of problems, but I didn't want to believe he was a killer."

"I agree with you there. What happens to him now?"

"I spoke to Lori Huff's family. They're willing to drop any charges related to the theft of the pendant in exchange for Charlie going into counseling. It turns out her father is ex-military and runs a support group for veterans. He'd like to see Charlie get the help he needs."

"That's good. Wasn't difficult to tell he's a troubled soul. Now that he's cleared in the matter, where does that leave us on the idea of two killers?"

"We need to continue to pursue all avenues, including the possible link to the murder in Alpine."

"Agreed. I keep hoping we'll get a lead on the composite drawing, but so far nothing. I'll keep you informed."

"Likewise," Randy said.

Jason ended the call, then turned to look out the window. Weeks had passed with no suspects. Would they ever catch a break?"

CHRISTINE SMILED as she looked at her friends seated around the table. For once, she didn't feel like the fifth wheel. She had Vince. Rachel had invited them to join her, Brian, Stephanie, and Matt for an evening out at Pinnacle, Brewster's most popular club.

Brian's band sometimes played there, but another group had the stage tonight. The place was noisy and crowded, but the music was good. The camaraderie among friends even better.

Christine hadn't seen Vince this relaxed since he'd returned from his recent investigation. She still didn't know anything about the case, but she'd sensed a lot of tension in him since then.

When the band began playing a slow song, Brian reached for Rachel's hand. "Want to dance?"

"Sure."

"You two behave yourselves." Stephanie smiled as the couple stood.

"I remember a certain dance at our wedding reception that had the whole town of Driscoll Lake talking. Do you remember it, Christine?"

"Oh, yeah. Probably everyone who was at the reception does."

Rachel shook her head, then looked at Brian. "We'll never live that down."

"Probably not, but it was worth it." He pulled her to the dance floor.

Vince put his arm around Christine. "How about it? Want to dance?"

She looked at Stephanie and Matt. "Do you mind?"

"Not at all. I'm perfectly content to sit here with my handsome husband. Besides, little one here tells me when I need to take it easy." Stephanie rubbed her slightly protruding stomach.

Matt grinned and squeezed his wife's hand. "We're fine."

Once on the dance floor, Vince pulled Christine into his arms. "Having a good time?"

"Yes. Being out with other couples is nice. I always felt like I didn't belong when they asked me along. I was okay if it was just Stephanie and Rachel, but I would politely decline if it involved the men."

"Felt like the odd person out?"

"Yeah."

"You don't have to worry about that now." His voice was low and husky.

"No, I don't."

Vince placed a light kiss on her lips and drew her closer.

For the first time in years, Christine felt like everything in her life was going right. Even Emily seemed to have turned around. Vince had recently joined them for dinner, and she'd been cordial.

Then again, Emily's mind had been on Ty Fuller the past couple of weeks. That could partially explain her change of attitude, but Christine liked to think the conversation she had with her daughter before the prom helped.

The song ended all too soon, and the band announced they were taking a break. Christine and Vince remained in each other's arms for a few seconds before Rachel and Brian approached.

"Careful, you two. You'll get a reputation like Brian and me." Rachel winked as she walked by.

Christine looked at Vince as he stiffened, then pulled away, glancing around the room.

"Ashamed to be seen with me?" She smiled as she said the words, but she couldn't ignore the sudden tension.

"Of course not. Why would you think something is wrong?"

"You seem... I don't know. Distracted."

He shook his head. "It's nothing. Everything's fine."

But as the rest of the evening progressed, Christine began to wonder if he had told the truth.

SOME OCCASIONS REQUIRED a person to be an extrovert. To mingle with the crowd. Other times one needed to blend into the background. Being able to disguise oneself had its advantages. The ability to be virtually unrecognizable.

Tonight was a time to remain hidden. To observe.

Three couples sat at a table close to the stage. It was a cozy little scene with lots of interaction among them. The women each had a distinct beauty, the men all tall and handsome. Talk about standing out in a crowd.

Who wouldn't envy the brunette and her six-foot-four husband? Or the auburn-haired physician and her successful man? But the third couple was the most intriguing.

What exactly was between them? Casual friendship? Something more? The desire to know had been festering for several weeks. It was the reason for tonight's visit to Pinnacle. To confirm what was already feared.

It didn't take long to determine the answer. The way Christine and Vince danced together wasn't something casual friends would do.

When the song ended, Rachel Nichols whispered something to them before leaving the floor with her husband. Whatever it was, caused a change in Vince. It wasn't hard to see he had gone into alert mode as if looking for something or someone.

Careful. He's been in law enforcement. Trained to be observant. Wouldn't take much for him to notice something out of the ordinary.

The inner battle began.

Calm down. Breathe. There's no way anyone would recognize you. Still, it's probably best you leave. Your mission is accomplished. You've got the information you came for.

The relationship between Christine Lawrence and Vince Green would have to end. There were lots of ways to ensure that would happen. But when it came down to it, there was only one way to guarantee success.

CHRISTINE LOOKED at Vince as he parked the car in her driveway. He was quiet during the drive from Brewster. Even though he assured her Rachel's teasing hadn't bothered him, something had caused a change in his attitude. He remained friendly and talkative the rest of the evening, especially to Brian and Matt, but he seemed to be on the alert for something or someone.

Maybe it was the memory of what happened the last time Vince was at the club. When they first arrived, someone mentioned the time Clay Abbott showed up, intent on killing both Brian and Rachel. Vince happened to be the one to wrestle the gun from him before he could inflict damage.

But Matt was also a trained law enforcement officer. He was at Pinnacle when the incident occurred with Clay, and the memory of what happened didn't seem to disturb him. Then again, tonight hadn't been his first time back at the club.

Whatever was bothering Vince, Christine had to know. "Want to come in?"

He took a deep breath, then quickly exhaled. "Uh, yeah, sure."

"If you're uncomfortable, Emily's spending the night with a friend."

"No. It's not that."

"Gossiping neighbors, then?"

"Christine. I want to come in." He opened the door, got out, then rushed to help her from the car.

Once they were inside the house, Christine asked, "Do you want anything to drink?"

He shook his head. "I'm fine."

"Are you sure? It's no trouble. I have wine, coffee, tea... Maybe you'd like a late-night snack."

Why am I acting like a nervous school girl? It wasn't like we haven't been alone before.

Vince took her hand and led her to the sofa. "I don't want anything to eat or drink. What I want is for you to sit here and tell me what's bothering you."

"Okay, back at the club—"

"When we finished dancing. You want to know why I acted a little strange."

"Yes."

"It had nothing to do with what Rachel said. I'm not ashamed to be seen with you and frankly, wouldn't mind if people thought of us the way they did Rachel and Brian. Everyone could see those two were meant to be together." He pulled her closer.

"You mean that, don't you?"

"Yes, I do."

"Then what was it?"

"Remember when you were at Cameron Park and thought someone was watching you?"

"Yes."

"I've had similar feelings the last few weeks. The first time was the night of Jenny's murder. Another time, we were in a restaurant in Brewster. I felt it again tonight. Don't know who, but someone was watching us. And I don't mean a casual observance."

"But who? Why? Have you ever had feelings like this before?"

"From time to time. But this is different somehow. The thing is, I don't know who it might be."

"Do you think it's related to Jenny's death?"

"It's possible. I don't want to spend all my time worrying about it. I'll be cautious, and I want you to do the same."

"I will. No more running alone for me." Christine couldn't help but remember the eerie feeling she'd had. It wasn't something she wanted to repeat. But neither did she want to dwell on the situation. Time to lighten the mood.

"Maybe you have a jealous ex-girlfriend out there somewhere."

"If I do, she's out of luck. I have what I want right here. Could be you have a jealous ex-boyfriend."

"Then he's also out of luck."

He pulled her into his arms and pressed his lips to hers. Then he managed a word at a time between kisses. "You are. The one. I. Want."

Christine nestled into his embrace. When he deepened the kiss, her pulse tripped. This was where she wanted to be and who she wanted to be with. After they broke apart, her eyelids fluttered open. "Vince?"

"Yeah?" His voice was low and husky.

"Stay with me tonight."

CHAPTER 22

*S*ean Armstrong never imagined he would return to the Brewster area. But when an eighteen-wheeler carrying an over-sized load struck an overpass, the bridge required immediate replacement. Sean's employer won the bid.

He was one of the more experienced crane operators for Ruckman and Wade Construction. It came as no surprise when his boss pulled him off a job in Florida and sent him back to Texas.

Almost two months to the day after leaving, Sean checked into Brewster Inn and Suites. As luck would have it, the clerk gave him the same room as before. The one-bedroom suite had served his needs during his previous stay. It was located on the ground floor and had an outside entrance that made coming and going easier. Most of the time, he was away well before daybreak and didn't return until dark.

Ignoring the curious look from the desk clerk, Sean took the key, then went outside to his pickup. The first order of business was to bring clothes and personal items inside, followed by a hot shower. Next, he'd grab a bite to eat, then get in bed early. Weariness set in after the long drive, and he had to be on the job at seven the following morning.

Not everyone was cut out for his kind of life. Highway construction jobs paid well, but they came with a lot of travel. Workers were often required to be away from home for months at a time. It was okay for a single person, but if he ever decided to marry, he would have to think about a different line of work.

An hour later, Sean had unpacked his things and showered. He considered driving to Hank's Tavern in Driscoll Lake. The food was good, and the variety of craft beers unmatched. But after being on the road the better part of two days, he decided to check out the diner next door.

The place was almost empty this time of the evening. "You can sit anywhere you like." The hostess smiled as she handed him a menu.

Sean chose a booth near a window but close to the television. He ordered a beer, then glanced at the menu, deciding on a club sandwich. While waiting for his server, he turned his attention to the screen and the local news broadcast. The headline story was about an upcoming bond election. Nothing interesting. Next, the newscaster reported on a rash of hold-ups at local convenience stores. Sean's curiosity picked up at the third story about the murder of two women.

"Weeks after the murders of Susan Mason and Lori Huff, Brewster Police still haven't made an arrest. Earlier this month, police questioned a person of interest in relation to at least one of the murders but now say they no longer consider him a suspect. Meanwhile, Driscoll Lake officials are also searching for a suspect in the murder of Jenny Allen…"

A photo of the third young woman flashed on the screen. Sean felt as if someone had punched him in the gut.

Impossible. It can't be her.

But the photo left little doubt.

Jenny. The woman he'd spoken with on several occasions at Hank's place. Maybe it was because she was new to the area and he was a long way from home, but the two of them had developed an instant rapport.

From all indications, she had faced a lot of pain and sadness. She didn't say a lot about her past but seemed to be excited about living in this area. Sean recalled her saying that being in Driscoll Lake was like having a fresh start on life.

Now she was dead. Murdered.

The reporter continued. "Investigators are still hopeful someone will come forward with information about a potential suspect. The unidentified man in this composite sketch was with the victim several times at Hank's Tavern on the outskirts of Driscoll Lake shortly before her death. No one has seen him since that time, and his whereabouts are presently unaccounted for. If you have any information, please contact Detective Jason Montgomery with the Driscoll Lake Police Department..."

Sean's jaw dropped as he stared at the television screen. It was like looking in a mirror. He was the man in the sketch.

～

CHRISTINE POWERED DOWN HER LAPTOP, then stretched her arms while waiting for it to shut down. The warm Sunday afternoon was too beautiful to remain indoors, but she needed to complete several tasks before her first Monday class.

Vince had headed to Dallas for a new case he was working, so she decided to spend the afternoon grading tests and reviewing lesson plans.

When her phone rang, she recognized Vince's number. "Hey, there."

"Hi, babe. What's going on?"

"Just finished grading some tests."

"Sounds boring."

"I usually don't bring work home, but it's been wild and crazy at school lately. Summer break can't come soon enough for me."

"So, you didn't have anything better to do?" he teased.

"Well, since someone had to go out of town... Are you still in Dallas?"

"No. Got home a few minutes ago. You there alone?"

"Yeah. Emily's at work."

Christine had seen numerous changes in her daughter in the past few weeks. She'd turned seventeen, began working a part-time job at a local restaurant, and announced she wanted to save money to buy a car. The teenager seemed to have a newfound maturity and sense of responsibility.

Curtis Lawrence, for all his faults and failures, had set up a trust fund for his only grandchild and named Christine as administrator. While the bulk of the money wouldn't be available to Emily until she turned twenty-five, he did make provisions for expenses such as a car and college tuition.

Christine decided to take some money and buy Emily a car. It wasn't brand-new. She thought Emily should learn additional responsibilities before entrusting her with something that expensive. But having a second vehicle took a load off Christine by not having to rearrange her schedule to accommodate Emily's.

"So, how about it?"

"I'm sorry. I was thinking about Emily. What did you say?"

"I asked if you want to come over. I'll grill some burgers."

"I'd love to. When should I be there?"

"Any time. The sooner, the better. We'll eat around seven."

"Give me half an hour." After ending the call, Christine went into her bedroom to change clothes. The weather was warm, so she chose a pair of denim shorts, a pullover top, and sandals.

After freshening her make-up, she grabbed her purse and keys, then hurried to the garage. Libby was outside again—this time doing something to her car.

Christine always took her car to the dealership for regular maintenance and routine oil changes. She would never attempt those things on her own. She hired someone to mow her yard and take care of the plants and shrubbery.

Libby was more self-sufficient. Christine smiled and waved as she back out of the driveway.

Libby returned the greeting with a half-hearted wave then turned away as Christine drove by. It was unusual for her to act in an unfriendly manner. But she also had a lot on her plate with the end of school and the upcoming art show.

Christine shrugged it off then turned her SUV in the direction of Vince's house.

∽

AFTER HE RECOVERED from the shock of seeing his face on the TV, Sean knew he needed to act fast. Had the hotel clerk recognized him as the man in the sketch? Was that the reason for the strange look she'd given him? If anyone in the diner noticed him and made the connection, police would soon swarm the place.

Stay calm. You'll get through this.

He threw a twenty-dollar bill on the table, thankful he hadn't already ordered his food.

The server approached as he stood. "Is anything wrong, sir?"

"Something has come up. I have to leave right away." He gestured toward the money. "Smallest bill I have. Keep the change."

Sean rushed out the door, then sprinted to his hotel room. Once inside, he pulled his cell phone from his pocket, then pressed the speed dial number for his boss. Doug Hollis was not only his supervisor but also a trusted friend. Ruckman and Wade also recalled Doug to the Brewster area for the overpass construction project.

One ring. Two. Three. Four. Sean tapped his foot.

Come on. Pick up.

Finally!

Sean barely gave his friend time to answer. "Hey, man. Are you in town yet?"

"I'm about five minutes from the hotel. You?"

"Checked in about an hour ago, but something has come up. I need to contact Driscoll Lake police."

"Police? What's going on? You been in an accident?"

"Remember me telling you about the woman I met at that tavern the last time I was here? Her name was Jenny."

"Yeah, I remember."

"She's dead. Someone killed her. I'm considered a suspect, or at least someone they want to question."

"What? No way!"

"A sketch of a guy matching my description hit the news. Can you freaking believe it? I'd gone to the diner next door and caught it on TV. Hurried back to the hotel before anyone recognized me."

"Okay, so you're there now?

"Yeah, room 118. I need to call the police or go there to talk with them."

"Want me to come with you?"

"Might need for to you vouch for my whereabouts the last two months."

"Hold tight. I'll be at the hotel in a couple of minutes. I'll drive you to Driscoll Lake."

"Thanks, man, I—" Sean's words were interrupted by a knock.

He didn't have to guess who was at the door.

JASON WOULD HAVE LIKED nothing more than to ignore the ringing phone. He'd had a relaxing Sunday afternoon. One in which he tried to put aside any thoughts of his job and the murder investigation. Most of all, he wanted to forget Tami.

He hadn't spoken to her since the day she came by the station with Vince Green. She hadn't attempted to contact him, which, for some reason, left him feeling empty. It was his fault. He'd been somewhat cold to her the last time they spoke.

Jason thought there might be something developing between them. Now he wasn't so sure. Yes, she was interested in solving her sister's murder. He couldn't blame her for that. But it hurt that she hadn't trusted him enough to tell him about hiring Vince.

When he recognized the number of the police station, he put aside his thoughts of Tami. "Montgomery."

"This is Dugan. Got a couple of calls from people with information about the person in the sketch."

"Figured that would happen. I saw it on the news. Might as well be prepared for the usual onslaught."

"Yeah, well, these are legit. The first call came from a desk clerk at

Brewster Inn and Suites. Said a man matching the description checked in there a couple of hours ago."

"What makes her so sure he's the one?"

"Said he'd stayed there before. Left the area in mid-February. Works for a highway construction company."

"Why didn't she come forward before?"

"Claims she'd forgotten about him. Said she sees a lot of people in her job, and it didn't occur to her until he showed up today."

"You said there was a second call?"

"Yeah, from a waitress at the diner next to the hotel. The man was there but rushed out after the TV broadcast. She's also sure he's the one in the sketch."

"He got away?"

"No. Brewster Police picked him up at the hotel. They took him in for questioning. Said he went willingly."

"Okay, phone Randy Somers, and tell him I'm on the way."

Jason ended the call. He debated on whether to phone Matt. Sounded like this guy could provide some answers. Then again, it could just be another in a long line of false leads. No need to mess up Matt's Sunday evening.

Jason made it to the Brewster police station in record time. When he arrived, Randy Somers waited for him in the lobby.

"Quick trip," Randy said.

"Yeah, anxious to hear what he has to say. What do you have so far?"

"His name is Sean Armstrong. Works for Ruckman and Wade. Has been on a job in Florida since the middle of February and arrived back in this area today.

"Mid-February?"

"He was specific. Left here the morning of February 14. A week before the murder occurred."

"Can anyone verify this?

"Yeah. Has a coworker with him."

Jason frowned. "Then why—"

"Did we bring him in? Because he admits to knowing Jenny Allen."

"Then I guess we'd better get in there."

Jason felt a sense of déjà vu as he entered the interrogation room. Nothing had changed since his last visit. The same dreary walls, a scarred table that had seen better days. The smell of burnt coffee still permeated the room.

He immediately recognized one of the two men seated at the table as being the person in the drawing. Hank Norton had a good eye for detail and provided an excellent description.

Randy made the introductions, then Jason sat opposite Sean Armstrong. He didn't waste time getting to the point. "Tell us what you know about Jenny Allen."

Sean cleared his throat. "We met at Hank's Tavern. I'd often go there after work. She came in a few times. Always alone, but she would talk to others. I think she was lonely. One day, we struck up a conversation. After that, I saw her there a few times."

"Did you meet with her anywhere else?"

"If you're asking if we ever went out on a date, the answer is no. If we happened to be at the tavern the same time, we'd sit together. That's it."

Jason began to write notes on a legal pad. "When did you last see Jenny?"

"The evening before I left town. Told her we'd finished the job here and that I was going to Florida."

"You left Brewster in mid-February, correct?"

"Yes. I had to be in Florida on the sixteenth to begin work on a new construction project."

"Then several people can verify you were out of state on the afternoon of February 21?"

Doug Hollis spoke for the first time. "I can vouch for him as can a dozen or so other people. If you need proof, I'll contact our main offices for payroll records."

"I don't think that will be necessary." Jason turned his attention back to Sean. "You didn't exchange phone numbers, emails, anything of the sort with Jenny?"

Sean shook his head. "No, the relationship never got that far. Anyway, she didn't talk much about herself. Told me she was new in town."

Where had he heard that before? "She never talked about her past?"

"Only to say she'd made mistakes. Done some things she'd regretted. Who hasn't?"

Jason nodded for him to continue.

"I got the impression there had been some sort of tragic event in Jenny's life. She didn't elaborate, and we weren't close enough for me to ask."

"Did she say anything about why she moved to this area?"

"Said she needed a fresh start and had fences to mend."

Jason furrowed his brow. Had Jenny moved here intending to reconcile with her family? If so, why did she leave San Antonio knowing her parents were close? Or was making amends with Tami the first step?

"Did she happen to say if she had any friends or family in this area?"

"No."

"What about enemies? Give any indication that someone might be trying to kill her? Or that she was running from someone?"

Sean shook his head. "Never. I wish I could be of more help, but that's all I know."

Jason pulled a business card from his pocket, then stood to extend his hand to Sean. "We'll get the word out to the media, so no one else will think you're still a suspect. Appreciate you telling us what you do know. If you remember anything else, give me a call."

AFTER MEETING WITH SEAN, Jason returned to Driscoll Lake. He decided to stop at the station to wrap up a few things, among them phoning Matt to fill him in on the details.

One mystery cleared up, yet the biggest one still unsolved. Jason glanced at his watch. It was half past nine. An officer had already informed the news outlets they no longer considered the person in the composite sketch a suspect. He'd also updated social media.

There wasn't much else he could do tonight. Might as well go home and try to get some sleep. Closing the file, he slipped it in his desk, then locked the drawer. He hesitated. There was one other thing he needed to do. Reaching for the phone, he dialed the now familiar number, almost hoping she wouldn't answer. No such luck.

"Hello?"

"Tami, it's Jason. We thought we had a lead, but like all the others, it proved false."

Her sigh was long and pronounced. "Then why are you calling?"

"Because I thought you'd want to hear about it from me—from us—rather than on the ten o'clock news."

"Okay, what is it?"

"We identified the man in the drawing, but he's not the murderer. Just someone who met your sister at Hank's Tavern a few times."

"How do you know he didn't kill her?"

"Because he was over a thousand miles away from here when Jenny died." Jason told her the story. "It all checks out."

"Did she… Did he say if Jenny ever mentioned my name?"

"I'm sorry, Tami. Like with everyone else, Jenny didn't reveal much about herself."

"I was afraid of that."

"Tami, there is one thing. Sean, that's the man's name, told me Jenny moved here to make a fresh start. Said something to him about needing to mend some fences."

Jason could detect the flicker of hope in her voice. "Maybe she did know I was here."

"I thought the same thing."

"If I hadn't been out of town… If I'd been home, she might still be alive today." Her voice broke.

"Don't go there. You don't know that. In the first place, your parents needed you. Secondly, you had no idea your sister was going to show up here unexpectedly. Even if you had been here, you have no way of knowing whether you could have prevented her murder."

"Yeah, I guess you're right."

"Tami?"

"Yes?"

"I wish I had better news."

"Me, too. Well, thanks for calling me." The line went dead.

Jason stared at the phone. Tami was hurting, and he was partially to blame. One way or another, he needed to fix what had gone wrong.

CHAPTER 23

A surge of excitement filled Christine as she neared the entrance of Driscoll Lake High School. Although only a few minutes past five, the number of cars in the parking lot indicated the art exhibit was already a success.

She held her head high as she walked through the doors. *My daughter is one of the featured artists.*

Once in the commons area, she scanned the crowd for Emily. It wasn't long before she heard the teen's voice.

"Mom. Are you here alone? I thought Vince was coming."

It was hard to believe this was the same sullen teenager from a few weeks ago. "He had to finish some things at the office first. He'll be here soon."

"Hope so. I really want him to see my drawings." Emily paused, chewing on her lower lip. "Do you think he'll like them?"

"I'm sure he will. It seems important to you."

"Yeah, well, Vince is all right." She lowered her head, then spoke in a softer tone. "I didn't give him much of a chance at first, but I'm glad the two of you are together."

"I'm glad we are, too. Now, why don't you show me around?"

Emily grinned. "Sure."

They wandered among the many displays. Christine had no idea Driscoll Lake High had so many talented students. A variety of media was represented—pen and ink drawings, charcoal sketches, paintings. Even a photography section. Other students worked with clay, and Christine marveled at the various shapes and sizes of pottery. Some students used a wheel, while others formed pieces by hand.

Emily was in her element as she laughed and talked with others in attendance. When they stopped beside her drawings, Libby approached them.

"Glad you could make it tonight, Christine."

"You didn't think I'd miss my daughter's first art exhibit, did you?"

"I've seen situations where the parents are too busy living their lives. Not that you would, of course.." Libby pointed to a drawing of an older woman. "Your daughter is very talented. See how she captures the woman's facial expressions? It's as if Emily breathed life into the sketch. You should be proud of her."

"I am." Christine reached for her daughter's hand, then watched as Emily's eyes misted. She couldn't help but feel melancholy over another lost opportunity for Kyle.

Yes, she had finally put his death behind her and moved on with Vince, but it saddened her to know Kyle would never experience moments like these. Emily's first date, first prom, her high school graduation. And sometime in the future, when Emily married, he wouldn't be there to walk her down the aisle.

Lost in thought, she didn't hear Libby's words. "I'm sorry, Libby. You were saying?"

"I asked if her talent came from you. I've never heard you mention an interest in art."

"Oh, I'm not the least bit creative. Whatever artistic ability my daughter has comes from her father's side of the family. More specifically, her grandmother."

"Oh, yes, the one who owns the art gallery. I'd love to meet her. Is she planning to come tonight?"

"Yes. Gigi should have been here by now," Emily said. "I hope she doesn't forget."

"She won't, honey. I'm sure she'll be here any minute."

"Then I'll get a chance to meet her," Libby said. "I'd love to ask her a few art-related questions."

"Only if you have time to spare. Darla loves to talk about art."

Libby smiled. "Not a problem."

Emily's face brightened as she nodded toward the entrance. "At least Vince is here."

Christine turned to see him stroll through the crowd. He wore jeans, a tan sport coat, and a button-down shirt with the top two buttons undone. Her pulse accelerated as they made eye contact.

"Libby." She faced her next-door neighbor. "I don't think you've met Vince. Now is the perfect opportunity."

"I'm sorry, but I really should mix and mingle among other parents. I'll try to get back this way before the night is over." She hurried away.

Why the sudden change? While it was true Libby should interact with other families, she had been all too eager to wait for Darla.

Christine's thoughts of Libby were soon forgotten when Vince walked up and placed a kiss on her cheek.

THE CROWD BEGAN TO THIN. Overall, the exhibit was a success. Vince stayed with Christine throughout the evening. He seemed completely relaxed. Anyone who didn't know would probably think he was a proud parent and not a thirty-something-year-old bachelor.

When Emily's boyfriend Ty showed up, he and Vince easily engaged in conversation. The two of them learned they had a lot in common—they liked the same sports and teams, and Ty expressed an interest in either going into law enforcement or joining the military.

When Christine glanced at her watch, it was almost eight. Time for the exhibit to close. In a small town, unless it was a sporting event, all school functions ended early, even on Friday nights. Nothing had changed since her high school days twenty years ago.

"Do you need to take your things home tonight?" she asked Emily.

"No. Ms. Gordon told us we could pick them up tomorrow morning."

"You kids hungry?" Vince asked, glancing between Emily and Ty.

Both nodded.

"Why don't we all get something to eat? My treat."

"Sure," Emily said.

Ty nodded in agreement.

After deciding on a restaurant, the four made their way toward the door.

When they reached the parking lot, Emily looked around. "Wonder why Gigi didn't come? She said she would be here."

Christine hesitated, wondering if Darla was slipping back into her "all about me" mode. But it was unfair to think that. She had been nothing but kind and considerate since moving to Driscoll Lake. There was probably a good reason she hadn't shown up. "I'm sure there's an explanation. Maybe she got tied up with a late customer and hasn't had a chance to call."

As if on cue, Christine's cell phone rang. "Wow! Talk about timing. This is her now." She swiped the screen to take the call. "Darla? We missed you at the exhibit. Is everything okay?"

"Yes, and no. I'm at Brewster Memorial Hospital. I had a little fainting incident at the gallery, and Kristen called an ambulance. I figured it was just low blood sugar, but they didn't like the results of some of my tests and are keeping me overnight for observation."

"Do you need us to come?"

"No, not tonight. Doctors want me to rest. But can you do me a favor?"

"Name it."

"I need to make a bank deposit. Had everything ready before all this happened. Kristen locked up and secured the alarm, but I don't want those checks lying around."

"I'll take care of it. We're leaving the exhibit now and are on our way to dinner, but I'll stop by the gallery first."

"No, go ahead with your plans. It can wait until after dinner."

"Are you sure? It's not a problem to handle it first."

"Don't be silly. Now, is my granddaughter nearby? I want to explain why I didn't come tonight."

"She's right here. Call if you need anything. Otherwise, I'll see you in the morning. You'll need a ride, and I'm more than happy to drive you home." She handed the phone to Emily.

A LONE FIGURE stood back to observe the crowd gathered in the commons area. Funny how these events brought out all kinds of people. Everyone from working-class families to the more affluent. All gathered for a common purpose.

But two people stood out from the rest. Christine Lawrence and Vince Green. As suspected, things were getting out of hand between them. It wasn't fair. The two of them, along with Christine's daughter and the boyfriend, seemed like a cozy little family.

If there had been any uncertainty before, there wasn't any doubt this time. Christine and Vince had crossed the line from friends to lovers. There was an intimacy in the way he placed his arm around her waist as he guided her from the building. Sure, most people would only see it as a polite gesture. But there were other telltale signs—casual glances, shared smiles. Those things spoke volumes.

Observing them had been easy. This time it wasn't from a distance like in Driscoll Lake Park or at Pinnacle. It was easy to blend in with the other families at the art exhibit and get a closer look. Everyone was there to have a good time and to support and encourage the students.

No one was the wiser. Wouldn't everyone be shocked to know a killer was in their midst?

"ARE you going to be all right?" Christine asked her daughter as they departed the restaurant. When she first spoke with her grandmother, Emily insisted upon driving to Brewster that night. It took a while to persuade her differently. But after receiving assurance she could visit Darla early the next morning, the teenager gave in.

"Yeah. I'll be fine. I'm just ready to go home."

"Okay, I'll be there as soon as I finish at the gallery."

"I'll follow her home and make sure she's okay," Ty said.

"Thanks." Christine had come to admire the young man who held her daughter's affection. He acted mature for his age and had a good head on his shoulders.

"Want me to go with you?" Vince asked.

"That would be nice."

"Why don't I follow you? That way you won't have to come back here for your car. We can go straight to your place afterward."

Christine chuckled. "Good thing we're not in the middle of an energy crisis. Amazing how four of us managed four separate vehicles to one event."

It didn't take long to drive the short distance to Cameron Place. Christine parked her SUV in front of the gallery, then waited until Vince pulled alongside her. When Darla insisted on giving Christine a set of keys to the building a few weeks ago, she wanted to refuse. Never thought she'd ever have a reason to put them to use. Now she was glad to have them.

After unlocking the door, she quickly turned off the alarm. "The office is in the back."

Vince followed her, then waited until she flipped on the lights. As Darla had said, the checks and deposit slip were still on her desk.

"This shouldn't take long. Darla said I could put it in the night drop. Would you mind checking to see if the coffee pot was turned off? The break room is through there." She nodded toward a door opposite Darla's office.

"Sure."

Christine sat at the desk, then double-checked to see that she had listed all the checks on the deposit slip before putting them into an envelope.

Vince strolled into the room. "Nice place here. I'm no judge of art, but it looks like some good stuff."

"Only the finest for Darla. She has an excellent eye." She glanced at the portrait, still sitting on an easel in the corner and wondered why her mother-in-law wouldn't display it in the gallery.

"I'm done here. I'll drop this at the bank on the way home. Still want to come over for a while?"

He smiled. "Of course."

Vince turned, then stopped suddenly, eyes transfixed on the portrait, his face ashen. "What the hell?"

Christine frowned. "Is something wrong?"

"Where did she get this, and what's it doing in her office?"

"I don't know. She's had it a few weeks. Why do you ask?"

He walked closer to the painting. A frown appeared on his face when he saw the artist's signature. "Saldana. I might have known."

"You know the artist?"

"Not the artist. The woman." His voice lowered to almost a whisper. "She was my sister."

Christine rubbed her forehead, trying to recall the conversation the two of them once shared. He'd seemed hesitant to talk about his family and didn't discuss the reason for the infrequent visits to his parents.

They had been in the beginning stages of a relationship then, but she sensed something happened to cause the estrangement. When she asked about siblings, he mentioned a brother—nothing about having a sister.

"I didn't know you have a sister."

"I don't."

"Sorry, but I'm confused. You just said—Oh."

"Yeah. I *had* a sister. She died a couple of years ago."

"I'm sorry. What happened?"

"I don't want to talk about it."

The pain in his eyes was obvious, but now Christine realized why the woman seemed so familiar. She and Vince shared the same hazel-colored eyes.

"She's beautiful. What was her name?"

"Sorry, I gotta get out of here. I need some time alone."

He turned, then rushed out the door. Christine came around the desk to follow, but when she got to the front door, Vince was already in his car. She could only watch as he drove away.

CHAPTER 24

*C*hristine pounded her fist on the steering wheel. How dare Vince leave without talking to her? Kyle kept secrets. His untruthfulness likely would have caused significant problems in their marriage had he lived.

It appeared history was repeating itself. What was it with the men she picked? Tears welled in her eyes, and she wiped them away.

If Vince was untruthful… She wrestled with her thoughts.

Don't go there. You don't know all the circumstances.

But he didn't want to talk to me.

He said he needed time alone.

Yeah, but why didn't he say anything about her earlier? What was the big secret?

Taking a deep breath, she forced herself to think of other things. Her mind drifted back to the painting. How had it ended up in Darla's possession? Why was she reluctant to display it? Had she been truthful when she denied knowing the woman's identity? Did she know there was a connection between the woman and Vince?

One thing was sure. She had questions for both Vince and her mother-in-law.

Christine drove home on autopilot. She barely remembered locking the gallery or making the bank deposit. When she entered the house, she found Emily at the kitchen table.

She swallowed a bite of brownie. "Hey. Where's Vince?"

"He… went home."

"You okay?"

"Of course. What makes you think I'm not?" Her answer came a little too quick to satisfy the curious teenager.

"Are you sure? You seem upset, and I thought Vince said he was coming over. What happened?"

"I told you, everything is fine. It's been a long day, and I'm a little tired."

"So that's the reason Vince isn't here?"

At times Emily was too perceptive. This was one of them. "I'll see him tomorrow."

Or will I?

"Okay. As long as you're all right."

Christine forced a smile. "It's just you and me tonight, kid. Want to watch a movie?"

"Thought you said you were tired."

"I am, but not too tired for my daughter."

"Mom, I'd love to, but I need to get up early. I want to see Gigi, and then I need to pick up my drawings before work. I'm going to bed."

"Guess that's not a bad idea. I'll see you in the morning." Christine walked to her bedroom, then closed the door behind her.

Tired. Who was she kidding? There was no way she'd get any sleep tonight.

VINCE SAT in his darkened living room with a glass of bourbon. Over the years, he'd replayed his last phone conversation with Alyssa. Time had done little to appease his guilt. Tonight, after seeing her portrait, the pain was almost unbearable.

She had reached out to him for help, and he'd failed her. All because he couldn't get past his judgment of her marriage. Why had it been so important to prove himself right? To remind Alyssa of her mistakes?

"What have you gotten yourself into Lys? You're a married woman. I may not like Travis, but you made your choice."

"I don't love him anymore. He's too possessive. He never takes me anywhere, and we never do anything exciting. Sometimes I feel like he's holding me prisoner in my—in his—home. The love I have for Jesse is unlike anything I've felt before."

"Then you need to decide what you want. You can't go on this way. Either divorce your husband or get over your feelings for this other man."

"It's not that simple. I can't just walk away without—"

"Gotten used to having a rich husband, huh? Can't bear to part with the fancy wardrobe and wealthy lifestyle?"

"Okay, I admit I've gotten used to having nice things, but can you set aside your feelings for a minute and listen to me?"

"All right. Talk."

"I think someone is following me. I'm not sure if Travis is having me tailed or not, but I'm positive the same car has followed me the past few times I've met Jesse."

"There's a simple way to find out. Stop visiting your lover and see what happens."

"I was hoping you'd call in a favor or two from one of your law enforcement friends."

"Oh, sure. What would I say? My sister's afraid her husband suspects she's seeing another man. Can you check it out so she can continue this tryst?"

"Forget it. I'll deal with it myself. I should have known better than to call you. You're too damn stubborn to see past your own feelings. Thanks for nothing."

Alyssa ended the call. It was the last conversation they had. How could he have been so insensitive? If he'd only swallowed his pride and listened, she might still be alive today.

Would he ever be able to get over his guilt? Or would those feelings haunt him the rest of his life?

≈

CHRISTINE AND EMILY arrived at the hospital early Saturday morning. After visiting with her grandmother and being assured she was okay, Emily left for work, leaving Christine alone with Darla. She was about to ask about the painting when the doctor came into the room.

"Good morning, Ms. Martel. I have good news. All your lab work looks good this morning. Repeat cardiac enzymes were normal, and we didn't find any problems with your EKG."

"I knew everything was okay, but it's good to hear it from you."

"We needed to be sure."

"Wait a minute," Christine said, looking at Darla. "Cardiac enzymes? I thought you told me you had low blood sugar."

The doctor looked at her. "And you are?"

"This is my daughter-in-law, Christine. You can talk in front of her."

"I'm Dr. Moreland. Your mother-in-law's blood sugar was extremely low when she arrived—a condition called hypoglycemia. That's the likely cause of her fainting, but we needed to rule out other possibilities."

"I gather you were checking for cardiac issues."

"A couple of her tests were a bit abnormal, and she complained of having some chest pain. We kept her overnight as a precaution." He looked at Darla. "There's nothing to indicate you have any heart problems. Do you often skip meals?"

"Sometimes I get busy at the gallery and forget to eat."

"That's not a wise idea. At the very least, keep some snacks readily available—something with protein. Your diabetes is well-controlled, and overall, you're in excellent health. I don't want to see you back here anytime soon."

"I don't want to be back."

"Okay, I'll write your discharge orders. You'll be out of here soon."

Christine was silent during most of the drive to Darla's house, her mood somber. The warm spring sunshine did little to brighten her outlook. She hadn't heard from Vince this morning. She could have easily phoned him, but pride and stubbornness held her back.

She debated on mentioning the painting to Darla, but even though the doctor assured them everything was okay, the timing wasn't right.

"You're rather quiet today," Darla said as they entered the house.

"I didn't get a lot of sleep last night."

"Hope it wasn't on my account. I told you I would be fine."

"No, it wasn't that—"

Darla motioned for Christine to sit at the kitchen table, then took a chair opposite her. "What aren't you telling me?"

Christine pressed her lips together. Darla brought it up. Opened the door. Might as well tell her now. "Vince was with me last night when I went to the gallery."

"And?"

"He saw the painting in your office."

"The woman's portrait?"

Christine nodded. "She was his sister."

Darla's eyes widened. "His sister?"

"You didn't know?"

"How could I? I never met Vince until I moved to Driscoll Lake, and I certainly didn't know anything about his family. How did he react?"

"Shock. Anger. Confusion. I'm not sure what he was feeling."

"You haven't talked to him?"

"Not since he left the gallery. He said he needed to get away and left without saying goodbye. I decided to give him some space."

"Think that was a good idea? The two of you have become close, and if he was upset…"

"I don't know. Maybe I should have gone to him. But he never told me he had a sister. We once talked about our families, and he never mentioned her. From the time we began seeing one another, I sensed he was holding something back. Kyle did that to me and… I don't want to become involved with anyone else who keeps secrets."

"Don't rush to judgment. Kyle was my son, but he made mistakes. You need to remember, though—in his mind, he had good reasons for keeping those secrets. Vince may, too. You don't know what's behind the story with him and his sister. There's probably a good explanation."

"I guess you're right, but it hurts. Why didn't he say anything when

I asked about his family? If he doesn't trust me enough to tell me about his dead sister, then what else is he keeping from me? I don't even know how she died."

"She was murdered."

Christine's eyes grew wide. "You knew her?"

Darla shook her head. "I told you I didn't. I knew her name, but I never met her. She lived on a ranch outside Marfa. My husband and I knew Jesse Saldana. He's the one who painted her portrait."

"Is that the reason you have the painting? Why would the artist give it to you?"

"No. I came upon it by accident. I had contacted another gallery owner about obtaining a couple of Saldana paintings. Her employee accidentally included it with the shipment."

"Why didn't you send it back?"

"The owner asked me to hold onto it for a while and consider trying to sell it here. I had no idea the woman was Vince's sister."

"If you planned to sell it, why keep it in your office?"

"Alyssa's death. It's a long story. Do you have time to listen?"

Christine took a deep breath. "I have all the time in the world."

CHAPTER 25

$\mathcal{A}$fter leaving Darla's house, Christine decided to purchase
groceries before going home. In the checkout line, she placed
the items on the counter, then looked at her cell phone for what seemed
to be the hundredth time. No texts, voice mails, or missed calls from
Vince. Okay, so he needed time alone. She'd given him all day, and now
it was time to act.

Or should I?

Christine was more confused than ever after Darla told her the story
of Alyssa Weber's murder. Her death happened around the time Vince
left the FBI and moved away. But why? He wouldn't have been
included in the investigation. What was the reason behind his reluc-
tance to talk about her death? Was he ashamed over her having an
extra-marital affair?

Not that she approved of that sort of behavior, but it was hardly a
reason to disown a family member. Christine didn't think Vince was
that archaic. The days of forcing women like Hester Prynne to wear a
scarlet letter were past.

"Christine?"

She turned to see Tami Sutton standing behind her. Gone was her
self-confident demeanor. Her complexion was sallow, and if the dark

circles under her eyes were any indication, she'd shed a lot of tears recently. Understandable, given the murder of her long-lost sister. Not knowing the killer's identity or motive had to be stressful.

"Tami. It seems inappropriate to ask how you're doing."

"I'm coping. Police still don't have any leads. The last one didn't pan out."

"You mean the man in the drawing? I'd heard police cleared him of any suspicion."

Tami nodded. "If my sister hadn't kept so hush-mouthed about her past, we might know the killer's identity. I'd hoped Vince could find something, but he didn't discover much more than we already knew."

"Vince? He helped you?"

"I hired him to check into Jenny's background. Took some persuasion given the similarities with his own sister's death. About the only thing he discovered was that my sister was involved with Jesse Saldana. Talk about coincidence."

"Jesse Saldana the artist?"

"Yeah, ironic isn't it?"

Ironic? Too ironic. "Uh, yeah."

"Ma'am?" The cashier's voice interrupted Christine's thoughts.

"Oh, sorry." She pulled her debit card from her purse and inserted it into the chip reader. As usual, it didn't work.

"Sorry, ma'am, you'll have to swipe it," the cashier said.

It took three tries before Christine entered her PIN correctly.

"You okay?" Tami asked.

"I'm fine. It's been a long day. I need to get home." After paying, she pushed the shopping cart outside.

Tears stung her eyes as she loaded the groceries into the back of her SUV. How could Vince confide in Tami about his sister but keep it a secret from her? Everything was so confusing. Jesse Saldana was connected to both women. Darla knew him but denied having ever met Alyssa Weber, even though they both lived in the same small town.

Did Vince suspect Darla might know something? She recalled his words the day he met her.

Marfa? You lived in Marfa?

What was it he said when Darla asked him about knowing someone from there? He mentioned a friend who was with the border patrol. Nothing about a sister.

It was shortly after that meeting when Vince began to show interest in developing a relationship. Was it only because he wanted to learn more about her mother-in-law?

She finished loading the groceries, then put the shopping cart into a stall before returning to her SUV. As she drove from the parking lot, she wiped away tears.

CHRISTINE TURNED at the sound of her neighbor's voice. She glanced to see Libby entering the garage.

"Need any help unloading those?"

"Thanks, but it won't take long. You're probably busy."

"Not too busy to help a friend. Besides, I wanted to apologize for my behavior of the past few days."

"Behavior?" Christine decided to play innocent. "What are you talking about?"

"I haven't been very friendly. It's no excuse, but I've been nervous about the show. It's my first one, and my contract is up for renewal. If the show hadn't been successful, I wasn't sure the school would hire me for another year."

"I understand. I know you were busy."

"I also promised to get back to you last night and never made it. By the time I was free, you and Vince had already left."

"Understandable. I'd say the show was a success. Lots of people attended."

"Yes, I was pleased with the turnout. I'm sorry I didn't get to meet your mother-in-law."

"She never made it. Had some problems and was admitted to the hospital."

"Oh? I'm sorry. Is she going to be okay?"

"Yes. They only kept her overnight. Doctors just wanted to make sure of a few things before they allowed her to go home." Christine picked up a couple of grocery bags, then went into the house.

Libby followed, carrying two more. After a couple of trips, the two women had everything unloaded.

"Would you care for a glass of iced tea? Some bottled water?" Christine asked.

"Water would be good."

Christine pulled two bottles from the refrigerator. She handed one to Libby and motioned to the bar stools before sitting down.

"I can't stay long," Libby said. "I have things to do, and I expect you have plans for the evening."

"No, I don't."

Libby arched a brow. "Oh? I just figured—"

"I don't have plans to see Vince tonight if that's what you mean. I'm not sure when I'll see him." Christine hadn't intended to say that last part. Libby was a neighbor, not a close friend like Stephanie or Rachel. But now that she'd said the words, she could hardly take them back.

"I'm sorry. You seemed happy with him."

"I was. I am." Christine shook her head. "It's probably just a silly misunderstanding on my part. But just when you think you know someone—"

"They do something that comes as a complete surprise."

"Yeah. I was married to my husband for fifteen years, and I still learned things about him after he died."

"My mother used to say you could live a lifetime with a man and not really know him." Libby brushed a strand of hair off her forehead.

"Unfortunately, your mother may have been right."

IT WAS late afternoon before Vince ventured out of the house, having stayed up most of the night drowning his sorrow in bourbon. He'd awoken around nine with a hangover, then staggered into the kitchen. He downed a couple of cups of coffee and managed to eat a slice of toast before returning to bed.

It was after three before he woke up again but felt surprisingly refreshed. He took a quick shower, then dressed. Sitting on his patio, he took his cell phone and scrolled through the missed calls. Not one was from Christine.

Vince supposed he should call to explain, but he was disappointed she hadn't attempted to contact him. Then again, maybe she was still with Darla.

Darla. How had she come to have a portrait of his sister? Why had she kept it hidden in her office? And how much did Christine know? Obviously, she'd seen the painting before.

Okay, he owed Christine an explanation. He punched in her, then waited for her to answer. Instead, he got her voice mail.

"Hi, this is Christine. I'm not available now. Leave a message at the tone."

Vince ended the call. Probably just as well. He needed a little more time to collect his thoughts. The last thing he wanted to do was hurt her. Had he been wrong about Darla? Maybe she did know something about his sister's murder.

He had a sudden need to get out of the house. Brian's band was playing at Pinnacle tonight. A perfect opportunity to be around people without getting involved in deep conversations. His decision made, he went inside to change.

As EXPECTED, Pinnacle was packed. Rather than wait for a table, Vince decided to sit at the bar. His seat provided a good view of the stage, and he'd still be able to eat a meal. He nursed a beer—nothing stronger tonight—and listened as Radical played a rendition of Tom Petty's "Refugee."

The crowd was lively, and the music enjoyable. Vince's mood had improved considerably since he first saw his sister's portrait. Coming here was a good thing. He couldn't help but recall the last time he was here with Christine. Not only had they enjoyed being with friends, but it had also marked a new stage in their relationship. He shouldn't be here without her. He should be with her.

Taking a sip of his beer, he glanced at the woman who slid onto the bar stool next to him. There was something vaguely familiar about her, but he couldn't decide what. She ordered a strawberry daiquiri, then smiled at him before turning to face the stage.

After a while, she spoke. "The band is great tonight. I've never heard them play before."

"Yeah, they are. The drummer is a friend of mine."

"He's talented."

"Brian takes music seriously."

She picked up her drink. "That's obvious. Do you come here often?"

Vince frowned. Why did he get the feeling he'd had this conversation before? "Not really."

"Didn't think so. Otherwise, I would have noticed you. I'm Simone."

Great. Just what I need.

He smiled but didn't give his name. The last thing he wanted to do was to engage in conversation with this woman and give her the idea he was available. "I was here a couple of weeks ago with my girlfriend and two other couples. First time in a while."

"But you're here alone tonight. Trouble in paradise?" Simone leaned closer.

Vince jerked his head and caught a whiff of her perfume. Exotic. Overpowering.

That's it. The woman who tried to come on to me at Casey's. He'd put a stop to it then, and he would stop it now. "It's none of your business."

She tilted her head. "Touchy about it, aren't you?"

"No. But since you're insistent, there's nothing wrong."

Simone plucked the cherry from her drink, then bit into it. Her voice grew sultry. "Your words tell me one thing, your eyes another. I think you could use some cheering up."

"Forget it. I'm not interested. Not now. Not ever." Vince rose from the stool, then strode from the club.

When he reached his car, he looked around to see if the woman from the bar was nearby. This time, she'd gone as far as to tell him her name. She was persistent, and it wouldn't come as a surprise if she tried to follow him. Vince had been around his share of flirtatious women, but there was something disturbing about this one.

She reminded him of the female lead in the movie, *Fatal Attraction*. A woman so obsessed with a man she would do anything to keep him —including murder. But that was Hollywood. This was real life. Except he knew those type of situations happen far too often.

What was I thinking? I should have been with Christine.

It was one thing to grab a meal at Casey's after work. Another to go to a club like Pinnacle alone on a Saturday night and sit at the bar.

He started his car, then drove out of the parking lot. Half an hour later, he rang Christine's doorbell.

"We need to talk," he said when she opened the door.

"Yeah, we do."

CHAPTER 26

Christine motioned Vince inside, then waited for him sit down. Rather than joining him on the sofa, she chose a chair.

What a difference twenty-four hours made. Last night she and Vince laughed and joked with Emily and Ty during dinner. Everyone enjoyed the evening. For a moment, Christine had allowed herself to imagine what it would be like if Vince was a part of their family.

Today the atmosphere was different. Not exactly cold, but not warm either—sort of like a spring day when winter can't decide to leave or stay.

Vince rubbed his forehead. "I owe you an apology for last night. I shouldn't have left without giving you an explanation."

"I guess it was a shock to see the painting of your sister."

"Yeah, but that doesn't excuse my behavior. Seeing her portrait brought back some painful memories."

There's a reason he hasn't talked about her, but can I trust him to tell me everything? Maybe I should give him another chance. "Want to talk about it?"

"Not really, but I need to. I've kept some things from you, and I don't want to do that anymore."

"Like Tami Sutton?"

Vince lowered his head. "How did you find out?"

Christine crossed her arms. "I saw her at the grocery store this afternoon, and she told me. Gotta admit the news took me by surprise."

"I didn't want to keep it from you, but Tami was insistent the investigation remain a secret. I had to abide by my client's wishes."

"Understandable."

"I almost didn't take the job."

"Why did you?"

Vince took a deep breath. "The similarities with my sister's death. That plus a lot of guilt."

"Why would you feel guilty?"

"Alyssa was the youngest in the family. She married a wealthy older man who lived near Marfa."

"Yeah, Darla told me about him."

"I didn't approve of her marriage for a lot of reasons—the difference in their ages, the fact he had two teenage children who were only a few years younger than Alyssa. Most of all, because I felt like she married him on the rebound."

Vince looked away. The silence in the room was palpable. Finally, he spoke again. "She and her long-time boyfriend were planning to be married in the fall after graduation. They had set a date, booked the church. She'd even bought her wedding dress.

"One day, he told her it was over. Said he couldn't go through with the marriage. Lys found out later he'd left her for another woman. She was devastated."

"I'm sure. She would have been vulnerable."

"Exactly. When I found out she was marrying Travis, we had words. Then we stopped speaking to one another. Both of us were too stubborn to apologize. But I've got to hand it to her. She stayed with Travis. They were married ten years when she died."

"But she wasn't happy." It wasn't a question.

He looked up at her, eyebrows arched. "You heard."

"Yeah, I talked to Darla this afternoon."

"Did she know my sister?"

"Not personally, but you know how it is in small towns."

"Yeah. Rumors and gossip. I'm sure plenty circulated about Lys."

Christine pounded her fist on the chair arm. "Damn it. You should know me well enough not to believe I'd resort to gossiping about your family. That's not what we talked about."

"I'm sorry. I know you wouldn't. Guess I'm still a little touchy about it."

She took a deep breath, then slowly exhaled. "Okay, tell me what happened."

"Alyssa was having an affair with the artist who painted the portrait. One night she was on her way home after meeting him. She never made it. Someone found her SUV at the side of the road, her body on the ground. She died from multiple stab wounds."

"You mean like—"

Vince nodded. "Like Jenny Allen."

"When did it happen?"

"Two years ago, this past December."

Now things are beginning to make sense. Two years in December. That's when he disappeared. He wasn't running from our developing relationship. He was running from painful memories. "I see."

"After Lys died, I pretty much dropped out of sight. Resigned from the FBI. Didn't think I had what it took to be a good agent. I felt like a failure."

"I don't understand. Surely you didn't investigate your own sister's murder?"

"No, but I could have done something to stop it. I failed her, and I didn't want to do that to anyone else."

"But you hadn't seen her in what, ten years? How could you prevent her from dying?"

"Alyssa called me that night. She was on her way to meet Jesse. Told me she suspected somebody was following her and asked if I could help. Wanted me to call someone to check it out. All I could do was go on about how she needed to decide between Jesse and her husband." Vince scrubbed his hand across his face.

"I acted like a sanctimonious jerk. More concerned people might find out she was seeing another man than for her safety. If I hadn't been so determined to make her see the affair was wrong, I might have been able to prevent her death."

"You were what, six-hundred miles away? Hard to protect someone from that distance."

"There were plenty of people I could have called. They would have followed up. Wouldn't have even asked questions."

"But if she died the same night, no one would have had time to investigate. Other than following her home, I don't see what anyone could have done."

Vince glanced away. "Maybe you're right, but I sure as hell could have tried. I've carried guilt from the minute I learned she was dead. Not sure I'll ever be able to forgive myself."

OFFICER TESSA HILL, the newest member of the Brewster Police Department, sat across from Detective Somers' desk, honored he'd requested her for a special assignment. Granted she wasn't a rookie, having worked three years in Dallas, but she thought the detective would offer the job to someone who had been with the force longer.

"This assignment is strictly voluntary," Randy said.

"I'll do anything I can if it will help solve the murders."

"We have no way of knowing when and if the killer will strike again or even if he's still in this area. What we do know is all the victims— including the one in Driscoll Lake—were either runners or attacked along a jogging trail."

Now the assignment made sense. Excitement mixed with a tinge of apprehension flooded through her. He was going to ask her to go undercover. She'd been a runner for years, having begun in high school. Truth was she enjoyed the many parks and trails in the area, but like most women, had avoided them except during daylight hours.

"As is the case with any assignment, this could be dangerous."

"I didn't choose to become a police officer because it was a safe line of work."

"Very well. I hear you are a runner."

"Yes. Best form of exercise if you ask me."

"Then this should be half-way enjoyable. We'd like for you to begin running in Fairview Park. It needs to be close to dark when the trails are less crowded. We'll have officers nearby, but for obvious reasons, they need to be in places where they aren't easily seen."

"You want to draw the killer out."

Randy nodded. "We've already mapped the area and identified places where we can have officers watching. However, you'll be alone on the trail. And part of the time no one will be near. Could be risky."

"Understood."

"I hear you have martial arts training."

"Yes, I'm a brown belt. Hope to get my black belt soon."

"Good. You might need to use it. You won't be able to carry a gun."

"Not a problem. When do we get started?"

"Tomorrow evening."

"I'll be ready."

JASON LEANED back in his chair, then tapped his pen on the legal pad containing various notes about Jenny Allen's murder. Funny how he always thought of her as Jenny. Not "the victim" or by her last name. During his years as a detective, he'd never allowed himself to become personally involved with an investigation.

Until this time.

Not the best situation. The academy covered cautionary tales of detectives who got too close to the victims in their cases. It often clouded their judgment and made them less effective.

He'd sworn it wouldn't happen to him.

But it had. All because of Tami. What had he told her? He would find the person responsible. A foolish promise. And with each passing week, he was no closer to learning the killer's identity than the day Jenny died.

He'd been arrogant and rude to everyone—including his boss. He treated almost everyone he questioned like a suspect—Christine

Lawrence, Vince Green, Darla Martell. Probably would have done the same to Tami if she'd been in town at the time of the murder.

Matt had every right to fire him after his first interview. Definitely after his first case of insubordination. Couldn't believe he was still employed. Thank God Bradford gave him a second chance. And a third. Probably a few more than that, too.

Somewhere along the way, he stopped trying to prove he was a top-notch detective and started to focus on solving the murder.

It wasn't that he never cared. It was that he cared more because of Tami. He cared about her. Then, when he learned she hired Vince to investigate her sister's background, it made him angry. Furious. Practically threw her out of his office.

He was still at a loss to figure out why.

The deal with Vince wounded your ego. You didn't think she had any faith in you to solve the crime.

The admission brought a sense of relief. Yes, he had changed, but he still had a long way to go. And the first step was making amends with Tami. He'd be crazy to let her get away. But instead of being with her, he was working on a Saturday night.

He looked up from his desk when an officer knocked on the door.

"Surprised to see you still here," Dugan said.

Jason glanced at his watch. It was nearly eight. "I lost track of time."

"A few of us are going to order pizza. Interested?"

"Thanks, but I'm about to wrap things up and go home."

"Understandable." The officer walked away.

Jason closed the file. He put it in his desk before picking up his cell phone to scroll through his contacts for Tami's number.

It would serve you right if she didn't answer.

He said a silent prayer she would, then sighed in relief when she did.

"Tami, it's Jason. Wondered if I could come over for a while. It's not related to your sister's case, but I want—need—to talk to you."

He smiled when she agreed and was out the door in under a minute.

～

VINCE CAME CLEAN WITH EVERYTHING—NOT only about his investigation into Jenny's background, but also Tami's reason for hiring him and their suspicion that Alyssa's and Jenny's deaths were connected. As he spoke, he'd been too focused on getting the words out to pay attention to Christine's reaction. Now, it was hard for him to gauge her emotions. She hadn't said much. Didn't show any anger.

Hadn't shown any signs of accepting his apology, either.

He was tired of secrets. Never should have kept anything from her. She had every right to be angry. But she simply listened, saying she understood.

And now, she chewed her bottom lip—something he'd seen her do when she was nervous or uncertain.

It seemed like an eternity before Christine spoke. "Thank you for telling me. Kyle kept a lot of things to himself. Most of which I didn't know until after he died. If he'd come clean—" She shook her head. "Guess there's no reason to rehash that now."

"I never should have kept things from you—no matter what Tami wanted. I didn't have to take the job."

"Yes, you did."

Vince jerked his head. "What?"

"Because of your sister. Her death has been tearing you up inside. You needed to learn the truth."

He leaned forward, placing his elbows on his knees. "But not at the expense of hurting you. I walked away from you once, and I don't want that to happen again."

Christine tilted her head. "Walked away? What do you mean?"

"When we danced at Matt and Stephanie's wedding reception. I wanted to get to know you better, but I sensed you were still grieving Kyle and didn't want to rush things. When Clay Abbott tried to kill Rachel, it made me realize life is short. I planned to phone and ask you out."

"But you never did."

Vince shook his head. "It was around that time when my sister died." He took a deep breath and forced the memories out of his head. "Well, you know the rest."

"Yeah." Christine stood, then walked to the window to look outside. Without turning around, she said, "There's something I need to know."

"Sure."

"The first time you met Darla, you made some comment about her living in Marfa. Then the night of Emily's prom I overheard you asking her a few things. Did you suspect she might know something about your sister's murder? Maybe even be involved?"

"I won't lie to you. Yes, I did."

"I see."

"But not enough to go to the police. Especially not Jason. You know how he was when the investigation started."

"All too well. But you and Tami later talked to him."

"I never mentioned Darla's name to either of them. I even asked Tami for some time before we talked to Jason. Told her I wanted to check on a possible lead. I didn't say anything because I didn't want you or Emily to get hurt. You're both close to Darla, and I needed to be sure.

"What convinced you she was in the clear?"

"Spoke to a friend with the FBI. Off the record. You and Darla were becoming closer, and I needed to be sure. I'm sorry for not being upfront with you about my suspicions."

Christine turned to look at him. "Don't be. With all the circumstantial evidence, even I would suspect her."

"Then, we're okay?"

"Yes." She closed the distance between them.

CHAPTER 27

*T*essa Hill took a deep breath as she exited her car. A prickling
sensation began at the base of her spine and went all the way
to her neck, causing her to shiver despite the warm evening air. It was
her third night to run in the nearly deserted Fairview Park. So far,
nothing had happened.

But butterflies had fluttered in her stomach all day. So much that
she'd barely eaten any lunch, something that didn't go unnoticed by
her partner. She had only worked with Steve Woods a short time, but
already they had developed a close professional relationship. Without a
doubt, she could count on him to have her back in any situation. That
he'd asked to be assigned to the undercover operation proved that. It
gave her comfort to know Steve was one of the officers positioned
nearby.

Tessa locked the car, then pocketed the keys before pausing to do a
few stretches. She wore a mic, the wire carefully concealed beneath her
t-shirt. Any of a half-dozen officers would be upon her within a couple
of minutes if she voiced even the slightest hint of danger.

But two minutes is long enough to die.

She finished stretching, then started to jog along the woodland trail.

It was longer, darker, and more isolated than many of the other paths. Had a lot of places where someone could hide. It was also the place where Susan Mason died. About half a mile along the trail, Tessa heard a rustling noise in the bushes. Her pulse quickened. She relaxed when a small rabbit bounded across the path and into the woods.

Concentrate. Don't become distracted. Stay alert.

She continued along the trail. Soon she heard the unmistakable sound of distant footsteps. Someone else was running, and the steps grew steadily near.

"Just another runner. Probably will meet in the vicinity of the duck pond." Her words, spoken softly, clued the other officers to move quietly in that direction.

The footsteps drew closer.

Pick up the speed. Else you won't make it to the pond.

"Guess I'm more tired than I thought. I probably won't meet my goal tonight."

When she turned a corner, the runner came into view—already well past the pond. He appeared to be around six-feet in height, with a muscular build.

Okay, maybe this is someone out of a late run. No need to be overly anxious. Just keep running. Act normal.

But as he grew close, he stopped.

She'd seen him before. But where?

Think, Tessa. Think. Of course. Right here in the park. Used to see him running before the first murder. He was always friendly.

"You're here late tonight." He smiled as he approached.

"Yeah, rough day at work. Needed to work off some stress."

"I know that feeling. Come here often?"

"Not as much as I once did."

"Let me guess. Because of the murder."

"Yeah. Probably shouldn't be here tonight." Tessa smiled.

"We all take chances."

"Yes, we do. Guess I'd better finish my run and let you get back to yours. I'll probably see you around sometime." She inwardly debated about continuing. If the killer was nearby, he wasn't likely to surface now. But she had a job to do, so she would see it through.

"Wait. Why don't we go for a cup of coffee or something? I've noticed you before, and I'd like to get to know you better."

A warning bell sounded in Tessa's head. She wanted to run away but forced herself to remain calm. "Maybe some other time. I have to be up early tomorrow, and it's getting late."

"No?"

"No." Tessa started to step past him.

"Reject me, and you'll be sorry." He reached out with one arm to grab her while at the same time pulled a knife with his other hand. In one swift move, Tessa whirled around, kicked her leg high, knocked him down. The knife fell beyond his reach. No time for her to grab it. Summoning all her strength, she dashed toward the pond, praying her fellow officers would soon appear. Her head start meant nothing. This guy's legs were much longer than hers. He'd be on his feet and chasing her down in a heartbeat.

He called out to her. "You won't get away from me. You'll die just like the others."

Please, God. Give me strength.

His footsteps drew closer. From the corner of her eye, Tessa caught movement. It was her partner, Steve. He raised his service weapon and pointed at the runner.

"Police, freeze!"

Three other officers appeared, all brandishing weapons.

"Drop it." Detective Somers barked.

"No," the man wailed. "No, I won't."

"You don't have a choice. We have you surrounded." Steve said.

There was a long pause. Then a clatter echoed in the stillness.

Tessa sent a prayer of thanks heavenward. The killer had dropped the knife.

~

JASON SAT IN THE RESTAURANT, waiting for Tami to return to the table. She had agreed to meet him at Casey's for a late dinner. Since their meeting a few nights ago, he was cautiously optimistic about their relationship.

He'd swallowed his pride and apologized for acting like a jerk about Vince. She'd admitted she should have been upfront with him but hadn't trusted him at first.

"You seemed too focused on blaminG everyone without trying to find the real killer. Alienated a few people along the way."

"I made a few mistakes. And it was wrong of me to be angry with you for hiring Vince."

"Stung your pride, huh?"

Tami had him pegged. She would challenge him. Wouldn't put up with his nonsense. Somehow the idea appealed to him.

The conversation had been pleasant, and it seemed as if they had regained their earlier camaraderie. One of these days, he needed to take her someplace nice. Probably sooner rather than later.

He smiled when she sat across from him. Their server appeared almost immediately, asking if they wanted dessert. Jason was about to decline when Tami spoke.

"I'd like the double-fudge brownie with ice cream." She looked at Jason. "Want to share?"

"Sure."

"Double-fudge brownie, two spoons. I'll have it out in a few minutes." The server walked away.

Tami grinned sheepishly. "Chocolate is my weakness. I keep a stash of peanut butter cups at home and in the office. I can eat an entire bag if I get stressed."

"Must not happen often. Either that or you have a fantastic metabolism." There wasn't an ounce of fat on her tall, willowy frame.

She smiled. "Oh, I get stressed all right. Even Madge knows to keep a supply of chocolate bars or cookies around. As to your other comment, I do have a good metabolism, but I also exercise regularly.

"Gym?"

"Sometimes, but I prefer biking."

"You're kidding? Me too."

"I don't get the opportunity often."

"We'll have to go for a ride together."

She smiled. "I'd like that."

The server returned with the dessert. Tami ate slowly as if savoring the delicious concoction. Jason took a few bites, but he was more interested in her than the brownie. They had almost finished when his cell phone rang. After pulling it from his pocket, he glanced at the caller ID.

"Sorry. I need to take this." Then he answered the call. "Montgomery... Yeah? ... When? ... He confess to anything? ... Okay, I'm on my way."

"What's up?"

"That was Randy Somers with Brewster Police. They arrested a man for attempted assault with a deadly weapon. Pulled a knife on an undercover police officer. It's possible he's the person responsible for the deaths of Susan Mason and Lori Huff."

Tami's eyes widened. "What about Jenny?"

"Too soon to know. I need to get over there." He rose from the table, then reached for his wallet."

"Go ahead. I'll take care of the check."

"But I—"

"Go. Don't worry about it. Your treat next time."

Next time? I like the sound of that.

"Okay. I'll let you know what happens." He bent down and placed a kiss on her cheek before leaving the restaurant.

CHRISTINE SMILED after Vince walked up behind her, put his arms around her waist, then nuzzled her neck."

"Mmmmm."

"You like?"

"Yes, but if you don't stop, I'm never going to finish preparing dinner, and I'm starving. Plus, you haven't seen how Emily reacts when she comes home hungry. I swear the kid turns into a bear."

"I gather she isn't working tonight."

Christine shook her head. "She'll be home any minute."

"Then I guess we'd better stop." He moved away from her. "Need any help?"

"Mind setting the table? Plates are in there." She gestured toward the cabinet.

"Sure."

The past few days, they had spent more time together. Most evenings, he stopped by the house, or she went to his. Tonight, she asked him to stay for dinner. She hadn't mentioned the painting again, although she did discuss it with Darla

"He's welcome to come anytime," she had said. "And I'm willing to answer any questions he might have."

The television played in the background. After Kyle died, Christine got in the habit of turning it on most evenings for background noise. She rarely paid attention to the programming. But with Vince here, she didn't need the distraction.

"And turn off the TV, will you? The remote is on the coffee table."

She was chopping tomatoes for the taco salad when Vince called out, "You might want to see this."

Wiping her hands, Christine stepped out of the kitchen in time to see the local news anchor.

"And now for tonight's top story. Brewster police have arrested a suspect in the deaths of murder victims Susan Mason and Lori Huff. According to a spokesman, thirty-four-year-old Brewster resident Ron Walsh was arrested last night for attempted assault in Fairview Park. The arrest came as a result of an undercover operation. It's unclear if the suspect is also wanted in connection with the death of Driscoll Lake resident Jenny Allen, but…"

When the station put the suspect's photo on the screen, Christine gaped.

"I've seen him."

Vince frowned. "Where?"

"At Cameron Park. He's a runner. Seemed nice. Smiled and spoke to me the last time I saw him there."

"The night I showed up? When you had the impression someone was watching you?"

A cold chill came upon her. "No. The night Jenny was killed."

"Are you sure?"

"Yes. I saw him."

"Near the lake?"

"No. He was on the other trail. It was before I met up with you. But if he did kill those other women, it's possible…"

"Yeah. He also killed Jenny. You need to talk to Jason."

JASON WAS on his second cup of coffee. It was early by his standards—he'd arrived at the office this morning before his usual time—and he wasn't fully awake.

Jenny Allen's case consumed him. After meeting with Brewster Police and listening to the interrogation of the suspect two nights ago, he still had doubts they were linked. While it was likely Ron Walsh was responsible for the deaths of the Brewster victims, Jason wasn't convinced the man killed Jenny. Too many inconsistencies to satisfy him. Her murder had more in common with one that happened in a town over six-hundred miles away.

Not surprising, the suspect denied involvement in any of the deaths. Randy Somers was still collecting evidence. He wanted a solid case before slapping a murder charge on Walsh.

Jason sipped his coffee as he read through his notes for what seemed like the millionth time. Scrawled in the middle of a page was one word. Motive. Who had a reason to kill Jenny?

Experience had taught him the number one motive in most killings was money. Tami said her stepfather was grooming Jenny to take over the family business. Upon his death, both women stood to inherit a considerable sum. But Jenny had few possessions when she died. It was likely Tami would inherit both shares. If money was the motive, she stood to gain the most from her sister's death.

Jason cursed himself for even thinking such a thought, but he needed to be objective. Tami was devastated when she learned of Jenny's murder. At any rate, she was out of town when it occurred. Murder for hire? Not likely, as Tami had no knowledge of Jenny's whereabouts for the past five years. If she did, she'd gone to great lengths to prove otherwise in hiring Vince Green. There was no way Tami could be involved.

Next, he considered revenge. But everyone he'd spoken with said Jenny had no enemies. She was quiet and reserved but well-liked by those who knew her. No reason anyone would want to kill her.

He shook his head. According to the FBI agent in charge of Alyssa Weber's murder, no one had been able to establish a clear-cut motive in her death, either. The one link in both killings, Jesse Saldana, was buried in a West Texas cemetery.

There was the possibility that Jenny was simply the victim of a crazed killer. Someone who targeted women and she had the misfortune of being in his path. If that was the case, then Ron Walsh was a prime suspect.

But if so, why had he used two different knives? Forensic tests were still pending on the weapon Walsh had in his possession at the time of his arrest. There was a high likelihood of it being the one used on Susan Mason and Lori Huff. But there was no way it was the same blade used to kill Jenny.

The buzzing of the intercom stirred Jason from his thoughts. He picked up the receiver. "Montgomery."

"Detective, there's a Christine Lawrence here to see you. She says she has some information that may pertain to the murder."

It had been weeks since he'd spoken to her. He couldn't help but wonder why she'd come forward now. "Send her back."

Jason stood, then walked to the door to greet her. "Ms. Lawrence. Please, sit down." He waited until she sat in one of the chairs before returning to his own seat. "What can I do for you today?"

"I saw the news report last night about the arrest of a suspect in connection with the Brewster murders. Is he also wanted for Jenny's murder?"

"We're still gathering information."

"Maybe I can help."

"Go ahead."

"I saw the man in Cameron Park the day Jenny died."

Jason sat up straighter. "You're sure about this?

"Yes."

"Why haven't you come forward with this information before now?"

"It wasn't until I saw his picture on the news that I remembered. He wasn't along the lakeside trail, but closer to the park entrance. That's probably why I never gave it another thought. Several people were running that day."

Jason paused for a moment before speaking again. "Sorry, but I have to ask you this. What makes you sure it's the same man? You didn't remember until after you saw his picture."

"I guess there's no way to be a hundred percent sure. As I said, there were lots of people there that day."

"Anything distinctive about him? Something that would stand out?"

Christine frowned. "He had a tattoo on his left forearm."

"Can you describe it?"

"Yes, it was an eagle with a snake clutched in its talons."

Jason nodded. "I see. Anything else?"

"Nothing I can recall now. Maybe I'm wrong about it being the same man, but I really thought it was and felt I needed to tell you."

"You did the right thing. If you remember anything else, please call."

Christine stood to leave. "Thank you. I will."

Jason waited until she had left before picking up the phone to call Randy Somers. He tapped his fingers on the desk while waiting for his colleague to answer.

"Somers."

"Jason here. Need to know something about Walsh. Does he have any tattoos?"

"Matter of fact he does. Has one of an eagle and a snake on his left forearm."

"Was it visible in any of the photos shown to the media?"

"No. We only released his mugshot. Why?"

"Then there's something you need to know."

CHAPTER 28

Simone couldn't believe her luck. He was here. In the grocery store of all places. Maybe she had another opportunity—one last chance—to make him want her. This time there would be no pretense, no overt flirting. She would be herself.

It was a matter of finding the right opportunity.

He seemed oblivious to anyone around him, but she knew better. The fact he'd been in law enforcement and was now a private investigator told her he noticed more than most people realized. Following him throughout the store would be foolish. Better to make it appear like a chance encounter.

She slipped around an aisle of the produce section, then positioned her shopping cart so it stuck out a bit, but not far enough that someone would easily see it as they rounded the corner.

If she guessed right, Vince would be coming this way anytime. It wasn't long before she felt a slight bump of the shopping carts colliding.

"Sorry," he said.

"No, it's my fault. Should have paid closer attention to what I was doing." She knew the minute recognition dawned on him. The look on his face indicated he wasn't pleased to see her. It was time to put her plan into action.

"You're the man who was at Pinnacle a few nights ago. I owe you an apology for my behavior. I just assumed—"

"I was there alone and was looking for companionship? You were wrong."

"Then, I'm sorry for giving you the wrong impression about me. Driscoll Lake is a small enough town that we're bound to run into one another again. I hope there are no hard feelings. Maybe you'll give me another chance. If you're not busy, I could take you out for a drink."

"Look, Ms.—"

"Simone. My name is Simone."

"Okay, Simone. There's already someone in my life. Sorry, but I'm not interested in pursuing a relationship with you. Now, if you'll excuse me, I have plans."

She could only watch as he walked away. There would be no more chances.

Rejection. She had lived with it most of her life. Would it ever end?

She finished her shopping then drove home, her thoughts and emotions blending into a toxic cocktail of depression and rage.

How many men had hurt her? Turned her away? Abandoned her. It began with her father shortly before her fifth birthday.

Alone in her bedroom, the memories flooded her mind.

"Daddy, why are you leaving?

"I have to go away, sweetheart. But I'll be back. Just because your mother and I aren't together anymore doesn't mean I'll forget you. We'll still see one another. I'll be here in a couple of weeks. We'll have the whole weekend together to celebrate your birthday."

As the time drew closer, her excitement grew. She must have pestered her mother with the same question a dozen times. "How many more days till Daddy comes?"

Finally, the day arrived. When she got home from preschool, she hurried to her room to change into her prettiest dress. Her mother had packed a small suitcase with enough clothes for the weekend. She gathered her things, including her favorite stuffed bear—a gift from her father.

Then, she went to the living room to wait for him. He said he would pick her up before dinner. But that time came and went. Soon it grew dark. Each time she saw car lights turn down their street, she held her breath in anticipation. And each time she was disappointed.

Something must have happened to him. Daddy always kept his promises.

But he never came. Heartbroken, she hugged her cherished bear and began to cry. Finally, exhausted by her tears, she fell asleep on the sofa. She didn't remember her mother picking her up and tucking her in bed, the bear still in her arms.

It was weeks before her mother told her the truth. "Your father isn't coming back. He's made a new life for himself, and we're no longer a part of it."

"But he's my daddy. He has to come."

"I know honey, but sometimes fathers don't always do the right thing. We're on our own now. Just you and me."

The man she idolized walked out of her life as if she never mattered. That night, after her mother was asleep, she went into the kitchen, got a butcher knife, and hacked the stuffed bear to shreds.

CHRISTINE PARKED her SUV but didn't bother to close the garage door. After grabbing her laptop and a couple of packages from the back, she hurried inside. She was excited about the weekend plans with Vince. He had purchased tickets to a concert for Saturday in Dallas, and they were driving up tonight.

They had seen one another every night the past week—either at his place or hers. Last night, the subject of the painting had come up. Vince was the one who initiated the conversation.

"I want to see Alyssa's portrait. What do you think?"

"I think it's something you need to do. You still have questions and need answers."

"Yeah, I guess you're right, but it isn't easy."

"I'm sure it isn't. By the way, Darla told me she stored the painting, but she'll make it available to you anytime. For what it's worth, she said Saldana was known for his landscapes. As far as anyone knows, your sister's portrait is the only one he ever did."

Vince had called to say he'd spoken with Darla and planned to stop at her place before going home. "Would you like to meet me at the gallery in an hour? We can go to my house from there, then leave for Dallas."

"I'd like that."

"Sounds good. I'll see you around five-thirty."

Christine unlocked the house, set her purse on the kitchen counter, then went into her bedroom. An hour would give her time to take a shower and freshen her make-up.

Twenty minutes later, she emerged from the bathroom, then donned a pair of jeans and a t-shirt. After slipping into a pair of sandals, she picked up her travel bag, then started back toward the kitchen. Someone knocked at the back door.

She wasn't expecting anyone, and not many people used the garage entrance. When she opened the door, she was surprised to see her neighbor. "Libby! What's up?"

"Sorry to bother you, but Emily left her sketchbook in the classroom. She'll need it for a weekend assignment." Libby smiled, then stepped into the kitchen.

Christine shook her head. "That girl! Sometimes I think she'd forget her head if it weren't attached. Appreciate you bringing it by."

"Teenagers sometimes get careless."

Christine took the pad from Libby and placed it on the kitchen counter.

"You must be going somewhere." Libby gestured to the travel bag on the floor.

"Yeah, I'm meeting Vince at Darla's gallery, then he and I are going to Dallas for the weekend."

"I gather things are okay between the two of you."

"Yeah, everything is fine. You might say better than ever. It was a misunderstanding."

"Oh, I see." She paused for a moment, a faraway look in her eyes. "Guess I'd better not detain you."

It wasn't the first time Christine had gotten the impression Libby was lonely. They had been neighbors for less than a year, but she hadn't gone out of her way to be friendly. "Sorry I don't have time to visit. Maybe next week we can get together sometime."

"Sure. I'd like that."

"Let me grab my bag, and I'll walk out with you."

Libby waited while Christine put her things in the back, then climbed into the driver's seat. "Need me to check on Emily while you're away?"

"I appreciate it, but she's staying with Darla."

"Then I'll see you when you get home."

Christine nodded, then turned the key in the ignition. Nothing happened. "That's funny. It was running fine when I got home an hour ago."

"Dead battery?" Libby suggested.

"Shouldn't be. I bought it a couple of months ago. And even if it were, it shouldn't have run down that fast. Guess I'd better call Vince and have him pick me up here."

"Don't bother him. I can drive you to the gallery."

"Are you sure? I don't want you to go to any trouble."

"It's not a problem. I planned to pick up something to eat, anyway. I'll grab a sandwich at the coffee shop across the street. Let's go."

VINCE SAT in Darla's office, listening as she spoke to Jensen Gallery about Alyssa's portrait. He wasn't sure if his parents would want it, given the circumstances, but he wanted to keep the option to purchase it open.

She ended the call, then turned to him. "Sue said I could keep the painting as long as necessary. Once you speak to your parents, you can let me know what they decide. Matter of fact Sue suspects the Saldana family would be willing to give you the portrait. They always felt it should belong to a member of her family. You can understand why they never offered it to her husband."

"I'm glad they didn't. Travis doesn't deserve anything of Alyssa's. Not after the way he trashed her name when news of the affair came out."

"Nothing he does would surprise me. My father never cared for the Weber family. But that's another story."

Vince glanced at his watch. It was after six and Christine had agreed to meet him a half hour ago.

"Something wrong?"

"Christine should have been here by now. It's not like her to be late."

"Probably got tied up at school."

"No, when I spoke to her, she was almost home."

"Then she's probably getting ready for your trip. I'm sure she'll be here shortly." She glanced up when Kristen tapped on the office door.

"Excuse me, but your granddaughter is on the phone. She sounds upset."

Darla picked up the receiver. "What's going on, dear?"

Vince frowned as he listened to Darla.

"No honey, your mother isn't here…Yes, she was supposed to meet Vince… What? Wait, let me put you on speaker. He's sitting in my office."

"Emily? Is something wrong?" Vince asked.

"I don't know where Mom is. When I got home, her car was in the garage, but she's not in the house. Her purse and travel bag are in the car, and her keys are in the ignition."

"Did you try her cell phone?"

"It's with her purse. I've checked outside. Ms. Gordon has been here because my sketch pad is in the kitchen."

"Slow down, Emily. What does your sketch pad have to do with anything?"

"I left it at school. She must have brought it because I need it for an assignment she gave me to do this weekend. And that's weird, too. It's not like I haven't done landscapes before and the place where she wants me to sketch is creepy."

"Maybe your Mom went next door."

"I called there, but no one answers. Ms. Gordon's garage door was open, but her car is gone, so she's not home, either. It's like Mom just disappeared." Emily sniffled.

"Honey, calm down. There's probably a good explanation. Stay put, and I'll be right over," Darla said.

"Everything will be all right. We'll find your mom."

Darla ended the call, then looked at Vince. "Something isn't right."

"I agree."

"Excuse me."

Vince jolted and whirled around. He hadn't realized Kristen never left.

"I couldn't help but hear Emily mention her art teacher's last name is Gordon. By chance, is her first name Libby?"

"I believe so. Why? Do you know her?" Darla asked.

"She taught art in Alpine. Rented a house from my parents."

Something struck a nerve with Vince. "Alpine? How long did she live there?"

"Two or three years. Left there a couple of summers ago to say she was moving to New Mexico. She was nice enough, but a little strange."

Vince frowned. "Do you know where she lived in New Mexico?"

"Santa Fe. She left town in a hurry, leaving my parents to clean out a lot of stuff after she was gone. They figured she followed Jesse Saldana there. Mom and Dad thought she was obsessed with him. Mom found a bunch of letters she wrote to him but never mailed. Pages and pages about them soon being together. Funny thing, though. Some she signed her name, Libby, but in others, she called herself Simone."

A sickening feeling washed over Vince. Simone. Could this be the woman who came on to him? He'd never seen Christine's elusive neighbor. Was she the connection between Alyssa and Jenny? She'd lived in both towns where the murders occurred, not to mention Santa Fe.

Was it only coincidence? He was beginning to hate that word. If Libby Gordon and Simone were the same person, Christine was in danger. He needed to act fast.

"Darla, I'll come to Christine's as soon as I can. In the meantime, I'm calling Jason Montgomery."

⁓

JASON SAT in front of Tami's desk, drumming his fingers. "Are you going to be ready any time soon?"

"Just a few more words. I want to finish this article about the high school art show. Lots of talented kids in this town."

"Can't it wait?"

She looked at him, then arched her brows. "The sooner I finish, the sooner we can get out of here. Besides, if I complete it this evening, I'm free until Monday."

"Then by all means, go ahead. Wouldn't want you to be thinking about work all weekend."

Tami turned back to the keyboard—totally focused on her task. Jason couldn't help but admire her work ethic. He'd been around his share of pushy reporters and had doubts about her in the beginning, but Tami was dedicated to learning the truth. She wouldn't print a story just for the sake of making headlines.

After a few minutes, he spoke again. "So, where do you want to go tonight?"

"Jason, please, I'm trying to concentrate."

"Okay." He sighed.

"And wipe that sad puppy dog look off your face. It's not going to work." She smiled as she said the words.

"You didn't even look in my direction. How did you know I'm trying the pitiful approach?"

"Let's say I know your type and it's not going to work with me. If you don't let me finish this, I'll banish you from my office. Madge is still here. I'm sure she'll be to keep you company."

He rolled his eyes. "I'll be quiet."

Ten minutes later, Tami hit the save button. "Done. Monday, I'll review it and have it ready to go to press on Tuesday. Now, you were asking where I wanted to go tonight."

Jason's phone rang. He frowned as he glanced at the caller ID. "It's Vince Green. I'd better see what he needs." He turned from Tami's desk and answered the phone. "Hello… She's what? … Who? … Are you kidding? … No, I don't think the idea is farfetched. You on your way to her house now? … Okay, make sure no one goes near the garage. Even though there aren't any signs of a struggle, we might need to gather forensic evidence. I'll meet you there in ten minutes." He ended the call.

"What's going on?"

"Christine Lawrence is missing."

"What? When did this happen?"

"Not long enough to file a missing persons' report, but Vince believes something's wrong. You won't believe who he suspects. I need to meet him at Christine's house. We may have found the missing link to your sister's murder."

CHAPTER 29

*C*hristine took several deep breaths, willing herself to relax. She didn't want to do anything to upset Libby further. She had threatened to harm Emily if Christine didn't cooperate. The risk of bringing harm to her daughter was real. After listening to the woman's tirade, she had no doubt Libby would try something.

Was this how Kyle had felt when Phillip Denton claimed to have taken her and Emily hostage? What did he think when he realized he was about to die?

Libby had severe emotional issues. Had there been telltale signs? Something she could have seen and possibly caused her to realize the woman needed professional help? Probably not. She didn't know her well enough.

To say she'd been shocked by Libby's actions would be an understatement. One minute, she was offering to drive Christine to meet Vince, the next she was holding a knife to her back.

"This is what you're going to do," Libby said. "We're going to get into my car, and you're going to act like everything is normal. Do something stupid, and your daughter will die."

"What have you done with her?"

"Nothing yet. She's in a safe place. At least for now. I won't hurt her if you cooperate."

Christine didn't have any choice but to do as Libby said. She wasn't sure where they were going, only that Libby drove east out of town.

"Where are we going?"

"You'll know when we get there. Probably not anywhere you'd ever go. You have no need. Some of us aren't fortunate enough to have a lot of friends. But you have Rachel and Stephanie. I'm told the friendship goes back a long time. What would they think if they knew you were in danger?"

Christine gasped. "You haven't done anything to them, have you?"

"Relax. I don't plan to harm your friends. *They* haven't done anything to hurt me."

"And what did I do? I've been nothing but nice to you."

Libby acted as if she didn't hear Christine's words. "I must say, your friends have excellent taste in men. But it's not their husbands I want."

"Libby, I no longer have a husband."

"That's true. You don't. And you won't have another one, either."

"What do you mean?"

"It didn't have to be this way. If you'd stayed away from Vince, things would have been different. It's you he wants, but I saw him first. I wanted him from the first time I laid eyes him. Funny. It was the same night Jenny died.

"Surprised me when I saw him in that diner. He was oblivious to my presence. You'd think someone trained in law enforcement would be more alert."

Try to remain calm. Make her think you're interested in what she has to say.

"Maybe he just didn't see you."

"He's had other opportunities. At Casey's, last weekend at Pinnacle, yesterday at the grocery store. Then there were other times when he didn't know I was there. I watched him in restaurants, at the park, another time at Pinnacle. But he was always with you."

Christine felt nauseated. The woman was obsessed with Vince. She had problems far beyond what anyone realized. Libby continued her rant.

"Like I was saying, Vince doesn't want me. I hoped to turn him around, but you got in the way. I'll take care of him just like I did Jesse."

"Jesse Saldana? The artist?"

"Oh, you know who he is. He betrayed me twice. I forgave him the first time. But not the second."

Christine shivered. The woman was insane. "You killed him?"

Libby slowed the dark sedan, then turned onto a winding country road. "I made his death look like an accident. I know a few things about cars. Had to learn. It's hard growing up poor because your father abandons you. But yes, I killed Jesse. And I took care of the two women who kept him away from me."

"Alyssa and Jenny?"

"How did you know about Alyssa?"

Instinct told Christine not to reveal too much. "My mother-in-law once lived in Marfa. She knew about the murder and thought it was similar to Jenny Allen's death."

"Smart woman. Yeah, Alyssa was my first victim. I tampered with her car just like I did yours. Killing Jenny was easier. When I found out she was in Driscoll Lake, I pretended to be her friend. It wasn't hard to lure her to Cameron Park. You should have seen her eyes when I pulled the knife. She didn't have time to react. I couldn't believe my luck when that copycat killer turned up in Brewster. Threw police off the trail."

Christine didn't respond.

A few minutes passed before Libby spoke again. "Yes, I stabbed them both to death. And I'm going to kill you the same way." She pulled into a dirt driveway where a dilapidated farmhouse stood far back from the road. Massive oaks, tangled vines, and overgrown weeds surrounded the place. Beside the house was a stone structure that someone probably once used as a barn.

Eerie was an understatement.

Libby nodded toward the building. "Charming, isn't it? That's where we're going. How long do you think it will take them to find your body? I gave your daughter a hint. She's smart. She'll figure it out."

～

VINCE ARRIVED at Christine's house a couple of minutes before Jason. Much to his surprise, Tami Sutton pulled into the driveway behind him. He raised his eyebrows in question.

"Tami and I were about to leave for dinner when you called. If what you suspect is true, the outcome affects her. She insisted on following." Jason said.

"Don't worry. I'm here not as a reporter but as a concerned friend."

"It's fine," Vince opened the door and motioned them inside. Darla was already there, sitting next to her granddaughter on the sofa.

Emily jumped up, ran to Vince, then threw her arms around him. "I'm scared. Mom doesn't do things like this. It's like when my dad... I can't take it if anything happens to her."

Vince patted her back and waited for her sobs to subside. "It's going to be okay. Detective Montgomery is here to help, and he'll do everything he can to find her." He wished he could be sure of his words. But he had his own fears for Christine's safety. He sent a pleading look in Darla's direction.

Tami must have noticed. "Emily, why don't you and I step into the kitchen while Vince and your grandmother talk to Detective Montgomery. We can talk about art. I saw some of your sketches last weekend. You're very good."

Emily managed a smile. "Sure."

After they left the room, Jason said, "While it's too early to file an official investigation, I've asked Officer Dugan to question the neighbors. Maybe someone saw something unusual. I also spoke with Agent Blake on the drive over. He'll check out any leads in Alpine. If what you suspect about Libby Gordon is correct, we need to act fast."

"But why would she target Christine?" Darla asked.

"She would go after anyone she perceives as a threat. In her mind, Alyssa and Jenny stood in the way of her being with Jesse. Now she has apparently set her sights on Vince, and that makes Christine a target."

"Why would a killer be interested in the brother of one of her victims?"

"My guess is she doesn't know there's a connection."

"Jason, Vince! Come here. You need to see this." Tami called out.

They rushed to the kitchen, followed closely by Darla. Emily and Tami stood beside the counter. Emily's sketchbook was open.

"What's wrong?" Vince asked.

"I asked to see some of her drawings. When she opened the portfolio, we found this."

Bile rose in Vince's stomach as he stared at the pages. What was once a drawing of Christine had been sliced to shreds.

"Honey, are you sure your teacher is the one who brought this?" Darla put her arms around her granddaughter.

Emily nodded. "I remember leaving it on her desk because she asked to see some of my recent work. When the bell rang, I was in a hurry and forgot to pick it up."

"Why would she bring it here knowing someone would discover the slashed pages?" Tami asked.

"To send us a message," Vince said. "She's desperate and doesn't care who knows."

Jason nodded. "I agree. This is more than a missing person's case. We need to find a murderer before she strikes again."

"But if she has Christine, where would she take her?" Darla asked.

"Somewhere remote. I think we can rule out Cameron Park this time since— I don't think she would choose the same place as before." Jason glanced at Tami.

Vince frowned, remembering something Emily said when she phoned the gallery. "Emily, you said Libby gave you a specific location for your assignment. Where?"

"The old Greer property east of town. She's fascinated with the place. Always talking about how peaceful and serene it is. It's scary if you ask me."

"You know the place?" Vince asked Jason.

"Never been there, but I know where it is. You thinking what I'm thinking?"

Vince nodded.

Jason's cell phone rang. "It's Dugan—" He answered the call. "Montgomery … Yes. He did? … When? … Okay, get a BOLO out for a black Hyundai Sonata. Possibly headed east. I'm heading out to the old Greer place off Tyson Road." He ended the call, then turned to Vince. "A neighbor claims to have seen Christine leave with Libby less than an hour ago."

"Then let's go," Vince said.

"Don't suppose it would do any good to ask you to stay here."

"No."

"Didn't think so. You carrying?"

"What do you think?"

CHRISTINE'S EYES widened at Libby's sudden outburst.

"Nnnnnoooo! They can't do this to me. It will destroy my plans." Libby pounded on the padlocked door of the stone building.

Someone had placed "No Trespassing" signs around the property. Based on Libby's reaction, it was probably a recent occurrence.

"Why, why, why? For once in my life, can't something go right for me? This is the place she's supposed to die!" She continued to bang on the door. Her voice broke. Uncontrolled sobs overtook her, and she sank to the ground.

Libby seemed oblivious to her presence. Christine took note of her surroundings. The derelict condition of the house made it appear unsafe for anyone to step inside. The porch looked as if it would collapse if someone stepped on it. At one end, a sapling grew through the rotting boards.

She doubted Emily was anywhere nearby. Libby's comment led

Christine to believe she wanted Emily to find her body. But if Libby was holding the teenager somewhere, the best way to save her was to get away from here. Find someone who could help her get back to town and notify Vince.

She might have a chance to escape. The car was less than a hundred feet away. Libby had the knife, but Christine was certain she left the keys in the ignition. She was a fast runner. Even though the sandals she wore weren't ideal, she could probably make it before Libby caught up.

Her decision made, she ran.

"Stop! Come back here."

Christine didn't have to look back to know Libby was following her. She sprinted toward the car.

Thirty feet. Twenty. Fifteen. The footsteps behind her grew closer. Libby had the advantage of wearing running shoes. Christine was almost to the car when her foot struck a rock. She tumbled to the ground.

"Can't you go any faster?" Vince asked Jason as he drove along the winding road.

"Not if I want to get us there in one piece. I'm already driving twenty over the speed limit. It can't be far now."

"I just hope we're in time."

"Me too. Backup should be along any minute." Jason glanced in the rearview mirror.

"Wait," Vince said as they approached a narrow, dirt drive. "I think this is it."

Jason slammed on the brakes, then pulled the car to the side of the road. "We'd better go on foot. It's our best chance at surprising her."

"If she's here." Vince jumped out of the car.

Jason followed.

The mass of tangled vines and underbrush made it difficult to see far, but about twenty feet from the road, they spotted a black sedan.

"Matches the description of the car," Jason said.

"They're here somewhere. I'd bet my life on it."

The sound of a woman's voice penetrated the stillness. "You won't get away from me."

Vince looked around an overgrown bush. Christine was running toward the car. Libby was close behind, brandishing a knife. He reached for his gun as Christine stumbled and fell.

"I've got you now!" Libby raised the knife over her head.

"Police! Freeze!" Jason pulled his weapon.

Libby never flinched. She plunged the knife as the sound of gunfire reverberated in the surrounding woods. The impact of two bullets sent her sprawling backward before the blade hit her intended target. She fell to the ground.

Vince rushed to Christine's side, then scooped her into his arms. "I thought I was going to lose you. Are you hurt?"

Christine shook her head and pushed away from him. "We have to go. I need to find Emily. Libby threatened to hurt her if I didn't cooperate."

"She's safe. Darla is with her at your house."

"Thank God." Her body deflated, and she slumped into his embrace.

Jason knelt beside the woman's body, to check for a pulse. He shook his head. "She's dead."

Vince helped Christine stand, then put his arm around her.

"Who would have guessed she was a killer? Besides her undoubtedly having psychological problems, who would have guessed she'd have reason to come after you?" Jason stood, then walked over to Christine and Vince.

"Jealousy, revenge. She wanted Vince, and I stood in her way."

"I never imagined the pushy woman who introduced herself as Simone was your shy, art-teaching, next-door neighbor."

"That's not all. Vince, she confessed to killing both your sister and Jenny."

"So, Alyssa's death was related to Jenny's?"

Christine nodded. "All because of their involvement with Jesse Saldana. Libby had her sights set on him, but he rejected her. She admitted to tampering with his car so his death would look like an accident. She planned to kill you next. I don't think she knew you were Alyssa's brother." Tears welled in her eyes.

Vince pulled her close, then kissed the top of her head. "Don't cry, babe. She can't hurt us now. It's over."

EPILOGUE

Driscoll Lake, Texas
May 2016

Christine placed a bowl of potato salad on the patio table, then glanced across the yard. Vince was grilling burgers and hot dogs. Brian and Matt stood nearby, the three of them probably talking about the latest baseball scores.

Stephanie and Rachel sat in lounge chairs. Emily and Ty splashed in the pool.

Darla was hosting a combination graduation celebration and beginning of summer party to close out the Memorial Day weekend.

Emily had graduated with honors three days earlier. Like her grandmother, she planned to attend UT Austin and major in fine arts. She was still seeing Ty Fuller. He enlisted in the Marines upon his graduation a year earlier and was home on leave.

A year had passed since the stabbings in Driscoll Lake and Brewster. Ron Walsh pleaded guilty to the murders of Susan Mason and Lori Huff. He was now serving time in a maximum-security prison. Ironically, Walsh also committed his crimes because he'd been rejected. But he'd killed the women who turned him down. Libby had done the same when she murdered Jesse Saldana, but she also went after the women she perceived as obstacles. At least Christine and Vince were spared the same fate as the others. After Libby's death, Jason learned more about her background. Her problems likely stemmed from her father abandoning his family.

Christine didn't want to think about the woman who nearly destroyed her life. Today was for good thoughts only. A celebration. Emily's best friend, Bethany, and her parents were there, as well as Jason and Tami.

Darla carried a pan of brownies to the patio.

"Anything else I can help with?" Christine asked.

"No. Everything is under control. Go have fun. Spend some time with your husband."

Christine and Vince married six months earlier in a small ceremony. Her long-time friends, Stephanie and Rachel, were her attendants.

Stephanie gave birth to a baby boy the previous August. He was the image of his father, Matt.

Two weeks earlier, Rachel and Brian announced she was pregnant with twins. She still maintained her medical practice, and his construction business was booming.

Christine took a beer from the cooler, then walked to where Vince stood beside the grill. Matt and Brian had joined Stephanie and Rachel. "Thought you could use something cold."

"Thanks. The burgers are almost ready."

After dinner, Christine and Vince sat together on the patio. Most of the guests were in the pool, enjoying an impromptu game of volleyball. Twilight had descended, and fireflies danced at the edge of the yard. The sweet fragrance of gardenias filled the air. Nearby, a mockingbird sang its last song of the day.

"Are you up for a swim?" Vince asked.

"Maybe in a while. I'm content to sit here and enjoy the evening. You can go ahead if you want."

Vince took her hand. "I'd rather be with you. What's on your mind?"

"Thinking about everything that's happened in the last year. Or rather, since we reconnected that day at the park."

"Yeah. What a way to begin a relationship."

Jason called to them from the pool. "Hey, you two. Get over here. The men are playing against the women."

"And whose idea was that?" Vince laughed.

Jason pointed in Tami's direction, which promptly earned him an elbow in his side.

"Hard to believe that's the same arrogant detective who dragged us down to police headquarters the night Jenny died," Christine said.

"Yeah. Matt said he's turned out to be one of the best detectives he's worked with. He's afraid he'll lose him, though."

"Has Jason said something about moving?"

"I don't think he'll move away without Tami, but I couldn't blame him for wanting to advance his career. And Matt's not going anywhere any time soon."

"What about you? Ever think you'd want to leave Driscoll Lake?" Christine asked.

Vince shook his head. "I'm pretty content right here."

"Yeah," Christine said. "Me, too."

AUTHORS NOTE

Thanks for going on this journey with me. It's hard to believe the time has come to say goodbye to Driscoll Lake. I have lived and breathed these characters for almost five years. Stephanie, Matt, Rachel, Brian, Christine, and Vince are all special to me.

It's also hard for me to choose a favorite of the three books. Unseen Motives was my baby. In Unknown Reasons, I listened to a character and allowed him to dictate the way the story played out. Unclear Purposes is perhaps the strongest of the three books but in many ways the hardest to write.

Speaking of characters, don't be surprised to see a couple of familiar faces in my new series. (There's a hint at the end of Unclear Purposes.) Like Driscoll Lake, these books are in the suspense/romantic suspense genre. However, there will be a bit of a twist in that I incorporate elements of folklore and legends.

Look for the first volume in 2020. To keep up to date on my latest news, visit my website (http://joanhall.net) and subscribe to my newsletter or sign up for my blog.

I hope you enjoyed reading this book. Would you consider leaving a review on Amazon or Goodreads?

Until next time,

Joan

WORKS BY THIS AUTHOR

Driscoll Lake Series
Unseen Motives
Unknown Reasons
Unclear Purposes

Novellas
The Stranger

Anthologies
Unshod
Macabre Sanctuary
Bright Lights and Candle Glow
Quantum Wanderlust

ACKNOWLEDGEMENTS

I'm grateful to the following people who helped make this book possible.

My critique partners, Staci, Mae, and Craig. Thanks for your valuable insight and feedback. You helped make this story stronger.

Alan Patton, Independent Investigative Consultant. A big thanks for answering my questions about forensics and DNA testing.

Sandi, Pam, Mary, Annette, Sandy, Sarah, John Mark, and Doran – as always thanks for your input and feedback.

Adam and the Writer's Detective Group for their help with my questions regarding jurisdiction in murder cases.

Adrian for once again reading the raw, unedited version (and for challenging me to have a different type of antagonist).

Michele Bosworth, MD, for answering my medical-related questions.

My friend Kathy who prompted me to keep writing and for spreading the word about my books.

The staff of AIW Press for publishing this novel.

As always, for the unwavering support of my husband, John. Thanks for understanding and your patience when I'm "in the zone."

ABOUT THE AUTHOR

Joan Hall likes to create character-driven fiction with strong, deter-mined female leads and enigmatic male characters. She has always enjoyed reading a good mystery or suspense story, so it's only natural that's her favorite writing genre. When she's not writing, Joan likes to take nature walks, observe the night skies, and explore old cemeteries. She also enjoys ghost walks and learning about local folklore. Joan and her husband live in Texas with their three cats.

You can connect with Joan at her website https://www.joanhall.net or on the following social media sties:

Facebook | Twitter | Pinterest | Bookbub | Goodreads | Instagram

Also By

Chronicle of Ceres Magical Realism Series

Beginning of Tomorrows, book 1

Denali Rising, book 2

Shasta Beckons, book 3

Bluestone Shadows, book 4 (releasing 2024)

Tales From the Crows

Horror short story collection (releasing October 2023)

www.ingramcontent.com/pod-product-compliance
Lightning Source LLC
Chambersburg PA
CBHW070633260626
47161CB00007B/2680